The monster propelled itself towards Frank (p. 142).

POLAR PERIL

LIONEL SURREY

Illustrated by A. S. Forrest

THOMAS NELSON AND SONS LTD
LONDON EDINBURGH PARIS MELBOURNE
TORONTO AND NEW YORK

THOMAS NELSON AND SONS LTD

Parkside Works Edinburgh 9
3 Henrietta Street London WC2
312 Flinders Street Melbourne C1
5 Parker's Buildings Burg Street Cape Town

THOMAS NELSON AND SONS (CANADA) LTD
91–93 Wellington Street West Toronto 1

THOMAS NELSON AND SONS
19 East 47th Street New York 17

SOCIÉTÉ FRANÇAISE D'ÉDITIONS NELSON
25 rue Henri Barbusse Paris Vᵉ

FOREWORD

I HAVE endeavoured to make all details of the background as accurate as possible in accordance with the maps published up to date, except the imaginary discoveries in the (so far) unexplored regions roughly south of Peter I. Island. Should any new knowledge come to light which appears to contradict the facts stated, these should be relegated to the sphere of the " might-have-beens."

L. S.

September 1938.

CONTENTS

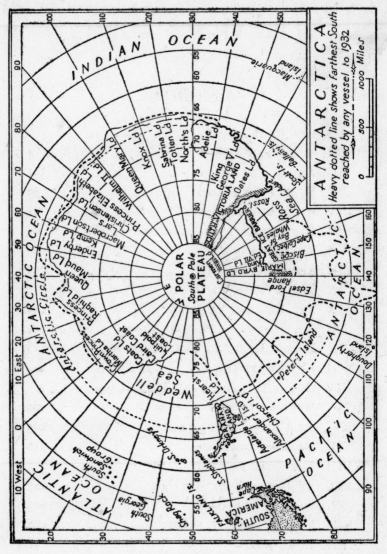

ANTARCTICA

Heavy dotted line shows farthest South
reached by any vessel to 1932

0   500   1000 Miles

POLAR PERIL

CHAPTER I

OFF TO THE POLE

A CHALLENGING blast from the siren and the Antarctic venture had begun.

To the casual onlooker Hobart might well have been celebrating a royal jubilee, so completely had the city gone *en fête*. All along the waterside, buildings were gaily decked with bunting, while every vessel within sight—from tiny rowing-boats to the ponderous ten-million-pound warship—was flying one or more additional flags. Stretched in the breeze, these flapped like wings until the air seemed full of a mighty horde of multi-coloured birds.

Noise too—as always—formed a large part of the enthusiastic send-off. Both on shore and on ship crowds cheered lustily in a generous farewell, while whistles shrieked, sirens wailed, guns boomed, and hooters blasted forth their " God-speed."

From a tug nearby Lord Castleton—the governor—and Lady Castleton waved their official good-bye, the concluding act of their visit to the plucky little vessel which might not enter that port again for several years —and then only providing she was fortunate enough to surmount the many and terrible dangers of the polar regions. To many of the crew, however, the main centre of attraction was the little crowd of relatives—actual or would-be—who gazed sadly at the disappearing ship.

Slowly the *Queen of the Antarctic* gathered speed and, escorted by excursion boats, the Harbour Board's yacht, and several vessels of the Royal Yacht Club, reached the open sea. Here, with a final pandemonium of farewells —vocal and mechanical—the captain rang down " full-speed ahead," and the helmsman set his course south-east.

In the bows stood a boy of fifteen. Despite his keen anticipation of the thrills of the voyage, there was an involuntary expression of sadness upon his face. Glancing up at his father on the bridge, Alan Baker wished that he had a mother, or friends, to wave to him as he gazed back at the last sight of land which he would see for some days. But his regrets were quickly forgotten as he noticed his two chums hurrying towards him. The taller, David Somervell, a strong, athletic youth of eighteen whose fair hair and laughing eyes surmounted a healthy glow, was struggling hard to find his sea legs as he placed first one foot and then the other firmly on the heaving deck, meanwhile allowing his body to sway with the movements of the boat. Frank Ingram, however, his junior by six months, dared not trust himself to walk unaided, and lurched along clinging to any available support. More than ever now he envied his chum his carefree nature.

" What-ho, Alan ! Isn't this great ? " David steadied himself against the anchor as he flung the question at him.

" Rather ! " beamed Alan.

With a final dash Frank fell rather than sat upon the anchor chain, and with a sigh of relief looked up to join the conversation.

" Tophole of your Dad to pick us out of all that crowd of chaps ! " he opined enthusiastically.

Alan glanced up at the bridge. " Well, you see he knew we three were great chums and he thought we'd be company for one another. Of course I shan't be able to see much of Dad—he'll be so busy with the ship, especially when we get into the danger zone." A dreamy look spread over his face for a moment, but a shower of spray, following an extra heavy lurch, made him exclaim, " Golly ! that was a good one. We'll have to look out or we'll get a ducking. Yes, I'm awfully glad he did. We'll have some topping fun together." Then as an afterthought he added, " Of course, Dad knew that we'd all been on that trip round the world when we were at school, so he said you two ought to know better how to make yourselves useful than most of those landlubbers who applied."

His reference to " those landlubbers who applied " was concerned with an advertisement which had appeared in several of the leading newspapers, stating that " Two healthy and willing boys . . . are required for a voyage to the Antarctic," for which opening there had been over twenty applicants. Captain Baker, to whom the final choice had been entrusted, had little difficulty in deciding when he saw the two well-known names in the list.

Very soon the position taken up by the three chums became untenable. Every yard the vessel travelled away from the shelter of the land the pitching and rolling grew worse, while the showers of spray which had been driving over the bows were replaced by huge waves which came curling over the side, swamping everything in their path.

Now that the excitement of their send-off had passed, and the difficulties of navigating the ship out of the harbour had been surmounted, Captain Baker found himself beginning to live in the past. His previous polar expedition, when his wife and little son had been at the starting-point to see him off, filmed across his mind . . . then came a mental picture of his only brother, who had been lost in the Antarctic while trying to fly to the Pole. How vividly he remembered his brother's only companion returning more dead than alive, and describing how the 'plane had been wrecked, their hopeless search for help, the dismal waiting in a snow-hut while food grew scarcer and scarcer, the death of the leader . . . and the almost miraculous escape of the survivor, through privations so terrible that his mind had gone blank and only a few misty details remained.

Fortunately his depressing thoughts, which could help no one, were cut short by the necessity for action. Out in the open the wind was blowing half a gale, and the sea, which was only "choppy" near land, was becoming rougher every moment. The *Queen of the Antarctic*, loaded right down to the plimsoll with stores and equipment, was unable to demonstrate her normal seaworthiness, and instead of riding easily over the huge waves, every now and then she fouled one with the result that a cascade of water went hurtling along the decks, washing her almost from stem to stern. This necessitated the utmost care in navigation, and Captain Baker quickly forgot his vain regrets as he concentrated every faculty upon his task.

As each wave deluged the decks the water penetrated into every nook and cranny; as it did so a chorus of dismal howls came from below, where nearly two hundred Eskimo dogs were housed in readiness for the long sledge journeys over ice and snow. Although used to the coldest conditions, these dogs hate water—so seldom met with in their native habitat—and were terrified at the novel surroundings in which they found themselves.

"Poor old Petz," exclaimed Alan as he heard the howls, "he will be scared stiff in this. I'll pop down and talk to him."

Conditions on deck were rapidly becoming worse, so all three boys made their way towards the dogs' quarters. Here, in a separate enclosure, slightly apart from the rest, Petz was howling loudly and looking the picture of misery. At the sight of his master, however, his howls ceased abruptly, and as Alan knelt down beside him, patting him and talking in a soothing tone, he quickly recovered his spirits and licked his friend's face. Ever since he had been a tiny puppy Petz had been Alan's special pet, and the two were almost inseparable.

The influence of human companionship was most striking, and, noting this, David turned to Frank.

"Let's go and see if we can quieten the rest of 'em, shall we?"

Before he could answer all three were hurled head-long, while water poured down every conceivable—and inconceivable—channel, half-drenching them and causing a fresh outburst of terrified howling.

Both David and Alan were quick to recover themselves. The latter hurried as best he could under the circumstances to his dog's side and proceeded to comfort him again. The former, with a grimace towards the canine chorus, sprang up, but was forced to grab at a support as another lurch upset his balance.

"Come on, Frank," he urged, "there'll be trouble with some of the brutes if we don't do something."

Realizing that there was no definite movement in Frank's direction, he glanced back over his shoulder. In one corner he saw a huddled heap, surmounted by an ashen face; a second look revealed tightly set lips and clenched hands, while a determined struggle to stand upright was obviously frustrated by paralysed muscles.

With a shrug of his shoulders David turned to Alan. " I'll go on and see what I can do," he called across. Then as he alternately ran and staggered forward he muttered under his breath, " Another attack of the blue funk, I s'pose."

For some years Frank had been an enigma to most of his acquaintances. At the first sign of danger he often appeared terrified and incapable of action. Yet at other times he would do the most foolhardy things and, quite unconsciously, hazard his very life. Only his parents and Captain Baker knew his bitter secret. When he was six years old his father had taken the family to live in Africa. Here, while they were exploring the bush, Frank had been carried off by a lioness and so badly mauled that his life had been despaired of. As the result of the wonders of modern surgery, however, he had been completely restored to health, except that no one could obliterate from his mind the ghastly memory of that time in a cave of lions. For years it remained a vivid nightmare, and when at last the picture became blurred the effect on his nerves persisted, with the result that he was quite unable to control himself on the sudden advent of danger. Nevertheless his constant and heroic efforts to overcome his nervousness resulted in a " daring " complex, which explained—to those in the know—his spasms of foolhardiness.

At the present moment he was a tragic demonstration of the all-too-frequent fact that " the spirit is willing but the flesh is weak."

Gladly would he have followed David and risked all the dangers, both imaginary and otherwise, but the storm had infused him with terror and he was practically incapable of movement.

As the day wore on the storm increased in fury. The wind shrieked through the rigging—the *Queen of the Antarctic* was a clever combination of the most up-to-date sailing vessel and steamer—while frequent gusts of wind buffeted the ship until it was forced, momentarily, out of its course. The sea, as most know it, had vanished, and they were travelling through a country of stupendous mountains, alternating with deep valleys, but all made of water and constantly on the move. At one moment they were making slow progress in an aqueous basin, surrounded by mountains of water which seemed to touch the sky. Then a sloping wall rushed towards them, and they began to climb up and up and up to the very clouds, tilting until to turn upside down appeared inevitable. The next moment the ship was balancing on the top of the mountain, only to dive head-first down the steep declivity and into another valley. As a variation, the mountainous wave would sometimes curl over before they reached the crest, hurling hundreds of tons of water on to the decks, creating widespread confusion and renewed outbreaks of howling.

No one was allowed on deck except those who were vital to the navigation of the vessel. In actual fact, few desired to be there. Of the twenty scientists and explorers on board, few could leave their bunks, while even some of the hardened crew failed to report for duty.

" How much of this is there before we sight land ? " asked Alan rather dismally as darkness began to blot out the wild seascape.

David had long since found that his bunk was the safest place. " 'Bout two days more, I think, before we reach Macquarie Island . . . at least, we were to be about eighty hours, but I expect this storm will delay us, so——"

His sentence was interrupted by one of the crew, who looked in to ask if any of the boys could help to man the pumps. " Stokehold flooded and steam-pumps choked," were his parting words.

CHAPTER II

THE FIRST BASE

THROUGHOUT the night the storm continued to rage with unabated fury. Meanwhile every available hand was needed to take turns at the pumps. Not until daybreak did the engineers succeed in finding the source of trouble and in removing it. Then, just as the steam-pumps were put into operation once more, the wind began to drop and conditions to improve steadily. Very thankfully all who were not actually required for duty returned to their bunks to turn the day into night.

It was a new world to which they awoke. From a cloudless sky the sun was shining brilliantly upon a blue sea—still running mountains high, but without the foam-crested breakers. The wind had sunk almost to a dead calm, and there appeared every prospect of the scene resuming its normal state within forty-eight hours.

Captain Baker, who had been on the bridge con-tinuously for twenty-four hours, was now able to hand over the responsibility to his second in command. On the way to his cabin he looked in on the three boys.

" Up again already ? " he asked approvingly, seeing that David and Alan were dressing. In the third bunk he saw a still helpless form, and called back cheerily :

" Buck up, Frank, we're out of the wood now. Sun-shine everywhere and sea's calming down like a house on fire."

As the door shut behind him David turned a smiling face to Alan.

" Bit mixed in his metaphors your Dad, isn't he ? "

14

Alan laughed. "'Spect you'd be a bit mixed if you'd been on duty for twenty-four hours in that storm."

With an effort Frank soon pulled himself together, and the three chums hurried to the upper deck to enjoy the glorious view of endless sea bathed in uninterrupted sunshine. Although the temperature was sinking steadily as they approached the northern limit of icebergs, the change was less noticeable owing to the pleasanter conditions, and, as the duties which had been allotted to them were so far light, the three boys proceeded to enjoy themselves in exploring their home-to-be and in energetic deck games.

Consequently when Captain Baker emerged from his cabin, the first sound he heard was the pattering of footsteps and a roar of boyish laughter.

"No need to ask who that is," he smiled to his fellow-officer. "You'll always know when David Somervell is about. His laugh would wake the Seven Sleepers."

His companion nodded pleasantly. "Sounds like it, certainly. Not a bad thing for us that we've got these boys on board, I reck'n. Laughter is infectious, and we'll be up against some pretty rough times on this trip unless I'm mistaken. . . . Help to keep us young, eh?"

"Yes, we'll need it as you say—there he goes again . . . just hark at that! You'd think he hadn't a care in the world." Both paused to listen to the high-spirited youths, then Captain Baker went on, "And yet, despite his apparent light-heartedness, he's really a most studious lad. Quite smart at science; carried off several prizes at school for chemistry and physics. And he's very thoughtful for others. What's more, he has the unusual virtue of being able to be perfectly serious whenever the occasion demands. Just my ideal of a boy, that. Hope Alan'll grow up like him. In fact that was one reason which influenced me in choosing him; I thought his companionship would be good for Alan. . . ."

"Why did you choose Ingram?" broke in his hearer. "He's so . . . well, quite different from the other two."

Captain Baker gazed pensively across the ocean wastes for some moments. " Yes, he is. *Officially* I chose Ingram because he has studied bacteriology, and, as you know, one of the aims of the scientists on board is to investigate the bacteria—if any—in the polar ice and snow. . . ."

" But could germs, or whatever you call them, live in such intense cold ? " interrupted the officer.

" Oh yes, easily. Bacteria are killed by heat, but never by cold as far as we know. Why, I read somewhere that they have been immersed in liquid hydrogen —about two hundred and fifty degrees below zero, that is—and they came out alive and kicking. But let me see, where was I ? Oh, I know. I was saying that I picked him on account of his knowledge of bacteriology. But unofficially I decided to take him because I thought it would help him. I know what you're thinking—that he's scared out of his life at the slightest danger. But there's a special reason for that. He's really making a splendid effort to overcome it, and I think that the constant companionship of the other boys, and the dangers of this trip, will help him more than anything else could do."

At this moment a ball came hurtling along the deck, followed by three flying forms who nearly catapulted into the officers. By dint of gymnastic contortions, however, an actual collision was averted, and as David turned to apologize Captain Baker waved a hearty greeting and the two officers continued their way towards the bridge.

Fortunately the weather remained gloriously fine and calm, with the result that, with deep sea all around for hundreds of miles, the difficulties of navigation were reduced to a minimum. Captain Baker foresaw in this fact an ideal opportunity to call every one together in order to explain the objects and duties of the voyage. Nor did he lose any time in putting his plan into action —he was, above everything else, a man of quick and

(4,766)

" Laughter is infectious."

accurate decision. Consequently, at 2 p.m. on the third
day after leaving Hobart, a large gathering collected on
deck, and, as soon as every one was settled, Captain
Baker addressed them.

At first the three boys found their attention wander-
ing while the speaker outlined the duties of the crew
and a number of technical details. It was not until they
heard the words " objects of this trip " that they began
to sit up and take notice.

"The objects of this trip," he was saying, "are, in the main, fivefold." Here he paused and consulted in low tones with the leader of the scientific party. "Before I go on to discuss our objects," he continued, "Doctor Elliot thinks that it might be as well if I say something first about the ship itself and the history of this expedition. It has, of course, long been public knowledge that the main scheme originated with the League of Nations. Realizing what a lot of nasty feeling had been caused in the past by competitive polar explorations, often resulting in international jealousy on account of annexation of new territory, and foreseeing increased difficulties arising from quicker modes of travel, the League decided to fit out an international expedition. Several important problems were selected for investigation, and the results of our experiments, as well as details of any land charted, will be submitted to the League, who will decide in the usual way as to whom is to benefit by the discoveries. From this you will understand that nothing of any importance must be communicated to any one until the League has published its report. Now, as I said, our objects are five in number and are as follows.

"Firstly, to search for and map out any new land ; but, especially, to decide the vexed question as to whether there is a definite Antarctic continent or not. Secondly, to check the exact position of the South Pole. Although this was reached by both Amundsen and Scott, there is some doubt in many people's minds as to the actual spot. Moreover, undoubted evidence was found by Shackleton, Priestley, and others of the existence of coal and fossilized wood in these regions, indicating quite clearly that there must have been a flora at some previous time. Scientists doubt, however, whether a flora could flourish when five out of twelve months would be in almost continuous darkness. From this some hold the theory that the Pole has shifted, and accurate determinations of carefully marked positions may at some future date throw interesting light upon this problem. Thirdly, we have been asked to make a detailed analysis of polar ice and snow with the special object of deciding whether it contains any ' heavy water,' as the new product of heavy hydrogen and heavy oxygen is termed. Fourthly, to search for and identify any bacteria which are to be found in these regions. Fifthly—and I think that this object will interest the non-scientists most—to investigate a new element. It appears that the Smith-Crayton expedition, which returned last year, brought back some specimens of a mineral deposit which they found near Mount Erebus —one of the two active volcanoes known in these parts. On analysis this so-called mineral proved to be an element. It is, in fact, an unknown metal very similar to platinum, only lighter in weight and very much more useful ; consequently it should be even more valuable. Our job is to find this deposit if we can, and discover its extent. The League has decided that all money resulting from the sale of any of this deposit which we may be able to take back with us will be divided among all those on the ship."

From a distance the *Queen of the Antarctic* was apt to present a twofold but very contradictory appearance. Under normal conditions she was an up-to-date steamer, although her masts and rigging were somewhat of an anomaly. With all sails set, however, the funnel was often hidden, and she might have been mistaken for a very large old-time sailing ship, which impression was augmented by the crow's-nest high up on the fore-mast.

It was from this crow's-nest that, shortly before midday on the fourth day, a cry rang out which sent every one rushing to the bows.

" Land-ho ! "

Shading their eyes from the glare of the sun, the anxious watchers saw what might have been a small cloud low down on the horizon. Very soon the outline grew more and more distinct, until those who had been there before recognized the twenty-mile long Macquarie

Island, bordered by a desolate coast rising abruptly to a height of about one thousand feet.

As they neared the shore, Alan was sweeping the scene with a pair of binoculars—borrowed from his father—when he suddenly exclaimed :

" What on earth—what—David, what the dickens are all those little people doing ? There's a terrific crowd on the beach."

So far David could see nothing except the dim outline of the beach, backed by higher ground.

" Can't be a crowd of people *there*. Lend us the glasses," he replied rather mystified.

A moment later he clapped the binoculars to his eyes, and as he did so he burst out laughing.

" *Little people*, that's good ! They're penguins, Alan ; not people. They always walk upright, and that makes them look like human beings from a distance."

Taking the glasses in turn they gazed fascinated at the beach, parts of which were literally covered with thousands of penguins, for which this island is famous. On landing the three rushed along the shore and examined them at close quarters, and many a roar of laughter rang out as they watched the queer antics both on land and as they plunged—or flopped would describe it more accurately—into the sea. Farther along they saw what they took to be a huge crowd of seals, but later they were joined by several of the scientists, who pointed out the difference between seals, sea-lions, sea-tigers, sea-leopards, and sea-elephants, all of which abounded along the shore but which differed only slightly in their anatomy.

Petz, who had landed with Alan, accompanied him everywhere, and quickly showed his joy at being on shore again by rushing about and barking (if barking it could be called). He was the only dog allowed to be free, on account of the risk of worrying the penguins and other animals, but all the dogs were taken off the ship and exercised.

For several days every one was kept busy, the crew

cleaning and reorganizing the ship, the scientists making copious notes, while all took turns to land the stores which would form a reserve for the return trip.

A strange quietness brooded over the scene as they left the island. Except for faint sounds from the penguins, or an occasional order by one of the ship's officers, the only sound came from the propeller. All who were not actually at work were lined along the sides, or standing at the stern, gazing half-longingly at the rapidly diminishing blur in the distance.

Frank expressed the almost universal thought when he turned to his chums as they sat on coils of rope just above the propeller.

" Seems curious to think that that's the last land we shall see for weeks, p'r'aps months . . . and that we may not touch habitation again for over a year."

David nodded. " 'Mm, yes, 'tis a bit weird. From now on we shall live in a world of ice and snow, 'normous bergs . . . continents of ice in fact . . . and we shall be the only living human beings within hundreds of miles. No trees, no grass, and very few animals except seals and penguins."

" Have you noticed how much colder it is since we left land ? " asked Frank.

Alan nodded. " Yes. I happened to notice the thermometer under the bridge. It's dropped ten degrees since we left Macquarie Island."

" And how early it gets light ! " added Frank. " I woke up this morning at three o'clock and it was quite light ; and I'm almost sure it didn't get dark until after ten last night. That meant there was less than five hours darkness."

Alan was stroking Petz. All sign of land had vanished while they were talking. After a brief silence he spoke.

" Dad says the days will get longer and longer rapidly now until it'll be light for the whole twenty-four hours."

" Light for twenty-four hours ! Great Scot, that'll be weird if you like ! " gasped Frank.

" And if we stop there long enough it'll be dark for twenty-four hours," continued Alan, smiling at the look of discomfiture on his chums' faces.

The *Queen of the Antarctic* had now entered the zone where icebergs were to be expected, and watch was kept continuously from the crow's-nest. At night-time speed was reduced considerably, and powerful searchlights assisted both helmsman and outlook. A drop of thirty degrees since leaving Macquarie Island provided an additional warning if such were needed.

Suddenly from the air above came the shout, " A large iceberg ahead, sir ! "

A rush was made for the bows, and a few minutes later a misty object was seen ahead which soon resolved itself into a huge mass of ice.

" What a whopper ! " exclaimed David. Turning to one of the crew at his side, he inquired, " What's the size of that one, d'you reckon ? "

The man addressed gazed at the iceberg as if measuring it with his eye.

" 'Bout half a mile long and nearly a quarter wide ; quite a small one that."

" And height ? "

" Over a hundred feet—above the water, that is. But don't forget that there's gen'rally eight times as much under the water as shows above. So you may reck'n that berg's nigh on a thousand feet from top to bottom."

Unknown to those below, the man in the crow's-nest had seen something else—something which might have surprised them had they been in his place.

From his perch aloft he could see miles beyond the horizon of those on deck, and, dead in their path, he had sighted an unmistakable wall of ice. It was not for him to decide whether this was merely a huge iceberg or whether it might be the ice barrier ; but, as it was the end of his watch, he resolved to report personally to the captain. With this end in view, he left the crow's-nest and began his descent immediately after handing over to the relief man.

Hearing a shout he—unwisely—let go with one hand and looked down. Almost simultaneously the ship collided with a large mass of ice, which had been unobserved in the growing mist, causing an impact which made it tremble from stem to stern. From the ship's point of view it was of little consequence—the bows were specially constructed for such, and worse, impacts—but to the man, taken unawares, it was critical. Jerked sideways, he lost his hold, and the horrified spectators below saw him come hurtling through the air.

CHAPTER III

AMONG THE BERGS

IT was a horrible moment of suspense. As their brains worked with cinematograph-like rapidity, they saw him—in imagination—fall headlong to the deck, there to lie crushed and broken. Then to their amazement they realized that he was still aloft, clinging desperately to a rope and swinging from side to side with every roll of the ship. As he fell the vessel had lurched sideways, with the result that his fall had been momentarily broken by one of the spars, from which he had again slipped. With wonderful presence of mind, however, he had clutched at the nearest rope, and had not clutched in vain. His hands closed over it, and after an arm-wrenching jerk he found himself hanging in mid-air, fifty feet above the deck.

At once all was commotion. Unless he could be rescued very quickly his arms would never stand the strain, and he must drop to almost certain death. But the problem of rescue was a formidable one. Owing to the angle of the ship when he fell, the rope to which he was clinging was not near enough to any mast or ladder for any one to reach him ; nor would it be of any use to throw him a rope—in his precarious position it would be impossible for him to do anything with it even if he caught it. The position seemed hopeless.

It was Captain Baker's alert mind which saved the man's life. A sharp order sent several of the crew hurrying below, to reappear a moment later with a large tarpaulin sheet. No second bidding was necessary to secure the help of every one within hail, and very soon the sheet, held firmly by over twenty pairs of strong arms, was underneath the dangling man.

Even so the chances against the unfortunate victim appeared to be enormous. It would be no easy feat to drop from such a height from a stable perch, but with the ship rolling from side to side the alternatives of the slightest misjudgment were to fall into the icy water or be mangled upon the deck.

But Captain Baker had his megaphone to his lips. With a few clear, curt words he warned the man on no account to let go until he gave the signal—and then to act promptly. The suspense to those watching was awful. Would his arms hold out until the crucial moment ? Would he be able to take full advantage of the captain's warning ? Even if he did, an unexpected lurch might frustrate all their well-planned efforts. Why was the captain waiting so long ?

Suddenly the word " Go " rang out clearly through the air, and they saw a body come hurtling down. At first it looked as if he would miss the deck altogether and fall into the sea. The next moment they felt the vessel rolling sharply, and realized that the captain had foreseen this and had judged the moment to a nicety. Just as the falling man reached the level of their heads, the sheet came exactly under him. Moreover, the captain's warning as to how to jump had been precise and clear—the man fell into the sheet with bent legs and landed upon his back. At first the strain upon those holding it was terrific and the man bounced high into the air. Then he was gently lowered to the deck and willing arms hurried him below. Twenty-four hours later he was none the worse for the incident except for strained muscles in his arms and back.

" Look at those gorgeous bergs ! " exclaimed David, slapping Alan and Frank on the shoulder and pointing southwards just as the men began to return to their normal routine. Almost unnoticed in the excitement,

the number of icebergs had increased rapidly, and masses
of ice of all shapes and sizes were floating around them.
Every now and then the bows fouled an extra large
ice-lump and with a grinding, crackling noise cleft it
asunder.

" Aren't they topping ! " agreed Alan, after all three
had gazed spellbound for some moments. Suddenly
Frank pointed excitedly, " Look at that one—looks just
like the Tower Bridge ! Wish we could go right through
that arch ! "

The object at which he was pointing was a magnificent
piece of Antarctic sculpture. Rising out of the sea to a
height of over a hundred feet was a glittering iceberg
more than a hundred yards long. Through the centre
was a colossal archway, large enough to allow the *Queen
of the Antarctic* to pass through, if the masts had been
shortened somewhat. Made almost incandescent by the
glare of the sun, it heaved sedately up and down, or
occasionally sideways, radiating as it did so the most
wonderful rainbows of colour—spectra caused by the
splitting of the sunlight by the unequal surfaces of the ice.

Alan's attention was riveted upon the spectacle.

" *Isn't it great !* " he murmured. " Yes, it would be
thrilling to go right through. Wouldn't do, though ; it
might be solid ice under the surface."

The remaining hours of daylight were spent by all
who were off duty in gazing awestruck at the marvellous
and ever changing ice panorama around them. Square
blocks, flat islands, atolls, pyramids, arched and turreted
masses, weird and fantastic forms, and much-crevassed
specimens floated by. Several miles away was what the
outlook had suspected to be the ice barrier. Completely
obscuring all further view, there stood up a wall of ice,
which, nevertheless, was nothing more than a monstrous
iceberg over twenty miles long and rising towards the
clouds to a height of one hundred and fifty feet.

As they rounded a medium-sized berg the watchers
caught their breath. For some moments they felt they

must be dreaming as the matchless spectacle burst upon their sight. Owing to the curious formation of a tall iceberg, the sun's rays were more than usually concentrated upon its sloping surface, with the result that parts of it had been thawed day after day, the process being arrested during the cooler periods. Instead of melting equally, tall columns of ice had been formed, leaving a cluster of pinnacles uppermost. As the sun shone upon these, its slanting rays were broken up by each ice-candle into all the colours of the spectrum, until from dozens of points the light was radiated in vivid beams of red, orange, yellow, green, blue, indigo, and violet. The resulting effect was as if some chandelier of giant and beautifully cut lustres had been placed in the brilliant sunlight, and as the ship steamed slowly past, the collection of ever-changing spectra flashed and scintillated until the very air seemed to be on fire.

None of the boys spoke until the vision had passed. Then Frank expressed a wealth of meaning in a few words.

" And they call that *nature* ! "

For the next few days there was not a dull moment. After the isolated bergs came the drift-ice with its large and small masses, through which at times they were able to steam rapidly by selecting channels of varying width, while at others they were compelled to force a passage slowly—often foot by foot—through extensive sheets of thick ice.

But if interest had not been lacking during this period they soon had a surfeit of excitement. A particularly fine berg drew the attention of the scientists, who decided to obtain some close-up photographs and to make a number of detailed observations by means of one of the small lifeboats.

" You three boys can come along," announced Doctor Elliot, adding, as if by way of explanation, " You can be more easily spared than some of us and you'll be less weight for the boat."

The chums needed no second bidding, and in due course the boat was lowered, filled with passengers and equipment, and pushed off.

Ten minutes' rowing brought them to within a few feet of their goal, and as they shipped oars they saw towering above them a sheer wall of ice over a hundred feet high, stretching for some distance on either side ; at such close quarters it was very painful to stare at the sunlight reflected back from the polished surface, which glare was unbroken save for a few multi-coloured points where a spectrum was produced by the chipped or partially melted exterior.

Without further delay the scientists got busy. Assisted by the boys, some photographed the berg from different angles, while others took measurements or noted the desired details.

During an interval Frank sat gazing at the summit. After a few moments he turned to Alan.

" Look, Alan ! *There's* a curious optical illusion, if you like. If you stare up at the top it looks just as if it was toppling over."

" Things often do when you look up at the clouds," replied Alan dreamily, quite oblivious of the fact that there were no clouds.

But a few stray words had reached David's ears as he wielded an oar to counteract the drift of the boat.

" What's that, Frank ? Toppling over ? Clouds ? There *are* no clouds, man ! "

As he glanced up casually he suddenly dropped the oar and shouted in tones of alarm :

" Look out—the berg's overturning ! "

Although most of the men concluded that his imagination was running riot, they one and all looked up. Then consternation seized them. To every one it was now perfectly obvious that the huge mass of ice was tilting away from them at a steadily increasing angle, and that in a few minutes it would turn partially or completely upside down.

And beneath them—rising rapidly—was a mass of ice eight or nine times as large as that in front of them! As the berg overturned, it would occupy an area of well over a quarter of a square mile!

"Back for your lives!" roared the officer in charge.

With commendable promptness each rower seized an oar and began to strain every nerve in a race with death.

With wild eyes staring at the receding wall, and muscles strained to breaking-point, each rowed with the energy of desperation.

Nevertheless the race was lost before it was begun. Despite their frenzied efforts, the rate of tilting increased rapidly, while the water around them began to heave and boil as if disturbed by a submarine earthquake.

David's brain was working hard. It was obvious now that catastrophe must overtake them almost immediately, and the only hope lay in being prepared. What would happen when the berg overturned? he asked himself. Something like seven or eight hundred feet of ice will rise rapidly beneath us and hurl boat and all . . . where? Would it hurl them in the direction in which it was revolving, or in the opposite direction? Or, would the wash of the disturbed water dash them sideways? If they were precipitated high into the air to fall spreadeagled into the icy water, there was little hope for any one. And what if they came down on ice? Anyway, he must be prepared.

"Take a deep breath when you are thrown into the water, and strike out hard immediately you go under," he advised his two chums.

Suddenly he saw the berg collapse, and prepared to follow out his own advice.

But as so often happens none of his "nicely calculated plans" came to fruition, and it was the unexpected which happened.

The iceberg was turning over because its centre of gravity had shifted. Collision with other bergs had

broken off large pieces of its under-sea structure, and
this, aided by the wearing action of the water—its
warmth augmented by an unusually long period of
sunshine—had reduced the weight of the under-sea
portion until it became top-heavy.

Even as he leant forward to shout a final warning
into his chum's ear, David saw the berg sink nearly
parallel with the water ; simultaneously the sea heaved
upwards, the boat began to rise, and he felt himself
jerked into the air . . . then falling, falling.

Plunged beneath the icy liquid, he involuntarily
began to gasp for breath. For a moment he felt as if he
were in a straitjacket, owing to the benumbing effect of
the intense cold. Then the desire to live reasserted itself
and he struck out vigorously. It seemed a long way up,
and he wondered how deep he had sunk ; another
energetic kick and his head struck something hard, after
which he rose, half-dazed, to the surface.

It took him an appreciable time to recover his full
senses and breath. At last he was able to look around.
To his joy he saw the boat still floating near him, and in
it were two men who were helping one of their comrades
over the edge. A little distance away he saw three
figures, among whom he recognized Alan, swimming
strongly for the boat—an example which he quickly
followed. Hardly had he taken three strokes, however,
when he noticed several more heads bob up ; then he
spotted something dark floating on the other side of him,
and to his horror recognized the inert form of Frank.

The sight of his chum quickly energized him and he
fairly leapt through the water ; just as Frank was
sinking he grabbed at his collar, and turning on his
back, swam to the boat, dragging his burden with him.

Several pairs of willing hands were waiting to pull
them to safety, and, after supporting his unconscious
chum until he saw him disappear into the boat, he
scrambled aboard.

There was no time to think about being tired or cold,

Helping one of their comrades over the edge.

and Frank claimed his immediate attention. Then there
were others needing assistance ; by throwing a lifebelt to
one, or extending a helping hand to another, he was able
to do much in the feverish attempt at rescue. Meanwhile Frank had regained consciousness and lay in the
bottom of the boat, where Alan was endeavouring to
chafe some warmth into him.

During a pause David was able to look around, and
as he did so his eyes opened wider and wider until he
ended by whistling softly to himself. The scene which
met his gaze, although explaining clearly what had
happened, was indeed an extraordinary one. At first
sight it appeared as if they were floating—rather uneasily
—between two icebergs. To north and south, at a distance of about twenty yards, he saw an ice barrier some
ten feet high. One suggestive fact struck him at once :

both bergs moved in perfect harmony. There was only one explanation—which was supported by the curved shape of the faces—namely, that it was really one enormous iceberg with a deep channel in the middle.

Every one was anxious to return to the parent vessel as quickly as possible, but some delay was caused by the disappearance of a seaman. After searching vainly for a considerable time all hope was abandoned, and it was presumed that he must have been stunned, or otherwise injured, when thrown out of the boat, and have sunk before any one had seen him.

Turning to row back they saw another boat approaching the channel. Captain Baker had followed their progress through binoculars, and had witnessed the whole tragedy. Immediately he was assured that there were some survivors, he ordered off another boat with supplies of hot drink, warm blankets, and first-aid requisites. Fortunately the last named were not required, but during the return journey the drinks and blankets proved very acceptable to those who had to sit still in their rapidly freezing clothes.

Doctor Elliot was quick to realize the importance of keeping up their spirits, and endeavoured to interest them in an explanation of the cause of the accident.

" I expect you are wondering what happened," he began. " It was a miracle we were not all killed. Had that been the type of iceberg we imagined, and had it turned upside down as one would expect it to do, we should of course have been thrown high into the air and hurled some distance into the icy water. The boat would have been smashed, and any of us who were not already killed by the impact would have been drowned before help could have reached us." Wrapping his blanket more closely around him, he continued : " That berg was no doubt originally about nine hundred feet high from top to bottom, but the lower part had melted until it became top-heavy ; it had not, however, as usually happens, melted sufficiently to cause the mass to turn upside down. All that had happened was that the centre of gravity had shifted just enough to make the berg turn on to its side. Simultaneously a very unusual thing had occurred. A deep trough had been worn in the side of the berg. Perhaps its equilibrium was disturbed by the wash from our boat. Be that as it may, it turned over, and as the under-sea portion came up we were washed into the said trough, with the result that, although the disturbance caused by the sudden movements of such a colossal mass threw us into the air, the actual impact was reduced to a minimum. Meanwhile our lifeboat, instead of being smashed, remained floating, thus giving us a sporting chance of being rescued. And, thanks to the heroic efforts of some of you, we were . . . all except poor old Bob," he added as a sad look spread over his face.

On reaching the *Queen of the Antarctic* all were glad to change into dry clothes, and those who appeared likely to be affected by their unpleasant experience were advised to rest in their bunks for a time.

Frank had quickly recovered on the way back, and soon rejoined his chums on the deck as they gazed at the ice, which was steadily increasing in denseness. Although the surface of the ocean was strewn with small and large lumps, with here and there an iceberg projecting high above the rest, the ice was mostly of a loose character, and they were able to steam at full speed when desired.

All three boys were now kept very fully occupied in scrubbing the decks, polishing brass, coiling ropes, washing up crockery, and a hundred and one of the other jobs which form an essential part of the daily routine on board ship.

As they reached the region of pack-ice, larger and larger floes were encountered, consisting of masses of ice which had been broken off large sheets by the swell, but had not yet been recemented by the frost. It was while watching these that Alan suddenly exclaimed :

(4,766)

" Just look at that—there's an ice garden for you ! "

Well might he term it an ice garden. The fragments of ice, of all shapes and sizes, had been pressed together again, piling up upon each other and assuming weird and wonderful forms. Many had been forced into shapes resembling beautiful flowers, while others looked like animals gambolling among the floes. To complete the beauty of the scene, the sunlight played fantastically over the figures, lighting them up with dancing rainbow colours.

" Isn't it spiffing ! " exclaimed Frank.

" Think we'll call it the ' Antarctic Zoological Gardens,' " suggested David.

Conditions had changed steadily during the last few days. Each night they saw the sun sink below the horizon, only to reappear a few minutes later almost at the same spot, with the result that it was light for the whole twenty-four hours. Temperature had continued to drop as they penetrated farther south, and seldom rose much above the freezing-point.

Absorbed in the beauty of the immediate scenery, the boys had not looked far ahead. When at last Frank lifted his eyes, he called his chums' attention to a thick mist in the distance.

" Crumbs, so there is ! And how oily the water has got suddenly," was David's astonished reply.

Alan looked up quickly. " That means pack-ice. Dad was telling me only yesterday that we should probably run into pack-ice fairly soon now, and that you always know when it's coming by thick mist and an unusually calm sea."

Not long after he had spoken another huge berg loomed out of the mist. Over a mile long and higher than any they had yet seen, the astounding feature of this specimen was that worn right through it were three huge arches, nearly a hundred feet high. The spectacle was rendered fairy-like by the presence of hundreds of stalactites hanging from the roof of each. Illuminated by the sun's rays these emitted a veritable kaleidoscope of colours.

Unusually beautiful was the sunset that evening—if sunset it could be called when it was always daylight. As the ball of fire approached the horizon, its slanting rays lit up the ice in every direction, while from the snow-covered top of a large iceberg it was reflected back with dazzling brilliancy. As the ice lumps rose and fell in the slight swell, the many-hued sunbeams danced merrily across the water, while the mist enhanced the scene by producing many kinds of unnatural tints, thus giving their surroundings a weird and uncanny appearance.

For some days drinking water had been growing short, and their arrival among the pack-ice presented a favourable opportunity to take in a fresh supply.

" Why are we going so slowly ? " asked David of one of the seamen who was temporarily unoccupied.

Ted Smithers, the man addressed, glanced up at the bridge, rolled the quid of tobacco which he was chewing to one side of his mouth, and replied in blunt tones :

" Cap'n's looking for a landing-place. Water's runnin' short."

" Drinking water, d'you mean ? "

Ted nodded.

David looked puzzled. " But how on earth can we get drinking water on the ice? Don't find ready-made springs out here like you do on the South Sea Islands, surely ? "

Ted's face relaxed into the nearest approach to a smile which ever illuminated his weather-beaten features. " No, nor cannibals either. You jest digs out the ice and melts it."

It was clear that his hearer did not even yet grasp his full meaning, so, always ready to help any of the boys, he added :

" As soon as cap'n finds a large enough berg, we shall heave-to and lower a boat. A party of us'll land and dig out chunks of ice with pickaxes ; this'll be tipped into the tanks below and steam let in. Then . . . well you oughter know what happens then, with all your larning, or science, or whatever you calls it."

David laughed heartily at his explanation. " Thanks, Ted. *Now* I understand. The ice, of course, makes fresh water when it melts—I ought to have thought of that. At home we should never think of eating ice off a pond or river because of the danger of disease—risk of infectious bacilli Frank would say—but out here it's all so different, and the ice is perfectly safe."

It was now Ted's turn to gaze round in astonishment. " Ain't there no germs out here, then ? "

" No. Frank and I were talking to Mr. Hawlet, the bacteriologist, only yesterday. He was saying that as far as is known there are no infectious germs in the Antarctic. In fact there are very few indeed ; he says that although they can live quite easily they can't multiply at such low temperatures, so it's quite safe to drink the water from melted ice and snow."

At that moment the captain's telegraph rang in the crew's quarters and Ted hurried off. While they had been talking, the *Queen of the Antarctic* had rounded a large berg, disclosing a high long wall of ice ahead. Whether this was ice-covered land or only an extra large iceberg they could not yet determine, but Captain Baker decided that it would serve his purpose. Consequently, the ship was hove-to and a boat lowered. Into this dropped an officer, six of the crew, two scientists, and the three boys.

Landing was not so easy as it sounded, but after exploring along the ice cliff for some distance an inlet was discovered from where they could ascend to the top with the help of ropes and ice-axes.

All were thankful to land and stretch their legs after the rather cramped quarters of their floating home ; but for the boys it was a thrilling experience. It was the first time they had ever landed in these regions—except for a few moments on the ice-floe to make scientific observations—and it was a very novel adventure to find themselves standing on a snow-covered sheet of ice, one hundred feet above the sea-level, staring in one direction across the pack-ice at the *Queen of the Antarctic,* and in the other across miles of snow and ice. Above them was the sky which, except for a few tiny patches, was obscured by cloud.

The men, enjoying the warmth-producing exercise, set to with a will, and soon big lumps of ice went bumping down the slope to the beach. Here they were loaded into baskets, placed in the boat, and rowed out to the ship. At set intervals the men below changed places with the diggers, while the scientists spent the time in making meteorological, geological, and other observations. Meanwhile the three boys helped each party in turn, or, as a variation, ran races with Petz, who was greatly enjoying the unusual freedom.

During the afternoon an officer signalled from the ship that one more load would be enough, and as the last voyage started orders were given for all to be ready to embark immediately upon its return.

A blast from the siren warned them when the boat left the ship, and all those who had not already done so began to clamber down the slippery pathway.

Just as the boat was within hailing distance, the officer in charge of the landing-party gave a quick glance round to make sure that every one was ready and that the tools were handy for reloading. Suddenly his brow furrowed.

" Eleven ? I must have counted wrong," he muttered. " I'll count again. One . . . two . . . ten, *eleven* . . . . hallo, some one's missing."

Overhearing the soliloquy, David ran his eyes quickly over the group.

" Alan's missing ! " he gasped.

CHAPTER IV

NEARLY ICE-BOUND

THINKING that he must have stayed at the top, not realizing that they were ready to start, he shouted to him to hurry down. When there was no response, and the boat was almost at the landing-place, David and Frank climbed up as hastily as they could to find him.

" Expect . . . he was . . . out of earshot," panted David.

Almost breathless, they stood once more at the summit and gazed across the white wilderness—a wilderness both of verdure and humanity.

" Where *can* he be ? " gasped David. " I'm sure he was with us when we were digging that last load of ice."

" The last I saw of him was when he set off over there with Petz," pointing away from the sea, " I think he wanted to give him a final run before we went back to the ship," volunteered Frank.

David started off in the direction indicated. " Let's follow up his tracks," he suggested.

But it soon proved hopeless. At first, near the scene of operations, the snow was trampled almost flat. Then they found one pair of footmarks which resembled Alan's leading off at a tangent. Beside the human track was a second one—indistinct, but obviously that of a dog.

" Why, Petz, of course. And he's vanished too ! " bewailed David.

Pressing forward in an attempt to follow the double trail they were quickly baffled. The strong wind had blown the loose snow along, completely obliterating the tracks.

For once Frank was the more practical of the two. " Let's call Petz," he suggested.

Uniting their voices, they shouted the dog's name as loudly as they could. For some time there was no result, but just as several men arrived at the top—anxious at the prolonged absence of the boys—a faint speck was seen in the distance, and very soon Petz rushed up to them. But of his master there was not the slightest sign.

It was obvious that the dog was in a state of great excitement. Barking and whining loudly, he jumped up at David and then rushed back several yards in the direction from which he had come. Finding that they did not follow, he trotted up to Frank and tugged at his clothes.

" I believe he's trying to lead us somewhere," suggested Frank, starting off after him.

Quicker and quicker grew the pace, until both boys were running as fast as their thick clothes would allow ; even then, the dog kept well ahead.

Suddenly Petz stopped, looked down at the ground, and barked excitedly. Hurrying up, the boys saw a crevasse in the snow several feet wide. Was *that* where Alan was ? they wondered.

Kneeling down, David shouted into the abyss. To his joy, an answering call came back.

" Hallo . . . I'm down here," and they recognized Alan's voice.

" Are you hurt, old chap ? " asked David anxiously.

" Not much, I think ; but I'm nearly frozen."

While Frank held him, David lowered his head into the crevasse and stared into the darkness. Very faintly he could discern the huddled figure of his chum.

" What on earth are we to do ? No ropes, no ladder, and we certainly can't climb down, and he can't get up," he moaned.

By this time several of the men had arrived upon the scene, and taking in the position at a glance, one of them rushed back for a rope.

It seemed ages before they saw him returning with a long coil of stout rope over his shoulder.

" I'll go down," volunteered David. Then seeing a rather mystified look upon his hearers' faces, he added by way of explanation, " Of course, we could let the rope down and leave him to tie it round himself ; but I think it would be safer if one of us goes down in case he's hurt. Besides, his hands will be numb by now, and he'll hardly be able to tie a knot safely. I'm the lightest, so you c'n let me down ; I'll fix a bowline under his arms and you can pull me up after he's safe at the top."

It seemed a wise suggestion, so David was lowered very slowly into the dark and eerie crevasse. Presently came the first signal—one tug, indicating that he was safe on the ledge beneath. To the anxious rescuers it was a long wait before three sharp jerks told them that the rope was securely fixed round the half-frozen boy.

Meanwhile, in strange contrast to the silent anxiety of the men, Petz was almost frantic. Looking down into the abyss into which his master had vanished, he barked loudly ; then, after running round in circles, he would gaze pathetically up at Frank as if imploring him to hurry up and do something, only to rush towards the edge again, where the onlookers expected every moment to see him dive headlong after his friend.

At last the rope, with its semi-conscious burden, was hauled to the surface, where willing hands hastened to examine the patient. Slight shock due to the fall, numbness and frostbite, were fortunately his only injuries, and after first-aid treatment on the spot he was able to walk, supported on either side, to the boat.

The dog's joy at seeing his master safe and sound again was most striking, and he resolutely refused to leave his side even when Alan was put to bed for twenty-four hours in his cabin.

During the water expedition Captain Baker had been growing steadily more anxious. When the first boat put off the ship was in fairly thick pack-ice, but a strong wind

He was able to walk, supported on either side, to the boat.

had kept the ice moving so that plenty of channels remained. Very soon, however, the wind began to drop and to shift to another quarter, the result being that the channels slowly disappeared while the ice was blown round the ship, there to cement together in ever larger slabs. The delay caused by Alan's mishap was at a critical time, and when he finally arrived on board, his father was in the crow's-nest surveying their surroundings for the best way out. A message flagged from the shore had informed him that his son's injuries were not serious, so he deferred seeing him until the *Queen of the Antarctic* was safely out of the danger zone.

At first it was difficult to make any headway against the imprisoning ice, but after backing and going full-speed ahead several times, a channel was slowly forged with much crackling and rending as the ice was split apart. Finally a moderately wide " lead " was reached and the ship was steered due south once more.

Christmas and New Year's Day—each with its own celebrations according to the nationality and customs of the international crew—had long since come and gone, and every day was bringing them nearer the Great Ross Sea. Despite occasional patches of well-channelled ice, progress was mainly very slow and difficult. After the pack-ice a larger kind of ice—ice-floe—was encountered. Standing in the bows were the three boys, one of the scientists, and the inevitable Petz.

" What's the difference between pack-ice and the ice-floe, sir ? " asked Frank.

The officer pointed behind them. " The ice we've been coming through for the last few days is pack-ice. Drift-ice, as you probably know, is just smallish pieces of ice which drift about freely ; when these are packed together in loose masses it is called pack-ice. But as we get farther south the sea is frozen completely over. Where the crust is only thin a swell will often crack the ice and break it into large pieces somewhere about a hundred yards square. The thickness, of course, varies tremendously—anything from a few feet to fifty feet or more. This is the ice-floe."

For several days after this they lived in a world of ice, with the temperature at twenty degrees below freezing-point. At times it seemed as if the vessel could never stand the long succession of shocks, as lump after lump was hit and either split into fragments or forced aside ; at others, the onlookers began to fear that the masts must go overboard. All around them, often within a stone's-throw, were huge icebergs towering above the floe, and sometimes above the ship itself, like colossal buildings of ice.

Then came a welcome change as the *Queen of the Antarctic* ran out of the floe into a stretch of open water —how large no one could say.

Simultaneously the weather improved, and a gentle breeze coupled with a sunny but cumulus-decorated sky made extremely pleasant conditions.

Suddenly a cry of " Whales ahead, sir ! " from the crow's-nest sent all who were free rushing to the sides. A few whales had already been sighted from time to time, but they always formed an attractive sight.   This time the watchers were well rewarded.

" There she blows ! " exclaimed one of the crew, who had been on several whaling trips.   " And there goes another ! " he added almost immediately.

At first many of them could see nothing, but as their eyes grew more accustomed to staring through the glare, they discerned the well-known spouting of a couple of whales.

" There's some more ! " shouted Alan in great excitement, pointing to the left of the others.   A succession of shouts proclaimed the discovery of more and more, until several dozen whales were observed ahead of them.   As they drew nearer it was seen that many of them were fine specimens of the giant Blue Whale, some of which were ninety feet long and must have weighed over a hundred tons.

While they were still watching the monsters of the deep, a curious phenomenon drew their attention towards the horizon.   The sky in the south-east was obscured by a thin layer of cloud ; this, near where the sea met the sky, was illuminated as if by the early sunrise.   Yet the sun was high in the sky !

For some time the three chums stared in amazement, thinking that it must be an optical illusion, but when the light grew steadily brighter and spread sideways and up-wards, they could stand the suspense no longer.   Turning round abruptly, David strode towards one of the crew— who had, he knew, been on several polar trips—and jerked out :

" What on earth's that light over there ? Looks like a sunrise or house on fire. Surely there's not *two* suns out here ? "

The man addressed guffawed loudly. " Two suns ! No, not unless . . . well, *you* know nothing about that condition, I hope. That's what we call ' ice-blink.' It's the light being reflected from a huge mass of ice . . . 'spect it's the ice barrier. We're nearly due there, any-way."

His remark was quickly confirmed by a shout from the crow's-nest, informing the captain that the look-out had sighted the Great Ice Barrier.

But before David could rejoin his chums a terrific impact sent them sprawling into the scuppers, while the ship heeled over sideways until it felt as if it could never right itself again.

" What happened ? " asked Alan with a wry face as he took David's proffered hand and struggled to his feet ; in this he was helped by the motion of the ship which, as the result of magnificent seamanship, was slowly tilting back to normal.

David was clinging tightly to a stanchion as he re-plied.

" Whales. I think one of the brutes mistook us for Carnera and tried to give us the K.O."

" Not a bad shot, either," smiled Alan as he rubbed his head ruefully.

" Wonder if it's damaged us ? "

Alan looked wise and shook his head. " No fear. Dad told me that this old bus would stand almost anything. You see, it's specially built to accept the challenges of all comers—in the iceberg class."

Although they said nothing about it, the impact had been so severe that it took the two chums an appreciable time to recover from the rough treatment. Presently, however, David glanced round in surprise, as if searching for some one.

" Where's old Frank ? " he rapped out.

Alan, too, had momentarily forgotten his existence. Now he failed to see any sight of him.

" I'll go and look," he volunteered.

His search proved to be an easy one. Peeping into the little deck-cabin close to where they stood, he saw Frank lying huddled up on the seat. His first glance showed him that his face was grey and that he was trembling from head to foot. As he had his face hidden in his hands, he did not observe Alan's entry.

Sitting down beside him, Alan gripped his hand and said sympathetically :

" Buck up, old chap. It was only a whale. No damage done."

" Only . . . a *whale*. I thought we'd been smashed by an iceberg and were sinking," was the tremulous rejoinder. With a plucky effort at self-composure he added, " Where's David ? "

Alan was not slow to read more into his question than appeared on the surface. " I'll fetch him," he offered with a cheery wave as he left the cabin.

An onlooker would have been sorely puzzled to explain the events of the next five minutes. As Alan disappeared, Frank sank back into the corner, a picture of misery ; but it was an upright, smiling youth who emerged a few minutes later with David and walked to the side of the boat to gaze at the ice blink, which was rapidly becoming more and more dazzling. Nevertheless the intense strain through which he was passing showed clearly in his eyes and the forced nature of his gaiety was not lost upon his chums.

Very soon their thoughts were torn abruptly from whales and accidents. Right ahead they could see the Great Ice Barrier rising sometimes to a height of over a hundred feet above the water-line.

It was a wonderful sight. In places, a sheer wall of ice barred their progress, above which they could see a mantle of snow as far back as the eye could reach. Farther east, however, the darker lines of a headland stood out clearly, the patches of snow showing up the land in sharp contrast.

All three were startled to hear a voice at their side. Turning, they saw Doctor Elliot smiling at their confusion.

" Wonderful sight, boys, isn't it ?   Interested ? "

" Rather, sir !   Can you tell us all about it ? " pleaded David.

" *All* about it ? " laughed the scientist.   " No, I don't think any one can tell you *all* about it.   In fact, no one knows very much.   The ice wall at which you are looking is called the Ross Barrier, after its discoverer, Sir James Ross, who first saw it in 1841—January 28th I believe was the exact date.   It stretches east for four hundred miles, and the barrier varies from almost sea-level to a hundred and sixty feet high.   I presume that you know that we are now in the Ross Sea ; from the headland we saw the day before yesterday—Cape Adare, I mean—it is four hundred miles to the barrier."

" Has it always been the same—the barrier, I mean ? " asked Frank, now absorbed in their discussion.

" That I can't say.   You see"—with a merry twinkle in his eye—"I wasn't here when Adam first saw it . . . but, to be serious, there seems a very strong probability that it does change more than one thinks—goes for occasional hikes, that is."

The speaker thoroughly enjoyed his hearers' mystification, and went on :

" According to measurements the barrier apparently moved back nearly forty miles between 1842 and 1911 ; what's more, it seems to shift quite frequently."

David was only too ready to link up with the doctor's humorous mood, and broke in, " Then if only it would be kind enough to shift far enough, we might reach the Pole by sea ! "

" That certainly *would* be convenient," was the jocose rejoinder.   Glancing at his watch, the doctor added, " Hallo, I must be off.   It's my turn of duty.   But quite apart from joking, boys, all I told you about the Ross Barrier is actual fact as far as these are known."

" Makes my eyes ache to look at it," remarked Frank as soon as their informant was out of earshot.

Alan looked up sharply. " Why, of course, what fatheads we are ! Dad specially warned us to start using our ice goggles as soon as we got to the ice barrier."

Before they had adjusted their green-glass spectacles they heard Doctor Elliot hurrying back.

" I quite forgot to show you the two volcanoes." Tapping Alan on the shoulder and pointing slightly west of south, he went on :

" See where the barrier face is fairly low, but above it the snow-covered surface rises steeply ? "

" Yes, sir."

" Well, that's Ross Island. Now look above that cloud over the island—can you see a conical-shaped hill ? "

" Ye-es, I think so."

" I can, quite distinctly," put in David.

"Good. Now that is Mount Terror, a dormant volcano. But if you look very carefully behind that you'll see another. . . ."

" Rather ! I c'n spot it," rejoiced Frank.

" The one behind is Mount Erebus, and it is still active."

The speaker was again turning away when David asked abruptly :

" Excuse me, sir, but how *big* is the ice barrier ? I think you said that the Ross Barrier is four hundred miles long ; but how deep is it ? "

Seeing that the boys were really deeply interested, the doctor ignored the rapidly passing time and proved a wonderful source of information.

" Yes, it is four hundred miles long—that is from South Victoria Land, or the land just behind Ross Island, to King Edward VII. Land over there "—pointing across the sea in a south-easterly direction—" but it extends inland, or southwards, I should say, for another four hundred miles. In fact, it stretches right to the mountains on the edge of what is known as the Polar Plateau. Some say that its area is a hundred and sixty thousand square miles—about the same area as France. It is, in fact, the largest ice sheet on earth."

David whistled in astonishment, but put still another question.

" One thing I'm not clear about, sir. Is it just a covering of ice on top of the land, or is it all one enormous . . . well, a kind of gigantic iceberg ? "

His question evidently intrigued the scientist.

" We should all like to know that," he explained. " Of course, there is a certain amount of land actually known ; also, even in the dreary wastes of snow and ice nearer the Pole, there are occasional jagged peaks of rock—nunataks, the geologists call them—which stick up out of the snow. But as for the rest, no one knows. Amundsen believed that the ice barrier rests on land, but Scott concluded that it is just a floating mass of ice. I think, however, that most of our scientists agree with Scott."

At this, Doctor Elliot hurried off at a trot, while the boys settled down to enjoy the scenery. The *Queen of the Antarctic* had now turned east, and was steaming slowly along within fifty yards of the barrier.

From this distance it was very noticeable how the different layers of ice showed, each seam being clearly defined. Moreover, the constant action of the sea had worn the face of the ice into caverns of all sizes, and in these penguins gambolled and dived.

" Great pip ! Just look at those ! " shouted Alan.

His excitement was called forth by the sight of the antics of a group of penguins, some of which were leaping along the surface just as a flat stone ricochets over calm water ; others dived from the caves or from blocks of ice, while many stared at the ship in a wonderfully tame and friendly manner.

In addition to the penguins, a number of seals and sea-lions were to be seen on the floating ice, most of which either gazed up with a " Queer fish those ! " expression or slid along the ice with a caterpillar kind of motion, finally flopping heavily into the water.

There was now little difference between so-called night and day, consequently it was thought that this would be a favourable opportunity to secure some views of Antarctic scenery, *taken in the midnight sun.*

Reaching a spot where there was a considerable amount of ice—forming a miniature ice-floe close to the barrier—it was decided to heave-to for several hours in order that the scientists might obtain some interesting photographs and make various observations.

Many others were glad of the chance to stretch their legs, among them the three chums. Alan was the most able photographer of the three, and almost immediately upon setting foot on the ice he blurted out :

" We're in luck ! There's a huge seal over there," pointing to a black object on the ice half a mile away. " Let's get a snap of it."

After being cooped up in the ship, David and Frank were only too keen on the idea. A walk over the broken ice always provided healthy and energetic exercise, while often it furnished them with unexpected adventure.

Setting off at a brisk rate they soon found that it was not so easy as it looked. Apart from the usual slippery nature of the surface, and the channels to be jumped, such ice has an uncomfortable habit of tilting with a sudden swell. This heaving may be due to the normal movement of the water beneath, or to the activity of some of the inhabitants of the ocean depths. Also, gaps too wide to leap may be encountered, necessitating a time-wasting detour.

Nevertheless, to the healthy adventure-loving youths these difficulties only served to add spice to the project, and puffing and blowing, they stepped eagerly towards the nine-foot-long specimen known as a Weddell seal. Alan had his camera, David was carrying a small bag for

(4,766)   4 specimens, and over Frank's shoulders was coiled the rope which they always took with them on such excursions —in case of accidents.

The photograph taken, they turned to enjoy the novelty of the beautiful Antarctic scene lit up by the midnight sun.

After conversing for some time about the main points of interest on land and ice, they turned their eyes towards the more open spaces of water.

" There's another seal," opined Frank, pointing to a small black patch which was moving slowly through the water.

No one answered for a moment. So little of the animal was visible that neither cared to express an opinion. Bit by bit the water seemed to fall away as, in reality, the object rose to the surface. Then a propeller-like fin shot up into the air.

" Whales ! " almost shouted Alan.

David's face was working with excitement as he turned to the speaker.

" You're in luck, old chap—they're killer whales or I'll eat my hat."

" No need ; they'll do that for you if they get a chance—and the owner," retorted Alan as he swung round and began to focus his camera.

But before he could do so the whale vanished. With a splash it dived abruptly into the depths and disappeared, leaving only a nasty swell which made the ice rock up and down.

" Oh, blow it ! Just my luck," complained the chagrined photographer. " Of course it *would* vamose just as I was ready. That's the first killer whale we've ever seen at close quarters, and it must go and try to show off how well it can dive just at the critical moment. It would have made a topping snap."

" Beastly swank, I call it. Jolly hard luck," sympathized David. " Never mind ; let's wait here and perhaps it'll pop up again."

Another was within six feet of David's leg.

They said afterwards that " it's not only walls that have ears—evidently the whale heard David's lament."

Just as he spoke the ice behind them shot into the air, some of it being splintered into tiny fragments, and the three boys were thrown violently on to their backs. As they struggled to get up—a very difficult proceeding while the slab of ice was heaving violently up and down—the blood froze in their veins.

Among the broken ice between them and the ship they saw six killer whales. Simultaneously a deafening hollow-sounding blare filled the air as the brutes all started to blow at once. Still more alarming was the fact that one of the killers had come up almost underneath them, and an enormous black and tawny head rose above the edge of the ice only a few feet away from where David was standing swaying dangerously from side to side. A pair of tiny, vicious eyes gazed hungrily at the prey, while a blast of fishy-smelling air enveloped them as the brute exhaled its pent-up breath. Mixed with the blast was the equally evil-smelling vapour condensing from its " spout." Uppermost was a cavernous mouth, each jaw of which was lined with terrifyingly powerful teeth. From head to fluke the monsters measured thirty feet.

To make matters worse, all six killers began to lash the water with their huge tail-fins, causing a bewildering convulsion of the elements and making the floes dance about like corks.

At first all three were paralysed at the sudden turn of events. If the floe should tip them off they would never be seen again—one bite from those ghastly teeth and all would be oblivion. The nearest killer was forcing its head higher and higher over the edge of the ice—another six feet and David's legs would be within its grasp.

CHAPTER V

FASCINATED, David stared back at the nightmare vision, then with an effort he spurred his brain into action.

What could they do ? There was little hope that their plight would be observed from the ship. Their direct line of escape was blocked by the six killers. Yet if they stayed where they were a few minutes longer . . . even now the floe was tilting dangerously towards the open mouth.

All at once he decided—and acted. After a feverish glance around he bawled to his chums :

" Follow me for your lives ! And don't slip or you'll be lost. One at a time on each lump."

With that he leapt on to the nearest slab of ice, in the opposite direction from the ship. From there he jumped from floe to floe, sometimes a distance of only a few inches, but at others as much as six feet, selecting a circuitous route which would eventually lead them back to the main party, while giving the killers a wide berth.

Partly to make sure of this latter point, and partly to assure himself that his chums were following safely, he paused in the centre of an extra large floe and looked round.

As he did so his heart sank into his boots. Only two blocks behind him were Frank and Alan, but close behind them were the six killers, hungrily chasing their prey.

David saw at once that it would be a race for life. When he started he had imagined that if they could succeed in finding a way round the whales all would be well. Now he realized that the position was far more critical than that. To this problem were added the dangers of slipping off the ice, misjudging a jump, or of a floe overturning.

" Hurry up for goodness' sake," he shouted back as he turned once more to pick out the least dangerous route.

The result of his urgent warning quickly became apparent. Alan and Frank, spurred to desperation, increased their speed. David, however, was forced to concentrate his attention upon the task of selecting a safe course. Consequently the two steadily overhauled their leader, and it was this fact which led to disaster—and nearly to tragedy.

Seeing that Alan was standing on the floe immediately behind him, waiting to jump, David failed to judge the next leap as carefully as usual. After a hurried spring he landed upon a rough part of the ice, slipped, and fell heavily with his foot twisted beneath him.

Alan paused anxiously, waiting for him to get up. Instead, he saw David rolling about, evidently in great pain. Then he struggled hard to rise, but only fell back with a loud moan. Trusting that the ice would hold two, Alan leapt across and knelt beside his chum.

" You two go on. I'm done. I've crocked my ankle. Can't move," gasped David.

Frank was already standing only a few feet away, not daring to jump lest he should endanger his two chums.

" What's up ? " he called.

A few words sufficed to enlighten him. While Alan was speaking, he had examined David's ankle, which had, he found, swollen to over double its normal size. He saw at once that it would be impossible for David to put his foot to the ground, let alone walk on it.

To all appearances they were up against a brick wall. Although only a short distance from the main ice-sheet, there was no way of transporting their injured comrade across the intervening stretches of water. Yet less than twenty yards away the swirl of water and crashing of ice heralded the rapid approach of their enemies.

Suddenly Frank revived their hopes. " I've got an idea. Jump to the next lump, quick, Alan ! "

Seeing no reason, but clutching at the new straw, Alan jumped across the three feet of water. Almost simultaneously Frank landed beside David.

Then Alan saw him slip the coil of rope over his head ; a moment later the curt command, "Catch it, Alan," was followed by one end of the rope. Hardly had he seized it when he saw Frank coil the rope round his body and sit down beside David, so that the latter could hold on to the rope.

" Pull for all you're worth," yelled Frank, pointing frantically.

Jerking round, Alan saw in a flash what was in his chum's mind. Between the floe on which he stood and the next one was a wide channel ; following this back, he realized that it led right up to the main ice. *If* he could pull hard enough, and steer the burdened floe correctly, he might succeed in hauling his chums to the edge, from where they could reach safety without difficulty.

Exerting all his strength, he drew the floe towards him. In a moment of inspiration he visualized the possibility of dragging the injured boy on to the adjacent floe and repeating the process. Equally quickly, however, he discarded the suggestion—the pressure on the edge of the lump would tilt it, and the patient, or perhaps all, might slip into the water with but one result.

Another moment and he was on the next fragment, pulling the burden into the wide channel. But for one boy to haul two heavier ones in addition to the ice soon proved hopeless. Already the nearest killer was forcing its way round the next floe but one.

" Leave *me* and save yourselves, quick ! " reiterated David.

" Never ! " affirmed Frank as he helped David to

wind the rope under his armpits and then leapt from floe to floe until he could catch the rope from Alan.

" You tear back and get help while I pull," he yelled. Noticing Alan's doubtful expression, he added, " We daren't both pull. These little floes won't bear two of us. Hurry up or it'll be too late," with an anxious glance at the turbulent water just behind him.

Fortunately, Alan saw the wisdom of this suggestion, and quickly leapt the few remaining gaps, after which he raced across the snow-covered ice towards the *Queen of the Antarctic.*

His thoughts were despondent as he ran. Long before he could hope to reach the ship the killers would have surrounded the floes and their burdens. Then what would happen ? A slip . . . a tilt . . . a heave from underneath . . . what would the rescuers find when they arrived ?

It was a terribly exhausting journey. After his recent exertions the half-mile over slippery snow and ice—the former sometimes a foot deep—seemed like ten, but as he reached a group of men nearly a hundred yards from the ship he gasped out his story.

The return journey was a blur. Exhaustion mingled with despair to benumb his senses, and it was only the shock of what he saw on reaching the water's edge that revived him.

Lying full length on the ice was David, while on the same floe stood Frank, deliberately shifting his position from time to time so as to balance the lump, around which four monsters were swimming, while two black snouts were actually resting upon the edge in an attempt to reach one or other of the boys.

Even in his dazed state he asked himself what had come over Frank that he could stand there in imminent danger of several kinds of death. Every moment he expected to see him pitch headlong into the water, instead of which he counterbalanced the downward pressure of the monstrous heads with amazing nimbleness.

The coil of rope lay at Frank's feet, and it took but a moment for one of the rescuers to leap to the nearest floe and catch the end as Frank tossed it across. Willing hands then united to pull the floe and its burden to the edge of the ice, where the injured boy was quickly dragged to safety and carried back to the ship.

Immediately he saw that David was out of danger Frank collapsed, and it was not until next day that he was able to relate what had happened after Alan had left them. Even then it was only David who could induce him to speak.

" I pulled my hardest but the brutes caught us up," he said with a shudder. " I saw that they would soon tilt David off the floe, so I jumped across and balanced it till you came," was all that he would say.

" Pluckiest thing I've seen for many a day," commented Captain Baker when he heard the full story.

Alan was looking forward to the afternoon. It was to be one of the rare occasions when Captain Baker would have a couple of hours off duty, and part of this he had promised to devote to Alan. Such times as these were nearly always spent in the tiny cabin—reserved for the captain's use—which had been specially built as a projection from the bridge. Here they could talk undisturbed, and at the same time have an almost uninterrupted view of the panorama around.

Captain Baker had been running over the past few days' events and telling Alan about some of the interesting discoveries which the scientists had already recorded.

" When are we going to land, Dad ? " asked Alan as he paused.

His father glanced unconsciously at the long wall of ice, the Ross Barrier, in front of which they were steaming. " Ask me another, sonny. Many an explorer has asked himself that question. The famous Scott expedition wanted to land at Cape Crozier—you know, that headland we saw the other day just before we reached Ross Island —but they found it was hopeless and had to go farther west. We could have done that, of course ; in fact, it's just what we want to do in order to search for that rare metal deposit near Mount Erebus, but we can't spare time now because the summer is nearly over and we must get through the ice before it closes. We shall, if possible, do that little job on our way back. We are now going to explore eastwards. You noticed, of course, that we turned round yesterday ? "

Alan nodded, and he went on, " We were then just off Ross Island, but now we're steering due east, and we shall continue to do so until we reach the little-known King Edward VII. Land. Look, Alan ! "

Breaking off abruptly, he pointed towards the barrier, and then stood up and pointed again.

At first Alan thought he was referring to a group of penguins who were disporting themselves on a large floe. A moment later, however, he saw lying on the tiny beach which they were passing a huge seal. Grey-green in colour, but with a number of lighter spots, it had a tiny head. As it lay with its two flippers folded against its side, it looked for all the world like a gigantic slug but for its length—twelve feet from snout to tail.

" That's a bull Weddell seal . . ." began Captain Baker.

But before he had time to say any more their attention was drawn to a fascinating picture of animal life which came into full view as they rounded the point.

" There's the mother and her twins," laughed the captain.

Close to the water's edge was another seal, chocolate-brown on top and fawn underneath. Some two feet shorter than the bull, this one was lying full-face, its expression and whiskers giving it a cat-like appearance. Just in front, two tiny but fat baby seals, each about two feet long, were rolling over and playing with each other. As they heard the sound of the screw they gazed up, and their looks of fearless astonishment made Alan roar with laughter.

" Looks something like a very fat snub-nosed mouse,"
he decided.

Farther on they saw many others, varying in colour
from dark brown to light fawn.

" Where was I ? " mused Captain Baker as they sat
down again. " Oh, I know . . . I said that we are going
to explore right along the Ross Barrier. Then we shall
probably have to turn north again, or north-east, for some
distance, to get round the land. You see our aim is to
find a way to the Pole from the east, where no one has
ever explored to any extent. Practically nothing is
known of the long stretch of eleven hundred miles between
King Edward VII. Land and Peter I. Island. We are
going to investigate that region. First we shall get as
far south as possible by ship ; then we shall land and
proceed by sledge, ice-yacht, aeroplane, or on foot, as
seems best at the time."

Several days were spent in exploring along the edge
of King Edward VII. Land, meanwhile mapping the
coast and making constant scientific observations. During this time all three boys were kept busy helping the
others and had little free time. They did not fail, however, to notice the slopes behind Cape Colbeck which rose
to a thousand feet, nor the wonderful sight of the ice-
packed Viscoe Bay, backed by the three-thousand-feet
peaks of the Alexandra Mountains.

On reaching what appeared to be the end of the land
—although it was realized that there might be terra-firma
underneath the ice—it was found that the barrier effectually prevented all progress in an easterly direction. More
than that, they discovered—much to their annoyance—
that they would be forced to proceed north-west for some
distance.

At last, however, the barrier again turned north-east,
and a week after leaving the Ross Sea they were able to
steer south-east once more.

On the approach of March conditions began to change
noticeably. The sun disappeared for several hours each

night, temperature began to show sudden downward spurts, while the pack-ice steadily increased in thickness. Progress became more and more difficult and speed correspondingly slow.

Seeing Doctor Elliot gazing across the ice, Alan approached him and inquired :

" Excuse me, sir, but why is it that the ice changes so much ? I mean, why is it that yesterday we were jammed in for several hours and couldn't move, yet to-day we have been getting along—slowly, it's true—ever since early morning ? "

When not too busy Doctor Elliot was always willing to answer reasonable questions. Turning with a smile, he pointed to the smoke from the funnel.

" It depends mostly upon the wind and temperature. At this time of year the temperature varies a lot. If you noticed the thermometer you would see that it's nearly twenty degrees warmer to-day than yesterday ; but more important than that, the wind's changed. Yesterday there was a light breeze off the sea ; that drives the ice into a pack against the barrier. To-day half a gale has sprung up *off the land*. That forces the floes away from the barrier and breaks them up. I'm afraid that it won't be long now before you see more pack-ice than you want."

His words proved very true. Each day the period of light grew shorter, gales became more frequent, and the less cold intervals farther apart. Many days showed only a few miles progress, and as the barrier suddenly turned almost due south, their joy was quickly damped by the advent of a blizzard, accompanied by low temperatures and an easterly wind. In a few hours they were brought to a standstill, completely hemmed in by impassable ice.

Despite ominous signs of a coming storm, no one had expected a real blizzard so early. In a very short space of time the sky was completely obscured by cloud, while the bitter wind was accompanied by terrific gusts of

whirling snow-dust. The cold became intense, and all
who could do so were glad to go below.

In less than an hour it was unsafe for any one to walk
the decks, and the few who were on duty were forced to
proceed in spasmodic rushes, clinging desperately to any
support available. The velocity of the wind had risen
to fifty miles an hour, and the fine snow particles were
forced into every nook and cranny. For those who were
exposed to the elements it was a most unpleasant time ;
the whirling, frozen snow found its way underneath their
hoods and goggles, causing painful frostbite, and even
lacerating the skin. The air itself was rendered opaque
by the density of the rapidly moving snow, and vision was
limited to a few feet.

It was indeed fortunate for all on board that the *Queen
of the Antarctic* had been steaming close to the ice barrier
when the storm broke. While the ice was being driven
inland and frozen over, the vessel was well sheltered under
the lee of a projecting promontory of ice, and was thus
protected from the inrush of huge icebergs. Had they
been a few miles farther out the vessel and its contents
must have been crushed in the warring ice-floes ; as it
was, the ship was quickly imprisoned in a pack of practically motionless bergs.

Nevertheless, above the shrieking of the tempest, they
could hear the crashing and grinding of enormous blocks
of ice as they pounded against each other.

Abating as suddenly as it had started, the snowfall
ceased, although the wind showed little sign of lessening.
Meanwhile visibility slowly became more normal ; hatches
were reopened, and one after another the bottled-up
passengers came up for a breath of fresh air.

Suddenly from the crow's-nest there rang out a most
unlooked-for cry.

" Ship ahoy, sir ! "

Almost mechanically every one within earshot stared
across the ice, endeavouring to pierce the still, murky
Antarctic atmosphere ; many rushed to the side of the

ship, but not a sign of any vessel rewarded their efforts.

" It's only a mirage, of course," concluded several old hands.

Even the captain began to doubt and sent another man aloft, who speedily returned quite definitely convinced that what he had seen was no mirage.

His report at once set tongues wagging and excitement ran high. What possibility was there, they asked themselves, of there being any ship in these unvisited and almost unknown waters ? As far as they knew they were the only human beings within two thousand miles.

While they were debating visibility increased. All at once an officer on the bridge was heard to shout :

" There she is, sir, south by west."

From that moment a succession of exclamations announced that one after another had sighted the objective.

Detailed examination with the aid of powerful binoculars and telescopes revealed that it was a vessel very similar in build to, but only half the size of, the *Queen of the Antarctic*. Hanging in shreds upon the masts were the remnants of sails, while a small flag at the masthead was unfortunately blowing directly away from them, and its nature could not be determined. The motion of the vessel as it rose and fell or rocked from side to side with the movements of the ice could be clearly discerned.

On the bridge a group of—inwardly—excited officers were discussing the strange sight.

" Can you make out her name or nationality ? " asked one.

" No, her bows are hidden by ice and her flag is flying nearly south."

" Fires damped down, or out, aren't they ? "

" Apparently. No smoke visible, anyway."

" Any one aboard ? "

" Just what's puzzling me. I've been watching some objects which look remarkably like men for some time . . . but I can't be positive that they're moving."

" She's doomed."

Turning towards the captain, his second in command inquired, " Fixed tight in the ice, isn't she, sir ? "

Several thought that he had not heard the question and wondered why it was not repeated. But the questioner knew his senior officer and remarked a well-known expression on his face. After a prolonged stare through his binoculars, Captain Baker lowered his arms, and with a serious expression, barked out :

" Yes, Mr. Ransome, she *is* fixed tight, *and she's doomed.*"

As his words bit the air his hearers turned horrified

faces towards him and waited anxiously for him to speak again.

Resting his left arm on the rail, and pointing towards the ship with his glasses, he continued :

" That vessel is caught in the ice just as we are. But there is a difference. We are in comparatively still ice, owing to the shelter of that promontory "—pointing away to the east—" but there's no shelter out there," indicating the unfortunate vessel. " So as long as this wind lasts she will be slowly but surely ground to pieces."

True prophet that he was, the captain's words were quickly vindicated. With their observation stimulated by the spectre of tragedy, many pairs of eyes watched every movement of the doomed vessel.

To all appearances she was on a rough sea, one moment going up and up until she appeared to be suspended in mid-air, the next rolling from side to side as if every jolt must be the last.

But their ears revealed the truth. A constant grinding and cracking sound told of huge masses of ice being compressed against each other, while frequent reports and crashing, rending noises came floating over the ice, informing them all too clearly that the ship was in the grip of Nature's ice nut-crackers.

Very soon it became obvious that the once-proud schooner could not live more than a few hours. Even as they stared spell-bound, the mizen-mast snapped off and disappeared. Then the ice suddenly opened and all but the masts disappeared ; the next moment a sudden gust of wind caught the floe and a terrible crash, followed by creaking, splitting sounds made the onlookers turn away sick at heart.

Several moving objects could now be discerned on the decks, in addition to dark specks on the surrounding ice. To those watching, it was a terrible feeling to think that these might be explorers like themselves, and yet they were powerless to help. Several wide leads in the ice proved, even to the ultra-venturesome, that any attempt would be suicidal.

Insistently through their brains thudded the question, " If those objects *are* human beings, how many more are there imprisoned beneath the decks ? "

This problem, and many another, remained un-answered. An hour later—it seemed an eternity as they listened to the heart-racking noise and watched the trembling vessel collapse on to its side—the wind changed; left in open water again, the wreck tilted bows uppermost and disappeared into its icy grave.

As if claiming those uncharted seas for its ruler, the brave little national flag paused momentarily a few feet above the surface, fluttered defiantly in the breeze . . . and dipped for the last time.

CHAPTER VI

LAND AT LAST

THE tragedy which they had witnessed, intensified by their own helplessness, cast a gloom over the inhabitants of the *Queen of the Antarctic* for many days. If the crew were still on board then it were stark tragedy indeed. Even if not a soul were on the vessel . . . the loss of a good ship is always a dire calamity in the eyes of a sailor.

Nor were their own circumstances too encouraging. Fixed immovably in the ice, there was the imminent danger that the wind might shift to a quarter from which they would be unsheltered. This anxiety was augmented by the fact that it was vital to reach land, or some part of the ice barrier where they could winter, before the long night set in. Already the darkness was twice as long as the light ; blizzards were more frequent and much more severe, while the temperature frequently remained close to the zero point for considerable periods.

With the boys, however, youth soon reasserted itself. After the first shock of witnessing the destruction of a ship very similar to their own, their naturally buoyant spirits quickly reacted.

" You were a true prophet when you said that it would be a good thing for us to have those boys on board," smiled Lieutenant Ransome as he and Captain Baker sat in the cabin—as they had done so many times already—to make and remake plans for *when* they should be able to land.

Captain Baker laughed heartily—at least, as heartily

as he ever did nowadays. " You're right. I don't know what would have happened to the morale of some of us if it had not been for their unquenchable optimism. In fact," lowering his voice to a whisper, " to be perfectly candid, their example has helped me not a little."

" The curious thing is that, latterly, it always seems to be that chap Frank who is the noisiest of the three. From what you told me about him I should have thought that he would have been scared after what we've seen and been through."

Captain Baker shifted his position, and as he looked up his eyes glinted with satisfaction. " That's just it. That's what makes him so boisterous. He's been waging a wonderful fight to conquer himself, and now we are seeing the result of his living with the other two. It is the very strenuousness of his struggle which necessitates an outward show of hilarity. If he once let himself go he'd probably collapse, then——"

" Lead forming ahead, sir," came the look-out's voice through the tube.

Both officers jumped up as if shot, and without another word rushed up to the bridge like two schoolboys ; from where they were able to survey their surroundings.

The slight rise of temperature which they had noticed that morning—but which they ignored in view of it having occurred so frequently of late—had continued, and a sudden warm spell, aided by a change of wind, was rapidly disintegrating the ice. Already water was visible around the stern of the ship, while a rapidly widening lead showed up ahead.

At a signal, or rather a succession of signals, from the captain all was hustle and excitement. Men hurried aloft to crowd on the canvas ; fires—which had been damped down during the enforced idleness—were refuelled, and active preparations made for restarting.

As the sails filled, the ship began to move slowly through the water. For some time it was necessary to proceed with the utmost caution ; the thickness of the ice made it essential to follow the narrow channels which were few and far between, and seldom led in the right direction.

The continuance of the " heat wave," however, made things much easier, and they were able to plough their way through the ice-floes.

Much excitement was caused a few days later when the cry of " Land ho ! " sounded from the crow's-nest. Rushing to the bows and staring ahead, they soon discerned a high headland rising out of the sea. All interest centred upon the view ahead. If only a landing-place could be found, all immediate danger would be over.

Under full sail, supplemented by steam, they forged ahead towards the welcome blur. Alan was busy with his camera.

" Wonder how far it is ? " queried Frank.

David tried to estimate the distance by letting his eyes travel backwards and forwards between the ship and their goal. " Difficult to judge out here. There's so little to go by. I should put it at ten miles."

" Must be more'n that, surely," put in Alan after glancing at his watch. " We've been over half an hour already since we first sighted it, and yet it doesn't look a scrap nearer."

" Alan's about right," agreed Frank. " It appears just as far off as ever ; and what puzzles me is that it looks so much up in the clouds."

And up in the clouds it was. After an hour the " land " was no nearer, and even the officers began to grow suspicious. When it suddenly disappeared every one realized that they had been badly had—the " land " was only a mirage.

The acute disappointment caused a sharp reaction which was only partially relieved when, later that day, the look-out sighted the ice barrier ; his warning was very soon confirmed from the bridge, and hopes rose again.

Feelings were, however, decidedly mixed. The ice barrier might mean a landing-place on the ice, or even land ; on the other hand, it did most certainly mean that all further progress towards the South Pole was barred.

Another hour saw them picking their way through the leads only fifty yards from the wall of ice, which rose sheer from the water to a height of a hundred and fifty feet. All along the base was a thick sheet of ice which projected from the barrier for some distance. Although only six feet above the surface, there was, they knew, between forty-five and fifty feet underneath.

" Any hope of landing ? " asked the captain anxiously as one of the officers returned from the bows after making a thorough examination of the ice cliffs with the aid of powerful binoculars.

" None whatever, sir. The ice face is absolutely vertical, and there's not foothold for a goat. What is more, the look-out reports from the crow's-nest that he can see the barrier for many miles in each direction, but that there's no sign of any break."

" Then I am afraid we must cruise along until we do find a possible place," was Captain Baker's disappointed rejoinder.

For nearly a week the search continued, while the situation grew daily more desperate. It was unreasonable to expect that the warm spell would last much longer, and the probability was that, once a change set in, it would be the beginning of the Antarctic winter, with its attendant frozen sea and darkness.

Then the unexpected happened. One of the officers had just returned to the bridge after working out their exact position.

" We are now in a region never before visited by any ship as far as the records go," he reported.

Before the captain could answer, a hail came from the crow's-nest, accompanied by a signal that the look-out wished to speak to the captain by means of the telephone which connected his station with the bridge.

" Captain Baker this end," called the captain.

" There's a gap in the barrier several miles ahead, sir,

and there appears to be open water beyond. I will report again as soon as we get nearer."

Delighted at the news, but discrediting the latter suggestion as a mirage, he kept his ear to the instrument and waited anxiously.

"It's quite clear now," came the voice again. "The opening is about a mile wide, sir, and it leads into a huge stretch of open water."

"I will come up," jerked out the captain as he replaced the receiver and strode towards the rope ladder which led aloft. As he did so he gazed at the cliff, but could see nothing except what looked like a gap ; this, he knew, might be only some curious marking on the ice.

Hurrying aloft, he was soon standing beside the look-out, absorbed in his examination of the scene ahead through his binoculars.

To his amazement he saw at once that the man's report was strictly accurate. There was now no longer any shadow of doubt as to the reality of the gap or of the open water beyond. Speaking with the glasses still to his eyes, he summed up :

"We must have discovered another sea, similar to the Ross Sea, but farther to the east ; and by the look of it, it extends much farther towards the Pole than does the latter."

On returning to the bridge, his report caused quite a stir among his fellow-officers. Not only had they made a most important discovery, but, if the weather held, they would be able to sail much nearer to the Pole and thus save many weeks—perhaps months—of extremely arduous and dangerous travel over the snow.

It was now a thrilling race against two factors—the freezing over of the newly discovered sea, and the coming of winter darkness. Already, the captain mused, it was phenomenally late for such open-water conditions, and once the sea froze, it was extremely unlikely that it would thaw again until after the long winter.

David was perched on a tall coil of rope in the bows,

so situated that he could obtain a clear view of the scene ahead. On his knees was a drawing-board covered with paper, while poised in the air his hand was fingering a well-pointed pencil. Just as he was about to start drawing Alan strolled up.

" Hallo, Dave, what doin' ? Charting the unknown seas ? "

" Not a bad shot," smiled the would-be artist. " As a matter of fact I'm making a sketch of the new sea ; I've just got the exact latitude and longitude from the chart-room, so I am drawing a plan roughly to scale."

" I'm too excited to do much. I met Dad just now and he says it's touch and go whether we shall be able to land or not. A change of wind might, so he says, freeze us up in a few hours, then——"

David jerked round. " Then what ? "

" We'd probably have to winter in this old tub. It's just poss, of course, that we might be able to drag all this stuff over the ice in the sledges, but as there's no sign of a landing-place yet, and we don't even know how big this bay is, the chances are all against that."

" Phew ! Shouldn't fancy being cooped up in this little bus . . . and four months dark too ! I'm just long-ing to get ashore, aren't you ? "

" Sh'd jolly well think I am ! "

" Same here," interrupted a voice. Looking up, they saw that Frank had crept up unobserved. Rather pleased at the way he had startled them, he added, " I'm dying to start on our bacteriological work."

Seeing that David wanted to get on with his map, his two chums strolled farther into the bows and surveyed the route ahead. The *Queen of the Antarctic* had now ap-proached to within fifty yards of the cliffs and was going dead slow, her bows aiming at the centre of the opening.

" Why are we going so slow ? " asked Frank with a puzzled frown.

" 'Spect it's in case there's ice under the water. You see, there might easily be a ledge of ice connecting the

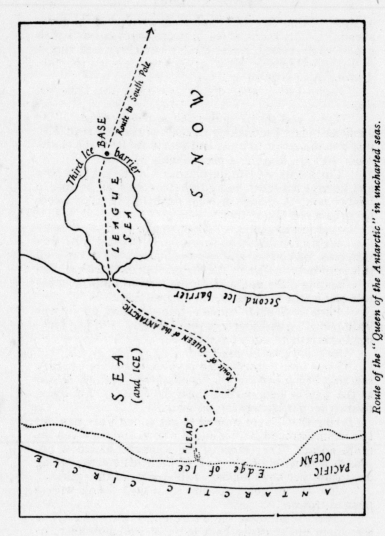

Route of the "Queen of the Antarctic" in uncharted seas.

cliffs across the bay—at least, I sh'd imagine so, shouldn't you ? "

" Ye-e-s, I s'pose there might be. Or, if it's really land, there may be a ledge of rock."

By this time they had reached the gap, through which they steamed very slowly without encountering anything larger than drift-ice, with here and there a conspicuous iceberg calved from the cliffs.

Ahead of them was what might have been mistaken for open sea. That it was not so was argued from common sense—the ice barrier and the known conditions round the Pole. In addition to this there were distinct traces of " ice blink " on the horizon.

Before they had gone far the look-out reported the ice barrier ahead. It was some time before those on deck could discern anything except the ice-strewn sea, but, first from the bridge and then from the bows, anxious watchers were able to make out the dim outlines of the ice barrier on the far-distant horizon. Before any details could be noted darkness had set in, and after proceeding carefully—their route picked out by searchlight—for several hours, it was decided to heave-to for the night rather than to undertake unnecessary risks when so near their goal.

Every one was up betimes at the first sign of dawn, anxious to see what daylight would reveal. As usual, the look-out had the first word ; soon after the vessel began to glide slowly through the water the watchers were astonished to hear a cry :

" Land ho ! "

The barrier was now plainly visible, and as the light grew stronger they saw above and about a mile to the rear of the cliffs a dark patch, mottled with snow, rising several hundred feet above the surrounding mantle of white.

" There's another patch ! " exclaimed David as the chums stood together waiting for orders.

Alan pointed excitedly. " And there's several more over there—why, it must be a range of mountains ! "

At that moment the captain's telegraph rang summoning every one to his station, and the boys each reported to the special science party to which he was attached.

Soundings were now taken frequently, and these revealed a fairly constant depth varying from sixty to eighty fathoms. In view of the short duration of daylight at their disposal, this was a very welcome factor.

The rising sun had also brought them cheering news. As it lit up the landscape ahead they saw a break in the cliffs, fronted by an easily accessible beach, and towards this the *Queen of the Antarctic* was steered. Only twenty yards from the barrier soundings decreased rapidly to ten fathoms, and Captain Baker decided to " anchor " the vessel to an ice platform which projected from the cliffs on either side of the beach. This rose about six feet above the water and was firmly attached to the barrier itself.

With intense interest the boys watched the anchoring party, which had landed on the platform, as they set to work to drill half a dozen holes in the ice, each about two feet deep; into every hole was dropped one end of a special anchor bent at right angles, the other end being formed into a loop. The holes were then filled with water which soon froze solid. Through all loops were passed strong wire ropes connected to the ship.

Once the vessel was securely fixed to the ice, Lieutenant Ransome, accompanied by Doctor Elliot, took a party ashore to reconnoitre. On his return, an hour later, his report was so favourable that unloading was started at once, and while one party went ashore to receive and unpack the goods, two boats were kept hard at work plying backwards and forwards.

Disappointed at not being chosen to go ashore, the three friends nevertheless worked with a will at sorting and packing the many scientific instruments, which were then handed to some of the scientists to transport.

But at last their turn came. Dusk was already settling down, and although some of the crew were to sleep aboard, the boys were among those deputed to occupy a tent on land. It was a thrilling experience as they approached the shores of a part of the polar regions never before—so far as they knew—visited by human beings. In front of them they saw a small beach, composed mainly of black volcanic rock resembling clinkers, but largely covered with snow. A steep slope led them to the top of the barrier—a flat, snow-covered expanse. A short distance inland they noticed hummocks, only partially covered, projecting from the white landscape like black ogres rising from holes in a sheet. Nothing could be seen of the more distant surroundings owing to the advent of darkness.

The next few days were very strenuous ones, as every moment had to be utilized if the race against darkness were to be won. Up before daylight, the boys returned to the ship at the first sign of dawn and worked with hardly any pauses, except for food, at their special jobs.

Fortunately for them this work was accomplished long before the main cargo had been unloaded, and it was decided that some of the scientific work ought to be carried out before daylight completely disappeared. Consequently the geologist and zoologist set off in the steam-pinnace to examine the cliffs, and to their joy the three boys were told off to accompany them.

"Do them good to have a little change; they've worked like Trojans since we arrived," explained Doctor Elliot to Lieutenant Ransome as they watched the pinnace disappear into the early morning twilight.

It was during this trip that a very unexpected and rather gruesome sight was met with. They had been at work for over an hour and were well out of sight of the *Queen of the Antarctic* when David, who was steering, suddenly called out:

"There's something ahead which glitters in the sun. What on earth can it be?"

Glancing in the direction in which he was pointing, they saw an unusually dazzling beam of sunlight reflected from some object just above the surface of the water. Steering so as to pass close to it, they recognized a small oblong iceberg.

" But it's black in the middle ! " protested Frank.

" So it is ! " exclaimed Alan, shading his eyes from the glare of the slanting rays.

A moment later gasps of horror escaped from all five occupants of the boat as they recognized a human figure. Frozen in the centre of the slab of ice, ten feet long by six wide, was the body of a man, fully dressed except for hat and fur gloves.

" Some poor explorer, less fortunate than we are, in a permanent tomb of ice," summarized the geologist.

" We'd better investigate and see who it is, hadn't we ? " inquired the zoologist in somewhat strained tones.

His suggestion would doubtless have been acted upon but for a remark from David.

" That's not a fog coming up, is it, sir ? "

Looking across the sea they noticed what looked like steam arising from the surface. Never had the boys seen anything like it before.

" Looks as if it's boiling," began Frank.

But both men had seen the phenomenon on previous occasions, and Mr. Slater—the geologist—quickly broke in :

" That's ' frost-smoke.' I thought it was turning much colder. We'll have to hurry back."

Without another word he restarted the engine, and as soon as David had turned the bows homewards, set off at full speed.

On the way Frank turned to Mr. Hill. " What *is* ' frost-smoke,' sir, and why must we dash back ? "

The zoologist was busy examining the contents of his drag-net and spoke without looking up.

" It's a warning that before many hours have passed we may be frozen-up. . . . What actually happens is something like this " (tipping the tiny animalculæ into a jar) : " A cold wind suddenly sets in and makes the tempera- ture of the air much lower than that of the sea ; consequently, the water evaporates rapidly, which makes it look as if it's boiling and causes that mistiness—' sea-smoke ' some call it. If you remember, we were saying how cold it felt soon after we started, and I've just noticed that the wind has changed. It's blowing right into the ice barrier now—that's a bad sign, for it means that the sea will freeze quickly and the ice will be driven in here. But we can't grumble ; it's mid-April already, so we've had several weeks more than we expected."

Even as he spoke the wind came in gusts of rapidly increasing strength and the temperature fell correspondingly. " Look there," continued the speaker, " you can actually see the vapour freezing and dropping back into the sea in tiny specks of ice . . . and the spray is freezing too."

On their way back they witnessed a beautiful—but ominous—process of nature. Seldom had they known the temperature to fall so rapidly. The wind seemed to pierce them through and through, and each felt as if he had suddenly divested himself of his outer garment. Then the wind dropped, and as they watched the water they could see needle-shaped crystals forming just under the surface ; on rising to the top these congealed and united into tiny patches of ice ; farther on, they encountered small, flat slabs, known as " pancakes," and these in turn froze together into larger masses.

" Jolly lucky we started back when we did," remarked Frank as they steered their way with the greatest difficulty through the network of ice which was rapidly increasing in thickness and area.

With hardly a moment to spare, the pinnace ran alongside its parent ship, from the bridge of which a group of officers had been watching their progress with the utmost anxiety.

For only a very few hours each day did the sun now rise above the horizon, and preparations for winter were pushed forward with all speed. Everything which might be needed was unloaded—there was always the risk that the *Queen of the Antarctic* would be crushed in the ice or rendered unfit for further use. Large sheds were built on shore, and shelters erected for animals and equipment as well as for the many scientific instruments. The sheds had been brought in sections all ready to fit together, and had been made specially strong and weatherproof. During most of the time the three boys were kept fully occupied, but one evening Alan rushed up to the other two and announced excitedly :

" News ! We've got a day off to-morrow. Doctor Elliot says we'd better have a final look round before it gets dark. What shall we do ? "

" I vote we visit those huge icebergs under the barrier which we saw when we were in the pinnace," suggested Frank.

" Agreed ! " shouted the others.

The ice was now thick enough for them to walk with safety anywhere within a mile of the barrier, and the whole of the visible sea was frozen over. As soon as there was sufficient light to see their way, the three set off across the ice, and before long were standing in awe among several icebergs of enormous size.

Suddenly David's voice came from behind the tallest of the group.

" Come here, quick ! "

Hurrying along, they witnessed the most intriguing spectacle which they had so far come across. Through the centre of the berg was a magnificent ice cavern, over forty feet high and of immense width. The recent warm spell had caused icicles to form, and these hung down from the roof, often for many feet, like magnificent lustres.

The sun had hardly risen when they entered, and as they stood inside the huge ice cathedral in the dim light the walls appeared to be transparent. All at once they heard Alan exclaim :

" Gosh ! Look at that ! "

While they had been exploring the cave the sun had travelled along the sky until its rays shone slantwise into one end of the tunnel, and now they observed that the walls had suddenly turned purple ; even as they watched, enraptured at the sight, the purple gave way to green and this in turn to blue. And so, while the sun moved in its orbit, blue changed to lilac, and this was superseded by amethyst.

But the climax was yet to come. When the sun arrived exactly opposite the centre of the opening it was slightly lower in the sky and shone full on to the drooping icicles, which immediately resolved the beams into a spectrum as if gigantic candelabra were hanging from the ceiling. Then bit by bit the beams focused upon the walls, and as they moved along the light played among thousands of tiny ice crystals which reflected back the dancing rays in every colour of the rainbow, making the walls appear to be made of all kinds of precious gems.

" How's that for Aladdin's cave ? " whispered Frank.

A few days later, in strange contrast to the beauty of this scene, the sun peeped momentarily over the barrier, only to disappear again for four months.

CHAPTER VII

WINTER GLOOM

BY this time all was as snug as human care could make it, and the party settled down to utilize the winter months to the best advantage. Long journeys were out of the question, but during their enforced stoppage there was much work to be done.

To those who had not been in the Antarctic before, the next three weeks were full of awe-inspiring mystery. From the moment that the sun disappeared for the last time a remarkable period of autumn, as it might be called, set in. Day after day there was no sunshine—yet it was not dark, but a prolonged twilight ensued as the sun moved along below the horizon. Each day the twilight grew shorter and darker; meanwhile the scenery assumed a ghostly bluish colour, while the icebergs turned green.

When they were not on duty, the boys took advantage of every opportunity to explore their surroundings. While on one of these excursions they had just made their way with the utmost care across a snow-hidden crevasse when David, who was leading, pulled up abruptly.

" What's that ? " he jerked out, pointing ahead.

" Looks like a patch of blood," frowned Alan.

" Must be the battlefield of the polar argonauts," added Frank with a grim smile.

Hurrying forward, they began to climb a gentle slope. Owing to the risk of falling into crevasses, it was impossible to keep their eyes ahead all the time, but at every available opportunity one or the other would pause and raise his eyes.

At each glance the expression of bewilderment deep-
ened, and when only a few yards away Alan pulled up
sharply.

"It *is* blood, or I'll eat my hat. How horrible!
Talk about the slaughter of the innocents!"

David did not reply. Instead he almost leapt forward,
stooped down, and plunged his hand into the red patch.

"It's red snow!" he gasped.

A brief examination proved that his words were true.
Over quite a large area the snow was tinted dull red, but
appeared brilliant red in sharp contrast with the
dazzlingly white surface around.

"What on earth makes it *red*?" puzzled Alan.
"Surely it doesn't snow red snow?"

David laughed outright. "Oh no, you chump! It's
always white when it falls, but . . . oh, I forget what it
is turns it red—we'll ask old Parkins."

Owing to the lower temperature—over forty degrees
below the freezing-point—this was easily accomplished,
and a tinful was taken back to the camp and shown to
Mr. Parkins, the biologist.

"Red snow?" he cogitated. "Well, it may be due
to one of three reasons. Usually it's caused by unicellular
algæ"—smiling at his hearers' faces—"but sometimes it's
due to red rotifers—or even the droppings of little
auks."

"Which is it in this case, d'you think?" pressed the
knowledge-hungry Frank.

Biologist Parkins shook some of the snow into his
mittened hand and examined it through a pocket lens.

"It's certainly not the third as there are no auks here.
I can't say yet whether it is due to algæ or rotifers, but
I'll take some into my lab. and examine it under the
microscope."

Later that day Frank was interested to hear the
report.

"About that red snow, Ingram. It contains crowds
of algæ but no rotifers."

(4,766)

6

Each scientist made the best use of the remaining days of twilight, setting up apparatus to record temperature, wind pressure and direction, snowfall, magnetic force and magnetic disturbances, conditions in the upper atmosphere and the depths of the sea, while physical, chemical, bacteriological, geological, and photographic laboratories were erected in order that a complete investigation of all scientific phenomena might proceed uninterruptedly—as far as would be possible during the months of perpetual darkness.

Conditions now became steadily worse. With the temperature never much above zero and sometimes forty degrees below (or over seventy degrees of frost), very careful precautions had to be taken to avoid frostbite. To expose bare hands for long would result in painful swellings, and those whose work required them to remove their thick fur gloves, even for a few minutes at a time, were forced to return to the hut every now and then to restore their circulation.

Fresh holes had to be cut in the ice each day for the purpose of marine observations and fishing, while terrible blizzards, sometimes lasting several days on end, often made it impossible to leave the huts.

Frank always said that one of these would remain in his memory as long as he lived. The first warning came from the dogs, who were invariably extremely restless before a storm, and on this particular morning even Petz refused to be quietened.

In the dim twilight ominous clouds could be seen completely obscuring the few stars whose brightness usually continued to master the faint light even at midday.

" Barometer's falling rapidly, and there's over eighty degrees of frost," warned physicist Walker.

" Batten down the hatches," roared Captain Baker.

Every one knew exactly what this order meant—that every individual must repair to his hut at once, and that every door and window must be securely fastened. In other words they were to " prepare for a siege "—the attacking enemy being a blizzard, and judging by all known portents, an unusually severe one.

Although the majority of the party were only too glad to hurry into shelter, there were a few who could not do so yet. The dogs had to be securely cloistered—Petz being the only one who was allowed to join his human friends—the store sheds to be locked up, certain instruments to be examined, and a host of last-minute jobs to be seen to.

For those still on duty it was a nerve-racking experience. A biting wind, blowing straight from the Pole, increased rapidly in force until it was raging at over fifty miles an hour. Fine snow, frozen so hard that it cut like tiny icicles, whirled along in ever-increasing denseness until all view beyond a few feet was blotted out. Meanwhile the cold was so intense that it could be acutely felt under the thickest clothing. Most uncanny of all, every angular object—finger-tips, head, roof of the hut, sledges and poles—was dimly illuminated as if it had become phosphorescent.

But at last all were battened in. Then, as if waiting to see them to safety, the blizzard burst upon them in all its fury. Pitch darkness had settled over the bleak Antarctic region ; even had it been daylight the impenetrable blanket of snow would have rendered all view from the windows impossible. The biting polar wind shrieked round the huts, and despite the strength and solidity of its structure, the building shook and trembled under the sledge-hammer blows ; at times it seemed as if the roof must be lifted bodily and whirled away. Higher and higher rose the needle of the anemometer until, at the climax, it recorded a wind-velocity of one hundred and twenty miles an hour, when it was practically impossible to hear any one speak even inside the hut.

Petz was nearly beside himself, and his terror was greatly increased by the piteous howling of the other dogs, plainly audible whenever a slight lull occurred. For the first time for many weeks Frank found his nerves getting the better of him ; making an excuse that he would look after Petz—who was now almost equally attached to each of the three boys—he led him away to an unoccupied corner of the building where each was able to console the other.

There was no sleep for any one that night as the hurricane continued with unabated fury. By 6 a.m., however, it appeared to be blowing itself out ; although the roof still shook violently, the lower parts of the building felt no shocks, and two hours later no sign or sound of any wind could be detected. Consequently, a hearty breakfast was consumed, after which every one prepared to turn in.

" Getting jolly warm in here, isn't it ? " queried Alan, turning to David, as they tumbled out of their bunks late in the afternoon.

" Just what I was thinking." As he spoke he walked away to examine the thermometer. On his return his face revealed his amazement.

" Great Scot, Alan ! D'you know the temperature's gone up forty degrees since midnight ? "

" What's that ? " asked a voice behind him. " Gone up forty degrees ? Surely not ! "

Jerking round, they saw Mr. Walker. A moment later he confirmed David's report. " You're right—there must be a sudden change coming for such a phenomenal rise to occur, especially inside the hut. I thought that there was something peculiar about the conditions because there's no trace of light yet. It should have been faintly light hours ago, but I can't even see out of the window. I think I'll pop out and read the thermometer."

Pulling on his fur outer garments, he unbolted the door and tugged it open. Instead of going out, however, he let forth a shrill whistle. His way was barred by a wall of snow ! In a very short space of time he had found the explanation of the sudden rise of temperature, the absence of light, and the apparent end of the storm. They were completely buried under the snow !

Digging his way out, he found that conditions had

" Great Scot ! D'you know the temperature's gone up ? "

changed but little. A terrific gale was still raging, the
temperature was rising slightly, but still showed seventy
degrees of frost, while the mantle of snow—already above
the roof of the hut—was being added to steadily by the
whirling flakes. Not until the fourth day did the blizzard
cease, when the snow began to melt away rapidly from the
warm precincts of the hut.

It was weeks before the scientists could renew their
outdoor experiments. In some places they were able to
dig down and uncover the instruments ; in others, where
the depth of snow was less, it was cleared away by the
frequently recurring gusts of wind.

By this time darkness had set in and there was practically no difference between night and day. Although each
" day " was fully occupied for every one in scientific work,
cooking, repairing, and preparing for a forward move

when the sun returned, the evenings were always free. It was during these periods that they thanked their lucky stars that they had brought gramophones and other musical instruments, games, and a well-stocked library. Despite the size of the party, it was a weird and lonesome experience ; each evening, when the time for recreation came round again, it was forced upon them anew that their world consisted of a few buildings in the centre of a vast and desolate expanse of snow, and that, however tired they might become of each other's company, there was not—as far as they knew—another human being within a thousand miles. However desperate their need, they could not move far from where they were nor could any one reach them for months.

Nevertheless, despite all its hardships and desolation, there were many consolations. Never would the boys forget the thrills of isolating bacteria previously unknown in polar regions, the analysis of snow and ice proving it to contain traces of the intriguing " heavy water," the microscopic examination of the contents of the drag-nets and study of the marine life from varying depths beneath the ice, the frequent opportunities to contemplate the stars by day and night, and their hilarious festivities to celebrate " turning the corner " on June the twenty-second—midwinter day.

More than at any other time during the whole expedition, it was while conditions were thus at the gloomiest that the older members of the party had reason to be thankful for the presence of the three youths. Their infectious enthusiasm over each new discovery, their irrepressible buoyancy, and the harmless practical jokes which they played upon every one in turn at every possible opportunity, all helped to leaven the monotony and drabness of their existence.

In addition, there were occasional incidents which, in view of their rare occurrence or beauty, did much to neutralize the unpleasantness of the long winter months. Several times the unusual spectacle of a full moon during the daytime claimed their attention, and the eerie beauty of the moonbeams shining on the spotless mantle of snow, or playing among the icebergs, was a never-to-be-forgotten sight.

Of all the miracles which they witnessed in the Antarctic, however, there was none to compare with what occurred only a week before the end of winter darkness. Immediately the sun had peeped its last farewell, a strictly regular routine had been enforced. Not only was there so much to be done to ensure a safe start and an efficient journey on the advent of spring, but Captain Baker—who always discussed such matters with Doctor Elliot—knew from past experience the truth of the adage that " Satan finds some mischief still for idle hands to do," and that the unavoidable ill-effects of the enforced stagnation are greatly lessened by a regular routine.

Breakfast was always at 8 a.m., and from Monday to Saturday every one had his allotted task which kept him fully occupied from 9 a.m. until 6 p.m., and sometimes later, except for intervals for meals. From 6 to 10 p.m. the evenings were given over to recreation —concerts, cinematograph shows, lectures, debates, and reading.

It was after an extra hard day's work that the three chums decided to go for their usual " exercise stroll," which they made an invariable rule, for health's sake, unless conditions rendered it impossible. The ever-present danger of losing one's way—especially in the advent of a sudden storm—had been overcome by a suggestion of David's. Each boy carried a spool of stout string half a mile long, and by this means they were able to secure a walk of at least three miles—or more if they chose to start off again a second time.

On this occasion Alan had just come to the end of his portion.

" Hitch on, Frank."

While the reef knot was carefully tied—a break in their guide rope might be disastrous—David fumbled in the large pocket of his fur over-garment to make sure that the third length was still in its place.

All at once the others heard him exclaim :

" Crumbs, look at that ! "

Frank tested the knot and looked up to see David glaring at the sky towards the south-east.

" Phew ! It's getting light or something ! " he blurted out, as he saw a greenish flush spreading up from the horizon.

Alan had joined them and was gazing open-mouthed at the spectacle.

" Walker must be wrong. He said we shouldn't see a trace of twilight until the first week in August, but *that's* twilight surely, and it's only July the twenty-fifth."

Frank gazed back at him for a moment with a half-puzzled look. " That's not *twilight*," he retorted, " that's the beginning of the Aurora Borealis."

It was now David's turn to jerk round. " Aurora *Australis*, you mean. It's called Aurora Borealis, or Northern Lights, near the North Pole, but Aurora *Australis* near the South Pole."

" Oh, I beg its pardon," said Frank with a low bow towards the south-east ; " I do hope it won't be mortally offended."

Further pleasantries were precluded by David's sudden remark :

" Look ! Now she's off."

An awed silence fell as they watched the celestial pageantry which followed. While the green curtain spread up the sky and became brighter, tongues of electrical flame shot up, disappearing and reappearing like coloured liquids. Then came a magnificent display of coloured streamers, all of which started from the initial glow, but which ran up the sky and dodged fantastically among the constellations as if playing hide-and-seek. At times the colours were intense and formed an archway over their heads, but the most characteristic feature was the way in

which these yellow, green, or lilac " merry dancers "
flowed across the sky, then retreated, only to flare up
again. Meanwhile the green light flickered, or darted
unexpectedly upwards, partially veiling the stars as it
did so. Suddenly a gasp was heard as the multi-coloured
lights dissolved away, leaving only starry points of light
in a dome of indigo.

" It's gone—my, what a sight ! "

Hardly were the words out of his mouth when David
exclaimed :

" No, Frank, it's coming back again, look ! "

Then, like a huge array of coloured searchlights exploring the sky for some lost aeroplane, the Aurora burst
upon their sight once more. Again the green hues spread
upwards, quickly riven by the fast-flowing rivulets of
molten glory, which dissolved into curtains draping the
heavens ; backwards and forwards fluctuated the beams,
chasing each other from east to west, while occasionally
an extra bright-hued ray would focus itself upon the
distant snow-mottled mountain range, lighting up the
dark crags with spectral hues, or reflecting back in
wondrous beauty from the snowy mantle. Backwards and
forwards, up and down, in and out, dancing and chasing,
flashed the miracle of nature until, when it finally disappeared, the three boys were left in inky blackness, speechless and reverent.

It was only the growing numbness which recalled
them to the fact that it is unwise to stand still for long
when the thermometer shows seventy degrees of frost.
Hurrying back, they found the rest of the party strangely
silent, and after supper all except those on duty were
quite ready to turn in.

It was not until next morning that they learnt from
physicist Walker that early the previous evening his
instruments had recorded the greatest magnetic disturbances so far met with during this expedition.

The first of August came on a Saturday. This fact
David always remembered because of a very happy event

which occurred on that date, and a contrastingly unpleasant one which happened on the following day.

Just as they were about to knock off for dinner on the
Saturday a shout was heard from the vicinity of the
physical laboratory. Hurrying out, David found Mr.
Walker gazing with a rapt expression at the sky. For a
moment the physicist did not observe his approach ; then
he pointed to the northern horizon and said in a joyous
voice :

" Look, Somervell—there's the first sign of spring ! "

A mystified look spread over David's face as his gaze
followed the direction of Mr. Walker's finger. He could
see nothing but a starlit sky. Then, realizing that his
snow-goggles were misty, he removed them and stared
again.

This time he saw what had caused Mr. Walker's jubilation. Just above the horizon was a faint reddish glow.

His companion turned to him again. " That is the
very first sign. I have looked for it every day for a week.
If you watch carefully you will notice that it increases
distinctly each day until we get twilight again, and then,
about the third week in August, you will see the good old
sun once more—if you're lucky, that is."

After three months of almost complete darkness,
every one was much cheered to know that they would
soon be able to see their way about again without the
aid of lamps. So intrigued was David that he decided
that, whenever possible, he would watch the advancing
signs of spring each morning.

As the next day was Sunday this provided an excellent
opportunity to start, all routine being cancelled. Consequently, immediately Captain Baker closed the morning
service, David hurried off to spend the time before dinner
in gazing at the " dawn of spring."

" It certainly is decidedly brighter," he mused. Then
the beauty of the scene caught him, and he found himself
complimenting Captain Baker upon the aptness of the text
for his morning sermon :

" When I consider Thy heavens . . . the moon and
the stars . . . what is man, that Thou art mindful of
him ? "

As he sat for a moment upon an upturned box, his
thoughts went back over the sermon. . . .

Alan looked questioningly at Frank on hearing the
dinner-gong (even empty biscuit tins and broken pick-axe
handles have their uses in the Antarctic !).

" Where's Dave ? " he asked.

Frank turned and walked to the window. " Dunno.
He said something about going to see the ' dawn of
spring.' Haven't seen him since."

Dinner, especially on Sunday, was always a welcome
diversion in the monotony of polar life, and it was seldom
that they had to wait for any one—Captain Baker was
always obdurate that no meal should commence until
every one was present. Some considered him rather
unnecessarily insistent upon this point, but those who
had been on polar expeditions before knew full well the
vital importance of fostering punctuality and all similar
attributes of civilization in the wilds of the Antarctic.
Moreover, Captain Baker perceived that, by thus making
every unit of the party of equal importance, he would
materially help to engender a community and family
spirit.

To-day, however, Frank and Alan gazed around for
David without result, and when all were seated, Captain
Baker at once spotted the empty chair.

" Where's Somervell ? " he rapped out.

In reply he was met by a blank stare, and it was then
that he fired his stock second question.

" Any one seen him lately ? "

Frank repeated his previous statement. " I saw him
just after the service, sir, and he said something about
going to see the ' dawn of spring,' as he calls the glow in
the north ; but I haven't seen him since."

Several others confessed to having seen him about

the same time, but no one had any idea as to where he was now.

Life is so uncertain, and there are so many pitfalls in the polar regions that, once any one is overdue or his whereabouts unknown, the gravest anxiety is quickly aroused.

" Mr. Hawlet and Mr. Walker, will you please take Ingram and my son and see if you can find anything of him. If you do not discover him in half an hour, report to me and we will all join in the search."

As the four left the table he announced, " The rest of us will start our dinner. In all probability our circle will be complete in a few minutes "—his anxious features did not appear to support his optimism—" but if not . . . well, we shall be better fortified for our task."

Frank and Mr. Hawlet at once made a circuit of the huts, looking in the stables, kennels, workshops, and laboratories. Meanwhile Mr. Walker and Alan steered due north, thinking that David might have forgotten the time in his absorption in watching the glow—still faintly visible near the horizon.

After walking for twenty minutes, Alan noticed that Mr. Walker was staring hard slightly to his left. Fifty yards farther on he pulled up abruptly.

" What's that dark patch on the snow ? " he inquired.

A moment later, without either expressing the fears which gripped his heart, both started to run towards the object.

CHAPTER VIII

SPRING AGAIN

BEFORE they had covered half the distance, it became evident that the dark patch was a human form, and on arrival they found David lying unconscious beside the empty biscuit tin.

At first they could not make out what was the matter. There were no signs of injury and no footmarks other than his own. He could not have fallen far—there was nothing from which to fall. But the sharp eyes of Mr. Walker quickly observed the " sign " in the snow and deduced the meaning.

" Look, Alan," he said, pointing down, " there's where he sat on the tin—and there's the marks where it overturned when he dropped asleep. Quick, Alan, it's the sleep of death. Unless we act smartly he'll never wake up. You rub his legs while I try to rouse him."

Alan had never seen Mr. Walker act so roughly before. Seizing David by the shoulders he shook him viciously backwards and forwards, every now and then interspersing several hearty slaps upon his back ; meanwhile he shouted loudly into his ear in an effort to rouse him from the stupor caused by the extreme cold.

At last David opened his eyes and began to mutter :

" Shurrup, Frank. Lemme alone. I want to . . . sleep."

Thinking that Mr. Walker was being very unsympathetic, Alan looked at him rather reproachfully.

" Think I'm being a bit unkind, eh ? " panted the physicist, as he renewed his efforts more vigorously than ever. Then, in very decided tones, he added :

" He's not really sleeping. The extreme cold paralyses all the muscles—and senses—causing an intense desire for sleep. Unless we can succeed in rousing him quickly he will die."

At this moment a group of four men was seen approaching, led by Petz ; hearing Mr. Walker's hail, they rushed forward and were soon helping to revive the patient. Captain Baker had thoughtfully insisted upon each party taking a flask of hot drink with them, and with the aid of this and more shouting and shaking, David was soon restored to sufficient consciousness to enable him to walk, supported on either side and with Petz running joyfully round in circles, back to the hut. Here he gave a brief account of how he had come to be in such a plight.

" Let this be a warning to every one," said Captain Baker as they finished dinner. " Remember that the extreme cold in the Antarctic—or the Arctic, for that matter—seizes hold of any one and very quickly produces a state of lethargy. While you are moving about it is usually quite safe, but once you sit down, even for a moment, the cold grips you and causes an intense desire for rest and sleep. Once you fall asleep you will never wake up unaided—in fact you would be dead in a very short time."

Every day the signs of the coming spring were more pronounced. Brighter and brighter grew the glow, while it spread over a larger area of the sky and lasted longer each time it reappeared.

The effect of this upon the spirits of the party was most marked. Although at no time had any one been unduly depressed or unsociable, it was inevitable that three months of perpetual darkness must affect their health adversely, and this, in turn, reacted upon their spirits. But the welcome signs of the coming of light gradually dispelled their gloom ; even those who were not on duty now spent less time in the hut, their gait became more springy and jokes increased proportionately.

By the second week in August the glow gave way to

a definite twilight ; at first lasting for only about an hour at midday, the period lengthened steadily, the sky meanwhile assuming majestic colours—blue, pink, and lilac. By the third week the mountain-tops were set on fire by the glow of the sun, which was only just below the horizon. But it was in the fourth week that the great event occurred.

August the twenty-seventh was Doctor Elliot's birthday, and great preparations had been made to celebrate it. It so chanced, however, that the sun decided to assist in the festivities, for on that day it rose sufficiently high above the horizon to light up the landscape and to warm the eager watchers with its genial rays. Needless to say the celebration at once became a double one, and the results of seeing the sun once more can best be summed up in Captain Baker's pithy remark :

" Never saw such a crowd of irresponsible schoolboys ! "

The daily reappearance of the sun acted like magic upon the camp. From a very restricted area of regular routine—mainly indoors—the scene was transformed into a hive of activity. Most of the winter tasks had already been completed, and except for the scientists who were engaged in regular experiments, every one concentrated upon the more immediate preparations for the start to the Pole.

The human beings were not the only members of the party who revelled in the gradually lengthening sunshine. Although they had all been exercised regularly, the dogs were overjoyed to see daylight once more ; more than this, they appeared to delight in the immediate prospect of work.

" Just look at those brutes ! " exclaimed Alan as, with Petz frisking at his heels, he stood beside his two chums. Not far away the Russian, Midoff, who, except for his assistant, was the only one whose language the dogs could understand, was opening the door of the shed where they were kennelled. A few of the tamer ones were let loose.

These immediately scampered wildly across the snow, some half burying themselves, while others rolled happily over and over or chased any near-by penguins. The majority, however, could only be let out on the lead ; if free, they might fight each other or attack the penguins and seals ; in the latter case they would often fall a prey to killer whales, or disappear entirely.

David was watching the scene eagerly. " Crumbs, aren't they keen on work ! Did you notice how the moment he brought out the harness they all went nearly mad ? "

Midoff, who had been chosen partly for his excellent English, overheard the remark in the still, clear polar air.

" They seem to live for work," he commented, " and nothing pleases them better than to feel the strain of the harness as they pull the sledges. They simply hate the idleness of the sea voyage or of the long winter months ; and it is wonderful what heavy loads they can pull."

Everything had to be carefully sorted and scrupulously overhauled. Ration bags were filled ; sledges, motor tractors, ice-yacht, and aeroplane were tested ; tents and clothes must be examined and routes planned.

These were only a few of the very necessary stages in the multitudinous and often monotonous preparations for the start of the great expedition. When they were nearing completion Captain Baker called a meeting in order to explain the final plans upon which he and Doctor Elliot had decided. Never a man to waste words, he had become more and more precise in his orders the farther they penetrated into the Antarctic.

" I want to remind you first of the main objects of our journey to the Pole," he began. Glancing round to ensure that every one was listening, he continued, " They are three. Firstly, scientific investigation ; secondly, to search and chart unknown lands ; thirdly, to obtain exact determinations of the position of the Pole. Now as to

" Just look at those brutes ! "

methods. To-morrow our three airmen will set off in
the aeroplane—or amphibian, I should perhaps say, as
it is built to land on water, ice, snow, or land—and while
one pilots, another will observe, while the third keeps in
touch with us by wireless. They will report on their
return as to our best route, the conditions, and any other
helpful information." During a pause the speaker's face
clouded momentarily. " I have arranged that if they are
not back within twenty-four hours we shall start.

"We shall divide into three parties. Doctor Elliot
will be in charge of the South Pole contingent, with
Mr. Walker as assistant ; in addition, this party will con-
sist of Mr. Hawlet, Mr. Slater, the ice-yacht in charge of
Mr. Le Brun, and the two dog-sledges with their drivers
Midoff and Zameneff."

All three boys were by now on tenterhooks to know
in which expedition they were to be included.

" The second party will be in charge of Lieutenant
Carmen, and will include Gutzberg, Carpini, and Arden-

holdt, with the two motor-trailers and their drivers. Each trailer will carry a load of nearly two tons, and it will be Lieutenant Carmen's object to proceed due south for three hundred miles. After establishing depots for the polar party, he will turn north-west and explore towards the Ross Sea."

" We're in your Dad's lot," whispered David, glancing at Alan.

As Captain Baker proceeded, a mystified look spread slowly over three faces.

" I shall take charge of the third party, and we shall endeavour to explore the huge tract between here and the Weddell Sea in our two newly designed motor-sledges which are also fitted with sails. Mr. Hill will be my assistant, and in addition to the two drivers I shall take Don Miguel and Vosziche."

Sudden gloom fell upon the boys as they heard him pause again. At that moment the speaker glanced up, noticed their blank expression, and added with a smile :

" I am sorry I forgot you three boys. I have decided that my son is too young to let him risk the rigours of the extreme Antarctic, so he will remain with the rest of our number who, under Lieutenant Ransome, will take charge of the *Queen of the Antarctic* and our depot here while we are away. Somervell and Ingram, however, will accompany Doctor Elliot as assistants to Mr. Walker and Mr. Hawlet respectively."

It was a great blow to know that they were to be separated. Upon Alan the shock fell heaviest, for to him it entailed a triple disappointment, separation from his two friends, temporary loss of his only parent, and the dashing of his long-cherished hopes of reaching the Pole.

Fortunately Alan had been brought up to face adversity bravely, and the thought of his father's courage in the face of past and future dangers helped him to put on a cheerful mien, despite his bitter disappointment.

For his chums it was a much easier matter. After the first blow, the excitement of the coming trip quickly overcame their regrets, while the rest of the day was fully occupied in putting the finishing touches to the preparations.

Next morning every one turned out to cheer the three airmen as they set out on their perilous journey. Even with their cleverly constructed under-carriage, there would be long stretches with no possibility of making a safe landing ; added to this was the extreme cold and the probability of sudden blizzards. The latter would not only reduce visibility to a few feet, or even less, but the wind might reach a velocity of anything up to one hundred and twenty miles an hour, creating impossible flying conditions.

Indifferent to the terrific odds against them, they set off with smiling faces, and half an hour later came the cheery message :

" All O.K. Speed one hundred and eighty miles an hour. Dropping weighted flags."

" Will they reach the Pole to-night, d'you think ? " asked Frank as he helped Mr. Hawlet to pack some bacteriological specimen tubes.

" I don't *think*—it's too much waste of time in this case," was the unexpected reply. " It's not like an ordinary flight, you see. There are so many pitfalls, known and unknown, in such a trip. All I *know* is that Doctor Elliot estimates that we are now about seven hundred miles from the Pole, so, as their aeroplane is capable of two hundred miles an hour, they should get there in under four hours. They started at nine o'clock and hoped to reach the Pole soon after midday ; as it will not be dark here before five, they should be back to-night. If delayed, they will camp at dusk and fly on as soon as it's light so as to be back before we start."

Although every one was very busy getting ready for the great exodus on the morrow, no one forgot to inquire each half-hour, " Any message from Collinson ? " and all were delighted to hear, time after time, " Yes, all O.K. still."

At one o'clock came the report: "All O.K. Now nearing the Pole." But the next message was rather disquieting. "Run into storm. Speed seventy."

"Which—the wind or the 'plane?" cogitated Mr. Walker.

With growing anxiety they awaited one-thirty. Five minutes late came the brief report:

"Blizzard . . . lost bearings . . . com . . ." but the rest was drowned by atmospherics.

From that moment no further message came, and the fate of the aeroplane and its passengers was left to the very dismal conjectures of those in whose thoughts it played a large part during that night and for many days afterwards.

It was fortunate for all concerned that in the bustle and excitement of the triple start next morning the gloom which had settled upon the party was largely dispelled.

Captain Baker, in his characteristic way, refused to start until he had seen the other two parties safely off. Shortly after nine, followed by hearty cheers, Lieutenant Carmen and his two trailers set off into the twilight and were soon travelling over the level snow at ten miles an hour. An hour later, Midoff gave the word to the dogs, and led by Captain Baker, those who were left shouted their "God-speed" to Doctor Elliot as the two heavily laden sledges slid over the snow at less than half the speed of the motors.

Alan continued to wave to his chums until they were out of sight and then turned with a sad face to watch his father as he gave the order to start. A final wave and the last party disappeared just as the sun beamed across the snow.

If only he could have kept Petz things would not have been so bad; but the dog was so valuable on such an expedition that he had to give him up to the other party. How were Dave and Frank getting on? he wondered. Would he ever see them again? If only he had been two years older . . . what experiences they would have and what sights they would see ! Would they find the missing aeroplane ?

Curiously enough David and Frank were talking about him at that very moment. The South Pole party had halted for the second time. Midoff knew from experience that the dogs would work best in short, sharp runs ; for this reason he drove them at a good pace—about three miles an hour with the present heavy loads—but stopped for a brief rest each hour. This was the second halt, and as before Petz was looking round for his master, whining and gazing up questioningly at David.

So far all had gone well. The route was fairly level, and in the deep snow, undisturbed by the wind, it was an easy matter for the drivers to follow the wide tracks of the caterpillar-wheel tractors.

A gentle breeze was blowing from behind them, and Le Brun and his ice-yacht—adapted to " sail " over snow or ice—had already come into his own. Skimming over the surface at ten miles an hour, he raced on and explored the route immediately in front of them ; then, turning, he was able to report to the drivers whether they could forge ahead without worry or whether there were crevasses to be negotiated—if so, which was the best crossing-place.

Petz, too, had proved himself invaluable. He was seldom harnessed, but acted as a leader of leaders. True, the leading dog of each sledge was quite capable of guiding his team and obeying the driver's orders as well as looking immediately ahead so as to pick out the best route. But Petz was a super leader, trained to the highest pitch of efficiency, combining the valuable characteristics of the wild Eskimo dog with a fuller understanding of human needs and their orders. He could always be relied upon implicitly, while his freedom gave him added opportunities. Racing ahead, he would run round in circles examining the ground. Should he scent danger he would pull up suddenly and communicate his warning to the other leaders in their own language ; otherwise, he would rush back, stir up any laggards with a bark—or even a snap—

and then trot up to the boys for a word of approval and a pat.

"Wonder how far the motor-trailers have got?" mused David as they made their third start.

Frank was occupied in trying to arrange himself more comfortably without falling off. As soon as he realized the import of David's remark, a question which had been on his lips many times recurred to him.

"Talking about motor-sledges, David, why didn't Doctor Elliot use motors for this trip, I wonder? They'd be ever so much quicker, surely?"

"Quicker, certainly—three times as quick, probably," was the reply. "But the doctor wouldn't trust any kind of mechanical transport; says they might break down; they did so pretty badly on the Scott expedition, I believe."

"Yes, but that's years and years ago. Surely motors have improved tremendously since then?"

"That's true of course. I know the doctor said he'd sooner trust dogs or Shanks' mare. If a motor breaks down you're helpless—it's far too heavy to drag; but you can trust dogs, and even if anything does happen to them you can always man-haul the light sledges."

Frank was obviously not satisfied. "That might all have been true years ago, but I reckon that you could rely on one of the most modern motor-sledges all right— especially if it had two engines."

"I'm inclined to agree with you, Frank, personally. But the doctor isn't as young as he used to be, and I think he's a bit old-fashioned. Besides, he isn't an engineer; if he was it might make a difference."

Both boys were gloriously happy. Not only were they on their way to the Pole, but the crisp, invigorating air as it brushed against their faces, the gentle crackling sound of the dogs' paws upon the frozen snow, and the awesome polar scenery, all helped to thrill them through and through.

At first their route had been over level, snow-clad

plains, while behind them rose mighty glaciers—already
beginning to feel the effect of the lengthening hours of
sunshine—and ahead, slightly to their right, were steep
snow-covered slopes through which grizzly patches of
mountain-top thrust their way here and there.

During the day good progress was made, and shortly
before the sun dipped behind the hills the first depot left
by the motor party was seen ahead.

" They should be at least fifty miles ahead of us by
now," remarked Doctor Elliot as he gave orders to camp
for the night.

His estimate proved over optimistic, however. Had
the motor-trailers worked as well as Frank had suggested
they should, Lieutenant Carmen would have been over
fifty miles ahead. But, on reaching the depot, Doctor
Elliot saw a message stuck in a conspicuous position.
Opening it, he read :

" Left here at 4 p.m. Trouble with motors on the
way. Twice delayed over an hour."

So the motors were only ten miles ahead !

Despite the disappointing news little anxiety was felt.
The advance party would travel on after dark with the aid
of powerful searchlights, and unless the motors broke
down altogether must keep well ahead of Doctor Elliot.
The arrangement was that depots would be left twenty
miles from the start and then every fifty, the last one
being four times the size of the others. The dog-sledges
carried full loads, and these would be used as they went
along until exhausted, thus lightening the loads each
day.

Barring exceptional delays, each sledge carried
sufficient provisions to last its human team of four—
Le Brun transported his own rations—for over three
hundred miles. Thus the depots should remain untouched
until they reached the last one. There the two sledges
would make further depots for another two hundred miles

towards the Pole, the lengthening sunlight allowing them to considerably increase their daily mileage if all went well.

Except for occasional blizzards which caused enforced camps, excellent progress was made, and at each depot a note was found stating the time of departure of the motor party. Despite a few delays, the latter were now forging rapidly ahead.

It was just six days after they had left the base that David suddenly dug Frank in the ribs and pointed excitedly to his left.

" What's that above the snow ?　Looks like a flag."

On his attention being called to the object, Doctor Elliot dug out his binoculars from the pile of personal luggage and focused them upon the fluttering something.

" It's a flag . . . and a red one by the look of it. . . . Wonder if it's one of Collinson's ?　Hi, Le Brun ! " he called.

The latter, in his ice-yacht, immediately steered across the snow, and a few minutes later returned with a red flag fixed on a long, weighted spear. Tied to the top was a message :

" Going fine.　Country ahead hilly.　Dropping these about every hundred miles.　Collinson."

Doctor Elliot gazed at the letter for some time ; folding it and putting it into a safe place, he remarked wistfully :

" I wonder . . . shall we see him again ? "

By the end of the second week they had covered nearly three hundred miles, and were eagerly looking forward to reaching the last dump which would be approximately half-way to their goal.　The motor-trailers were now a week ahead of them, and two more messages had been picked up from the aeroplane.

David and Frank had from the first cast envious glances at the ice-yacht, and before they had been travelling for a week had persuaded Le Brun to " show them the ropes." Such apt pupils did they prove that, with Doctor Elliot's permission, Le Brun now frequently changed places with them. While he walked by the sledge, the two boys would skim happily over the snow and return with their reports to Doctor Elliot—reports which he quickly learnt to trust implicitly.

It was their report " that although they had prospected several miles ahead of the main body, no sign of the two-ton depot was to be seen," which decided Doctor Elliot to camp for the night.

" Golly, it's good to lie down and get snug," said Frank emphatically, as he gave Petz a final pat and told him to lie down.

" Rather ! " grunted David. " And we'll see that jolly old depot to-morrow morning."

His words were early fulfilled. Only two hours after they had started Le Brun returned with the news that he had spotted it, and by midday they were seated around the huge cairn listening to Doctor Elliot reading two messages.

" The first," he began, " is from Carmen. He says that all is well and that they made a good start for their objective just ten days ago. So they should be, let me see, nearly eight hundred miles away by now. The other is from Collinson. This is an extra message to warn us that there's crowds of penguins only a short distance ahead." A cheer interrupted him. " Yes, it's good news, certainly. The dogs' food is very low and I fear there won't be enough here to last us out. Now we can make several extra depots of penguin-meat for the dogs, and, incidentally, for ourselves if necessary. But we've got to find our penguins before we can catch 'em and eat 'em," he smiled.

David glanced hastily towards Frank, and at an answering nod from him piped up :

" May *we* go, please, sir, on the ice-yacht ? "

Half an hour after dinner saw the yacht, with its

burden of two boys, preceded by a dog, tacking carefully over the increasingly difficult surface. After searching for some time without success, they began to make ever-widening circles until, at a spot several miles off their route, and some five miles from the depot, they were confronted by an impassable barrier of rock. Steering round the nearest end of the ledge, they saw a fairly level snow-plain stretching along the other side of the mountain range.

Hardly had they turned the corner when David gasped out :

" What on earth's that sticking out of the snow up the hill ?   Looks exactly like an aeroplane wing."

CHAPTER IX

THE MYSTERIOUS RECLUSE

FRANK shaded his eyes and stared towards the object, finally raising his snow goggles for a moment and looking again.

"So it does, Dave. I could swear it was! And there's something else to the right . . . kind of black lump . . . may be a rock, but looks to me more like a tank or engine."

"I'm off to find out."

With that David tried to steer the yacht towards the spot in question. After crawling for a few yards, however, he had to give it up as hopeless, because the hill cut off every scrap of wind.

"We'll have to foot it!" he jerked out.

Throbbing with excitement, not unmixed with a trace of anxiety, they hurried—as far as the treacherous surface would permit—forward.

Half-way there, Frank pulled up and grabbed his chum's arm.

"Dave, it *is* the wreck of an aeroplane," he almost shrieked. "Look, you can see two bits of wing quite clearly now, and the British mark on the underside. That thing just beyond is the petrol tank, I'll bet. Dave, d'you think it's . . . "

"I know what you mean," interrupted David. "Yes, I wonder if it's Collinson's 'plane."

"But I thought he was quite near the Pole when he sent the last wireless?"

"Yes, so he was. He obviously couldn't have crashed here on the way out. . . . "

" Perhaps he was on his way back," put in Frank.

" 'Mm, yes, he might have been.   He said they'd lost their bearings. . . . They might not have been as near the Pole as they thought . . . then, if they turned back . . ."

" But what about the wireless—there were no further messages, were there ? "

" No. It might have broken down owing to ice on the aerial, or they mightn't have been able to get through. The magnetic disturbances are terrific during a real polar blizzard. But we'll soon see what the identification mark is."

While they were talking they had arrived at the base of the slope where, from the rugged surface some fifty feet above them, the end of an aeroplane wing stuck out conspicuously.

That fifty feet, however, took a lot of climbing. Jagged rocks, mixed with ice and snow, made a very slippery foothold, but at last David succeeded in reaching the place ; meanwhile Frank contented himself with waiting for his friend's verdict, but held himself ready to climb if need be.   From where he stood he could see David examining the wing, tugging at it and then edging along towards other portions of the wreckage.   After poking among the snow and rocks for some time—not without considerable danger to life and limb—he hung on to the wing-end and called down :

" No go, Frank. It's hopeless. There's two pieces of wing, a tank and some metal-work. But the rest's hopeless—too deep in the snow. Can't find any sign of the identification mark either."

" Shall I come up ? " shouted Frank.

David shook his head.   " No use, I'm coming down."

His intentions were fulfilled quicker than he intended, for at the first step he slipped and half fell and half rolled, until he lay nearly buried in a deep snowdrift at Frank's feet.

For a brief moment Frank's heart seemed to stop as he watched his chum bounce over the rocks and crash to

" I'm off to find out."

the ground. Then, realizing that he might need help, he pulled himself together with a jerk and dropped on to one knee. To his joy, before he could turn him over to examine him, David sprang to his feet.

"Where did that one go to, 'Erb? Answer, into the snow!"

But the shock had been too great for Frank, and instead of laughing heartily at the joke—as the maker was doing—the positions were suddenly reversed. Noticing that Frank had gone deathly white and was trembling from head to foot, David quickly became serious, laid him down on the snow and spoke firmly to him.

"We must hurry back, Frank, and tell the others

about our discovery, or it'll be getting dark before they can come and examine the wreckage."

The days had lengthened out considerably since they started, and he knew that they still had nearly four hours of daylight before them, but he thought that by diverting Frank's attention to the urgency of helping others he could best assist him to conquer the spasm of fear by which he had been gripped. In this he was right.

Glancing up into David's strong face, with its tightly set lips and look of determination, Frank clenched his teeth and struggled up.

" I'm all right, thanks, old chap. Let's get on," was all he said as the two hurried back to the yacht, and were soon speeding back to the depot.

A few words sufficed to explain to Doctor Elliot all that was necessary, and before long a team of dogs—happy at being in the traces again—were making their best speed towards the mountain range. Behind them was the sledge with four occupants, while guiding them was the ice-yacht navigated by the two boys.

On arrival at the scene of disaster an unexpected disappointment awaited them. Willing hands quickly set to work to dig out the wreckage, despite the extremely difficult conditions under which they were forced to work. But instead of salvaging two wings as they had hoped, they only succeeded in removing two half-wings ; the other ends had been so damaged by fire that nothing remained but blackened metal. With the burnt-out portions had disappeared the identification marks. Moreover, after several hours work, the only other débris recovered consisted of a battered petrol tank, the remains of the engine, and a heap of fire-twisted wire and metal. Beyond the fact that the machine must have been a British three-seater 'plane, no evidence whatever could be found of its identity.

Perhaps the most mysterious fact of all was that no trace of the occupants could be discovered, despite the obvious fact that—unless completely consumed by the fire—their bodies would be preserved, almost unchanged, by the snow and extreme cold.

Work had to be suspended owing to the failing light, and before they reached the depot darkness fell. All were only too glad to turn in, tired out—physically by the hard work entailed and mentally by the haunting thoughts of the unsolved mystery.

" We'll pay our call on Mrs. Penguin—if she exists—to-morrow," were David's last words as he wished his chum " Good-night."

Next day, after a hearty breakfast—all were making the fullest use of the plentiful supply in view of the probability of scanty rations in the future—permission was obtained from Doctor Elliot, and the boys set off once more for " Wreck Point," as it was now known. On the way they discussed plans for the day.

" I can't make up my mind whether it would be better to keep on this side of the range or to explore beyond the wreck," cogitated Frank as he adjusted the sail.

David was consulting a small compass. " It seems to me that a direct line from where the flag was picked up to the Pole would pass behind, or to the right of Wreck Point. If so, that would be Collinson's route, but it doesn't follow that the penguins—or whatever he mistook for penguins—were actually *on the route*. He said " ahead "; but that might mean one or two miles on either side when judging from an aeroplane, perhaps several thousand feet up. What we really want is to be able to get up somewhere and look all round." A moment's silence was abruptly broken by David's fist coming down with a loud bang on the top of the box which contained their day's rations. " I've got it ! " he exclaimed. " What a fool I was not to think of that before."

" What ? " asked Frank.

" Why, the hills. I'm almost sure I can climb up to the top of that ridge and then I shall have a fine view "

Although he saw that Frank was rather nervous at the proposal, nothing could daunt him, and immediately he had selected a possible-looking starting-point he began to climb towards the summit, which, at that point, was only a few hundred feet above the snow-level.

After a slow and difficult ascent he stood at last at the top, and removing the binoculars from their case which hung over his shoulder, began to search the surrounding landscape.

All at once Frank saw him become rigid, with the glasses focused upon one spot near the base of the steep slope. His next action was to point excitedly along the range of hills, on the same side on which Frank was standing, and then to start the descent.

"I've spotted 'em, Frank," he ejaculated joyfully as soon as he reached the level once more. "We'll have to steer well out from the range or Wreck Point'll keep all the wind off," he added, meanwhile jumping on to the yacht and hauling up the sail as his chum joined him.

Before long they were crawling slowly—far too slowly to satisfy their impatience—over the rough surface, but for two miles they could see nothing of any interest ; moreover, they were too preoccupied in avoiding projecting rocks or half-hidden crevasses to pay much attention to the scenery. Farther on they began to ascend a gentle slope, and ahead of them the white blanket appeared to meet the sky.

Frank was at the front acting as look-out to warn David of obstacles ahead.

"Looks as if there's a sudden drop at the top—something like when there's sea beyond," he said.

David adjusted the sail and then glanced up. "Corks ! So it does. We'll have to keep our weather-eye open—must be prepared for *anything* in these benighted parts. Be ready to help douse the sail when the time comes, Frank."

"Right-o, cap'n," came the cheery response.

The slope, as so often happens, proved to be much

longer than it appeared, and the log attached to their yacht registered four point seven miles from Wreck Point when they began to climb the final stretch—a steep slope about a hundred yards long.

It was well that they were both prepared to act instantly. Without the slightest warning Frank's voice rang out through the cold air :

" Round with her sharp, Dave ! "

Good leader that he was, David was an equally good follower. Without as much as glancing up to see what was the danger, he swung round the snow-rudder and sprang forward to help Frank drop the sail.

Losing way rapidly, the yacht answered promptly to the rudder and swerved round at right-angles to its previous course, finally coming to a standstill on the ridge which formed the top of the slope.

Only then did David turn his head to see what had caused the look-out to give such an exigent order. But when he did he had a shock.

They were, he realized, almost on the edge of a precipice, and from where he stood he could see the nearly vertical cliff face dropping down into a huge valley of snow and ice. A cursory glance showed him that on his right the valley stretched away into the distance and was lost among the limitless white. Opposite, and some half-mile from their present position, was another ice-covered precipice, while slightly to their left the mountain range crossed the two ice cliffs nearly at right angles.

The grandeur of the scene gripped them, and for some time precluded all desire for conversation. At last David spoke :

" Guess it's worth all our little troubles just to see that ! "

Frank had torn his eyes away from the majestic exhibition of Nature's sculpture and was staring down at the sheet of ice eight hundred feet below.

" Lend me your binocs, Dave," he said in urgent tones. Hardly had he focused them when he swung round

"Penguin Cove."

and announced triumphantly, " I thought so ! There are the penguins, Dave."

Without replying, David seized the binoculars and clapped them to his eyes. Sure enough, as he turned the focus-screw, the tiny blurs resolved themselves into moving objects . . . then he saw that they walked upright . . . and as both eyes and glasses collaborated, he could distinguish the dark heads, lighter backs, and white fronts, as hundreds of penguins, varying from three to four feet high, strolled sedately over the ice.

" It's not going to be too easy to get them, I'm afraid," cogitated Frank. " I don't see how any one can ever get down to catch them, let alone up again."

David's face showed that he also was puzzled. " No. It looks pretty hopeless, certainly. But they'll be awfully disappointed if we go back and tell them that ' penguin steak is off.' I vote we explore along a bit and see if there's any possible way down "—consulting his wristwatch. " We've got crowds of time."

Frank quickly agreed, as he usually did to anything which David suggested, and taking care to " anchor " their yacht securely, they began to walk along the ridge to their right.

Progress was slow and extremely difficult. In fact both realized, although saying nothing, that they had undertaken a very perilous task. The more or less flat part of the ridge was only six feet wide ; on their right it sloped downwards with moderate steepness, but on their left the precipice was almost vertical, with a treacherous icy edge.

Fortunately they did not have to go far. Hidden by the snow, a gap extending inwards for nearly fifty yards crossed their path, and this, they found, formed a descending gully which wound down the cliff in a steep but quite scalable slope. To their surprise, they saw rocks projecting here and there and knew that these would greatly simplify their task.

" Shall we try it ? " asked Frank, pausing at the edge.

"I think we ought to. You can't see the bottom from here, so we'd better make sure before we send them on a wild-goose chase."

"I'll go first," replied Frank, and before he could stop him David saw his chum hurrying down the slope.

"Take care!" he yelled, expecting every moment to see Frank slip and go hurtling down.

Luckily for both—and for those who were to follow—the descent not only continued right into the valley, but proved much easier than they had anticipated. A quarter of an hour's exhausting—and often none too safe—climbing over rocks and snow found them standing on a ledge only fifty feet above the ice, and from there they could see the remainder of the way down, at the same time obtaining a clear view of the cliff-end of the valley.

"This'll do us, I think," decided David as he sat on a rock to recover his breath ; "we know now that we shall be able to get down quite easily, and we can see all we want to see from here. My! what a spiffing day!"

It was a never-to-be-forgotten scene. One of the rather rare cloudless days, the sun was shining full into the valley, reflecting back from the sheet of ice like a searchlight, and lighting up the rugged end of the valley. With the coming of the longer days, temperature had risen, and although occasional snatches of severe cold still occurred, at the moment it felt quite pleasant basking in the sunshine.

"No doubt about them being penguins now, and plenty of 'em," mused David as he watched the queer amphibians strutting about, every now and then stopping to squawk to each other.

Frank was examining the scene through the binoculars, but after letting them rove from penguin to penguin he focused on to the other side of the valley. Here he paused and stared fixedly at one point.

"Look, Dave, there's water over there," pointing

across the ice. " Look, just there, near the opposite cliff. And what's that black thing on the ice—looks like a seal."

David took the binoculars and confirmed his chum's suspicions. " It *is* a seal, Frank. My ! We're in luck to-day, old chap—penguin and seals. That means lots of reserve food, and a choice too. Fresh seal-meat fried in butter, yum yum ! Makes one's mouth water after all the preserved meat we've been having, eh ? "

Again Frank's eyes wandered back to the top of the valley as he searched along the rugged surface, picking out rocks here and there amid the patches of snow.

David stood up and stamped. " I'm getting cold, Frank ; anyway, I think it's time we got a move on. We've got a stiff climb in front of us, and then a longish run back on the yacht—with the wind on our beam too. We'd better not be late or they'll be getting anxious."

" Half a mo', Dave," called Frank, focusing and re-focusing on a dark patch where the cliffs met the ice.

" Say, Dave, isn't that a *cave* in the cliff over there ? You look ! "

" I think you're right," agreed his chum a moment later. " Looks like a large one too."

Frank took the glasses back. " I believe some of the penguins must be nesting in there. They keep on going in and out anyway. Hallo ! What's that ? " His voice suddenly became vibrant with apprehension.

" Dave, I believe it's an animal. Yes, it's . . ."

David had already begun to climb, but noting the abrupt break in the sentence he looked back. Frank was in a heap, the binoculars beside him.

At once David recognized the—now less—familiar symptoms. His chum was in the grip of an unusually severe attack of his old trouble and was lying absolutely helpless, trembling from head to foot.

A glance at the cave mouth showed him that Frank's halting suggestion was fully justified. Standing nearly upright was an animal about five feet high, but unlike anything he had ever seen before. In the momentary and distant glimpse were mixed the confused outlines of a gorilla and a gigantic penguin.

While he knelt down to do what he could to restore his chum, the reasons for the unusual violence of the shock slowly pieced themselves together in his mind.

> " A cave . . . an animal . . . Antarctica.
> A cave . . . a lioness . . . Africa."

At once he saw it all and his deepest sympathy went out to his companion. There was no time for reflection, however ; something must be done immediately. There was the animal—whether fierce or not he had no idea, nor could he forecast its climbing powers—and Frank was ill and must be got back to the depot.

With a supreme effort David dragged him foot by foot up the steep and slippery track, and at last had the consolation of laying him in the yacht ; but it had been a terribly exhausting task, and he sank down beside him, breathless. As soon as he could sit upright he noticed that Frank was slightly more self-controlled, and spoke to him reassuringly :

" Buck up, old chap, you'll be back at the depot in a jiffy."

Frank raised his head and stared wildly around. " W-where is it ? " he groaned.

To his chum, who knew him so well, it was at once apparent that he was speaking almost unconsciously— prompted by his gripping fears ; never in his normal moments would he have allowed himself to reveal so clearly what he felt.

" 'Spect it's gone back into its cubby 'ole," he replied cheerfully ; then, as an idea struck him, he added, " I'll go and see."

Any one watching would have noticed that David glanced ahead somewhat anxiously as he neared the edge ; but one glimpse down into the valley reassured him—the

" There's something moving inside the cave ! "

animal was standing in a crouching position surrounded by
penguins.   Hurrying back, he called across the snow :
    " It's all right, Frank.   It's still where it was.   Seems
to be holding a council of war with the penguins. . . .
Don't suppose it's even seen us."
    The news certainly had a drug-like effect upon Frank.
Nevertheless, his heroic struggle to regain control of him-

self was not lost upon David as he steered the yacht back to the depot. Before their arrival Frank had recovered sufficiently to avoid letting the others see what he had been through, but he insisted upon keeping close to his partner's side as they accompanied one of the dog-sledges, containing four men, back towards Wreck Point.

Led by the two boys, the party climbed down to the ledge from where the strange sight had first been spotted. Although a crowd of penguins surrounded the cave, and several seals could be seen on the ice not far away, there was now no sign of any other denizen of the valley.

Several of the party began—either openly or secretly— to doubt the boys' story, and to presume that it was only the product of their excited imagination. Doctor Elliot, however, with his customary sympathetic insight, had seen through Frank's mask, and had read in his face evidence of the shock so determinedly hidden. Raising his binoculars to his eyes, he studied the entrance to the cave and two minutes later rapped out :

" There's something moving inside the cave ! It *may* be a penguin, but I think not."

His words were quickly verified as the tall figure came slowly out.

" That's no penguin. Looks more like some new kind of gorilla," remarked one of the watchers.

Then every one within earshot had a shock. With his extra powerful lenses Doctor Elliot was able to observe details unseen by the others.

" That's no animal—it's a human being ! " he averred.

CHAPTER X

THE MYSTERY DEEPENS

THE news came like a bolt from the blue to both boys and men. All that they could see, even with the aid of glasses, was a fawn-coloured, hairy skin, a curious head surmounted by a circlet of fur and a small, very hairy face. But the doctor watched the " animal " walk, noted its anatomy and studied its eyes and mouth, with the result that his scientific knowledge enabled him to say definitely that " it " was a human being, though whether civilized or otherwise, and of what—if any—nationality he could not yet judge.

Before any one could offer further conjectures their attention was absorbed by the scene in front of the cave. As the tall figure emerged, the penguins halted in their progress and bowed low. This fact in itself would not have surprised those of the onlookers who had studied the habits of those queer inhabitants of the Antarctic, for they knew that whenever a penguin sees a person approaching it almost invariably comes forward and bows, in apparent greeting, before beginning to talk to the stranger in its queer squawks. But on this occasion not one penguin, but the whole assembly, bowed in unison, while the tall figure acknowledged the gesture in similar manner. After these preliminary greetings the main actor sat down upon something—what it was no one could see—while the remainder continued to stand, and perfectly still at that.

What was happening then it was difficult to see, but the one sitting appeared to be addressing the others.

Suddenly a babel of squawks reached their ears, the man stood up and waved his arm, and the penguins, after bowing low, turned round and walked sedately away from the cave, followed at a short distance by their "leader."

Before the procession had advanced twenty yards David noticed an unusual commotion among the seals. Raising their heads they stared for a moment at the cavalcade, and then, as if picking out an enemy amongst them, turned and wallowed along the ice ; on reaching the edge each animal flopped into the water and disappeared, until there was not a single seal left within sight.

"That's curious, Frank," he remarked, seeing that his companion was also following the pantomime.

Frank was leaning against a snow-covered ledge, staring intently down, his face free from the haunted expression which David so dreaded to see.

"Crumbs, what a goggle-eyed show ! Just like a lot of mummers ! Yes, those seals are evidently properly scared of something. Can't be the penguins, 'cos seals and penguins are quite good friends. So, by the Sherlock-Holmesian method of elimination, it can only be—well, ' IT.' "

David smiled as he grunted his assent. " 'Mm, yes—and yet he, or it if you like, seems a kind of blood-brother to the penguins."

By this time the queer crowd had reached a spot near the nesting-haunts of the birds, and while they formed themselves into a large semicircle, their leader—for such the spectators now realized him to be—walked towards a heap of snow and sat down upon it.

"Bless my whiskers ! " ejaculated the normally clean-shaven Doctor Elliot, whose binoculars again gave him the advantage, "blowed if he isn't sitting upon a snow-throne."

Noticing the bewildered looks of one or two of his hearers, he added, " That heap of snow has been carefully made into the shape of a throne."

The scene, which had been rapidly increasing in

interest, now gripped them one and all with its comedy-interest. Not a word was spoken, while each of the six faces reflected its intense absorption.

As the leader took his seat the penguins nearly prostrated themselves, but rose again at a signal from him. Then came the most amazing act yet. From his gestures it was perfectly obvious that he was addressing them—occasional remarks in the form of squawks could be heard from where they waited—while the penguins kept rigidly upright. Immediately he paused a chorus of squawks ran round the semicircle, after which he went on with his address. This continued for some little time, but at last he rose—the penguins again bowing—and made his way back towards the cave. At the entrance he turned, received the homage of his subjects, and vanished into his " palace." As he disappeared from view the penguin group dispersed, each becoming an individual again instead of one unit of a crowd.

Doctor Elliot removed the glasses from his eyes, and as the gasps subsided, exclaimed :

" Well, of all the extraordinary sights I have ever witnessed, that beats the band ! "

" What d'you make of it, sir ? " asked Mr. Slater.

" *Make of it ?* " The doctor's face, such of it as could be seen, was a picture. " Why, the chap's dotty—that's the only thing any one can make of it. Think's he's king of the penguins, by the look of it. But we'll go down and investigate."

" Think he's dangerous ? " asked a voice, rather hesitantly.

" Dangerous ? Why should he be ? . . . At least, he may be, of course . . . oh, is he armed, you mean ? How do I know ? What does it matter after all ? *If he is a human being, we must rescue him.*"

With this typical but very dogmatic conclusion the speaker led the way down ; or, rather, tried to. Very soon, not knowing the best route, he began to get into difficulties. Frank at once sprang forward.

" This way, sir. David and I spotted an easy pathway down this morning."

With that he led the way, while David followed closely on his heels, stamping down the slippery snow in places or giving a helping hand to others where necessary.

At the bottom the whole party made tracks for the cave. Fortunately, the penguins were busily engaged some distance away, so the intruders' arrival was unnoticed.

Just as they approached the entrance their quarry emerged from the cave. For a moment he stared vacantly across the ice towards the penguins, then, observing the figures on his right, looked straight towards them.

The onlookers held their breath. Would he attack them or retreat to his cave ? Then they saw him draw himself erect, raise his arm, and make a signal. Most of the party were completely mystified at his actions, but seeing Doctor Elliot bow, they realized that he had understood and knew that the man had taken them for a new variety of penguins and expected them to bow to him. Consequently, five other heads were solemnly lowered.

" Wish Hill were here ; he understands animals better than I do," muttered Doctor Elliot. " Oh well, something must be done, so here goes."

With that he walked towards the man. He had already utilized the opportunity to note that he was unarmed. Again the remainder of the party waited in mute expectation. *Was* it really a man ? they asked themselves a dozen times, and if so, what would he do ? If not . . . they must be prepared to rush to the doctor's aid at a moment's notice.

While all this was going on they had time to take stock of the extraordinary figure in front of them. Standing upright it was taller than they had imagined—about five feet six, as far as they could estimate. Perhaps the most remarkable thing was that no trace of its body was visible except a circular view of the face extending from just above the eyes to the top of the chin, and sideways, from the centre of each cheek. Even this portion was thickly covered with hair, and the only features really evident were two very dreamy eyes, a much frost-bitten nose, and a gap in the hair where the mouth should be. Every other part of the body was covered with fawn-coloured sealskin, the short furry surface of which gave him a realistic animal-like appearance. In addition to the sealskin hood which encased his head and part of his face, a circlet of silver-coloured fur was fixed on the top of his head ; this, especially in the sunshine, resembled a silver crown at a short distance.

When only ten yards away, Doctor Elliot addressed the strange being, purposely speaking very deliberately.

" Good-morning, I am pleased to meet you ! " True it was late afternoon, but he did not presume that his hearer would argue that point. As he spoke, Doctor Elliot held out his hand.

At first the seal-man stared at the unaccustomed sounds ; then a rapid volley of unintelligible squawks poured forth.

Each squawk proved to the onlookers that he was some kind of man. A distinct mouth, with two rows of decayed, but obviously human, teeth were revealed.

Whether by intuition or of set purpose the amazed spectators could not determine, but, regardless of the answering squawks, Doctor Elliot started a slow conversation with the man.

Gradually the squawks grew less frequent, and as the long-forgotten sounds began to penetrate into his almost inactive brain, his eyes showed that an internal conflict was in progress.

At last they heard isolated words interspersed among the squawks ; then, just as they were marvelling at the doctor's consummate patience, there was a brief silence, broken suddenly by the words :

" King of all penguins ; bow when you meet me."

That sentence revealed the secret. Doctor Elliot

was still master of the situation, however, and bowing towards the speaker, he asked :

" Will you show us your palace, your majesty ? "

His ruse succeeded immediately. The man turned, and beckoning the others to follow, made towards the cave.

Inside it seemed almost pitch dark as they left the sunshine behind them, but after a few minutes their eyes began to grow accustomed to the altered conditions, and after removing their goggles, they were able to pick out the most prominent details.

Even before they could see anything one curious feature struck them. It was very much warmer inside the cave ; in fact, on entering, the heat felt oppressive. Space was the next condition of which they became conscious ; everything was still very blurry, but it was obvious that the cave was a large one, although the roof was less than a foot above their heads. Then came the realization that they were standing on a sandy rock-floor and not on ice . . . an indistinct heap of something loomed up in one corner . . . several variously shaped objects lay in another . . . something partially covered the entrance, leaving only a narrow doorway.

Then some one remembered his flash-lamp and a brilliant beam cut the darkness, throwing into relief the farther end of the cave as the rays diverged. A few jerks of the holder's wrist and every detail of the recluse's dwelling was laid bare.

Across the entrance had been fixed a heavy curtain of sealskins, effectually keeping out most of the cold wind and leaving a space only three feet wide. Even this, they discovered later, could be closed at will by dropping a flap. The cave was a long oval apartment, although it did not extend inwards for more than twenty feet. In the most protected corner was the owner's bed—a thick layer of sealskins, with a pile of extra skins to pull over him as required. At the other end was a large pile of ashes, surrounded by the contents of several boxes of long-used-up matches, evidently the remains of ancient fires, while near-by were his " kitchen utensils "—a composite billy-can, plate, and mug, knife, fork, and spoon, and other oddments ; in still another corner was his larder, consisting of a few tins of meat and a small quantity of frozen seal-meat. A large heap of empty tins which had originally contained meat, fruit, milk, sugar, coffee, etc., told their own tale, and it was these which re-stimulated their curiosity as to the previous history of the occupant. All the tins bore the name of a London dealer . . . among them were two spent flash-lamps.

While they were inspecting his " palace " the man followed them round dreamily ; now and then—as when the torch first threw its beam across the cave—something seemed to stir a chord in his memory and he would pull up with a jerk to stare at his visitors, while wistful, searching expressions filmed across his face ; but, putting his hand to his forehead, he relapsed once more into the rôle of recluse.

"Been having a pretty thin time of it lately, by the look of it," remarked David to his chum, adding by way of explanation, " No fire for ages—those ashes are very old. Practically nothing to eat except seal-meat, and that raw, I s'pose ; nothing to drink except water . . . and, by the way, how does he prevent that from freezing, I wonder ? "

As if to demonstrate the answer to his question, the man began to push his hand into the pile of skins ; a moment later he drew forth an uncorked flask and began to drink.

"There you are, Frank ! Kind of him to answer my question so promptly, although I don't suppose he even knew what I was talking about ! See how he does it ? Just fills that flask with snow, lets it melt in the cave, and then tucks it among the folds of those sealskins. The warmth melts the snow and probably keeps the water slightly warm as well."

"Brainwave that ! " laughed Frank. " Wonder why it's so warm in here, Dave ? "

"Just what I was wondering. I'll ask old Walker—he should be able to explain it."

His hopes were justified. "I don't wonder you're puzzled," began the physicist. "I was myself at first. But I think I've got it now. You know, of course, that the deep-earth temperature remains very constant, just as an underground railway is always cool in the summer and warm in the winter. . . ."

"And fuggy all the year round," interrupted David.

"That is so, usually," laughed Mr. Walker. "Now this cave is really a long way underground, as far as the normal surface of the globe in these parts is concerned. This valley, I imagine, is really a frozen-over inlet from the sea ; fortunately the cave is protected on three sides, so, unless the wind happens to be directly off the sea, there is usually a dead calm here. The result is that this cave, especially with its artificial door, is, to all intents and purposes, an underground cavern. I doubt if the temperature ever drops much below the freezing-point, nor would it vary much—possibly a few degrees below in the winter and a few above in summer. Meanwhile, as you see, he's well protected by day and night by those wonderfully non-conducting sealskins. When you remember that seals *live* in water which is practically always just below the freezing-point, but have to come up into temperatures varying from about a hundred degrees of frost to well above freezing, you'll see that their coats must be marvellously effective in keeping out both cold and heat."

At that moment the man glanced anxiously at the narrow doorway, and then stepped outside. To their astonishment they saw that the sun had disappeared. So engrossed had they been that the flight of time had been unnoticed, and it would soon be dusk.

Further thoughts were precluded by the reappearance of the recluse, who stood in the doorway pointing along the valley. At the same time he uttered several loud squawks. Seeing that none of the visitors took any

notice of this signal, he—possibly quite unconsciously—
relapsed into their language.

"Time—to say—good-night," he called.

Utterly mystified, Doctor Elliot bowed and followed
him out of the cave. Once more the whole party traversed
the ice towards the "throne room," as Frank had
christened it. Near his "throne" he pulled up and
uttered a number of raucous squawks, similar to those
they had heard in the cave. The result was almost
magical. The crowd of penguins, who were at that
moment standing quietly about fifty yards away, gave
a chorus of squawks and hurried in a body towards
him.

Then, as their "king" took his seat, they all bowed
reverently. Suddenly, to their horror, the man noticed
that his newly arrived subjects had omitted to show their
loyalty. Standing up again, he glared and pointed
straight at them.

"Evidently we had better copy the others or there'll
be trouble," smiled Doctor Elliot. At a signal from him,
the party of six bowed solemnly, and were relieved to see
the king reinstall himself upon his throne.

Then came the most extraordinary comedy they had
so far witnessed. Raising both his arms, the man uttered
a string of squawks as if blessing his charges. As he
finished, his subjects bowed and squawked back their
"good-nights."

The visitors took good care to bow this time. But
this was not enough. Somehow the king had detected
that they had not answered his message vocally and again
pointed at them.

"Imitate their squawks as well as you can," warned
the doctor.

Once more their leader harangued them from the
throne, and as the penguins bowed or squawked his
human subjects did likewise—as far as they could succeed in imitating the penguin noises, that is. Then the
king answered in two very deliberate and impressive

(4,766)

9

squawks, rose from his throne—to the usual accompaniment of bows—and, with a majestic gesture, dismissed the assembly.

"I didn't know what on earth to do with myself ; I was simply bursting with laughter," said David, as they followed the king towards his palace.

"Same here," agreed Frank. "What on earth d'you imagine it all meant ? The birds seemed to understand. I wonder if they really do ? "

While they were talking, Doctor Elliot had overtaken them and heard their conversation.

"It was humorous," he broke in. "But I think I've got the hang of it. That man has evidently lived among these penguins for some time. The privations through which he has passed have affected his brain, and his insanity has taken the peculiar form of imagining that he is king of the penguins. Living among them so much, and being entirely cut off from human beings, he has almost forgotten his own tongue, but has succeeded in learning—to some extent at any rate—the penguin language. They are some of the most friendly creatures on earth, and by dint of kindness and constant friendship he has trained them to regard him as their leader and to obey certain commands. I *think* that the ceremony which we have just witnessed is their ' Grand good-night.' If you remember, he said something about it being time to say good-night."

"So he did ! How wonderfully he imitates them, and they seem to follow him blindly," marvelled Frank.

Doctor Elliot nodded his agreement. "The fact is that he has become one of them, as far as any human being can, that is."

They were now faced with two problems. The most immediate one was caused by the fact that it was rapidly growing dark. There would be no chance of getting back to the depot before dark. After a short consultation, Doctor Elliot and Mr. Walker agree that the only thing to do would be to sleep in the cave.

" What about food ? " asked Mr. Hawlet.

Their leader looked blank. " Nothing doing. I had no idea of being away for long, so we haven't brought any."

" How about that box, sir ? " asked David.

" Which ? "

" The one we used for a seat in the ice-yacht. I think that's full of ship's biscuits."

" Good for you," congratulated Doctor Elliot, " I had forgotten that." Glancing at the sky—" There will be just time, I think, to send up and fetch them. It'll be a poor supper, but it will keep the wolf from the door."

Suddenly another idea struck him. Walking up to the recluse he bowed, pointed to his mouth, and asked :

" Can we have some food ? "

A flash of enlightenment spread over his hearer's face as he hurried to a corner of the cave where he picked up a coil of rope and an axe. On emerging from the cave he made a circuitous route towards the edge of the ice where a number of seals were lying at varying distances from the water. At his approach most of them propelled themselves along the ice with their flippers and vanished into the sea. By a clever movement, however, the hunter outflanked a group of four, and ran between them and the water. His next move astounded the watchers because of its artfulness and rapidity. Throwing a noose over one, he attacked another with the axe, and in a remarkably short space of time he was on his way back dragging three dead seals behind him.

These he proceeded to cut up with his axe and a large knife, and before it was quite dark he presented to his visitors a number of fine seal-steaks, as well as other edible parts. These he doubtless expected them to eat raw, as he always had to do nowadays since his fire-making materials had given out.

Fortunately several members of the party possessed matches, and with the aid of these—supplemented by the

Dragging three dead seals behind him.

wooden box, spent matches, and blubber—the steaks were soon sizzling merrily over a good fire.

Both boys were more than ready for the appetizing meal, and chatted as they munched.

"What we saw just now, and his lavish supply of seal-skins, clears up our puzzle as to why the seals vanish so quickly when he approaches," remarked Frank.

David paused in the act of breaking off a lump of ship's biscuit. "You mean when we first arrived, when we were squatting on that ledge?" A nod answered him. "Yes, I remember, we were puzzled because, although the penguins seemed so friendly, the seals hopped it immediately they saw him."

It was a picture to watch the recluse as he tasted hot, cooked meat again. But he ate ravenously, almost animal-like, and had finished long before any one else.

While they were eating, he collected the skins of the seals, cleaned and dried them and placed them, together with a bundle of his own, for the use of his visitors.

The second, and more difficult, problem to be solved was what they were to do with the penguin-man.

This, however, was left to solve itself while they slept —or remain unsolved until to-morrow—and less than an hour after dark every one was fast asleep except Doctor Elliot.

CHAPTER XI

EXCITEMENT IN PENGUIN COVE

DOCTOR ELLIOT could not dismiss the queer man from his mind—his eccentric appearance, his penguin language, and his curious delusions. Who was he? How did he come there? But the most difficult problem of all—what should they do with him?—completely baffled him until its insistent recurrence lulled him to sleep.

David woke up in a perspiration. At first he could not understand why he was so hot; slowly it dawned upon him that he was sleeping in a sheltered cave instead of in a tent in the open. Seeing that Frank was stirring, he called across:

" Morning, Frank; how goes it? "

" Phew! Baking hot! "

" Same here. I'm all in a bath. It's the warmth of this cave. We're not used to such luxury."

Frank looked around at the " luxury " with a wry smile. " No, we're not. Life in a tent with the mercury at thirty below zero is not exactly luxury, certainly. I'd no idea these sealskins were so warm though, and I piled several on top of me. By the way," with a prolonged yawn, " what d'you imagine we're going to do to-day—about the K.O.P., I mean? "

" K.O.P.? " puzzled David. " Sounds like a new petrol."

" No, chum! Him, I mean," jerking his finger towards the still-sleeping mystery man. " King of the Penguins, of course. Shall we rescue him like a fair maiden in distress, or leave him to his fate—and his rookery or penguinery, or whatever you call it ? "

David rose and stretched himself, rolling the skins into a neat little heap. " Blowed if I know. Can't leave him here to his fate, I shouldn't think . . . Robinson Crusoe isn't in it. And yet I'm jiggered if I can see how we can take him with us—or send him back. Give it up."

By this time there was a general stir. As the processes of dressing, washing, and shaving did not enter into their schedule since they had left the base, " getting up " consisted of two very brief items—waking up, and pushing the sealskins into a heap. After this, one good stretch and every one was more than ready for breakfast. Fortunately there was enough left over from the previous evening's meal, although cold seal-meat and ship's biscuits did not provide too appetizing a meal.

During the night Doctor Elliot had advanced one step further in his wrestling with the problem. He would question the man about himself ; perhaps that would throw some light upon the mystery and help him to decide on some definite action.

Immediately after breakfast, he walked across to where the man was standing and began :

" I say—what's your name ? "

But he might as well have spoken to the air. A glance from the mouth of the cave had informed its owner that the sun had just risen, and with a look as if he had some urgent duty to perform, he strode out on to the ice sheet. Following him, the doctor made his way along his last night's tracks until he saw the penguins a short distance ahead. Very soon he was watching the " Good-morning " ceremony, an exact repetition of the evening performance, except that (he presumed !) the words were different.

Back in the cave, he tried again. " Who . . . are . . . you ? " he asked very deliberately.

" King of the Penguins," came the decisive but un-looked-for answer.

He tried again. " What is your name ? "

" Squawk-squaw-squaw-w-w-awk." A repetition of the question brought exactly the same reply, as did a third attempt. " No doubt that is his name among the penguins," thought Doctor Elliot ; but as it was useless for his purpose, he tried his next query.

" Where do you come from ? "

This was too much for the recluse's memory, which catered only for the present, and could not dive into the past ; a blank stare accompanied by a shake of the head, was the sole reply.

" Are you an Englishman ? " was his last shot, and the one which brought the only informative reply—a vigorous nod.

After this mainly ineffectual cross-examination, a conference was called to discuss their action.

" Although I am frankly puzzled as to what is best to do," began Doctor Elliot, " I think I can now piece together the mystery pretty completely. The man is evidently one—perhaps the only—survivor of a party of explorers. Somehow he found himself here alone—perhaps too ill to go on, or believed dead, perhaps abandoned by some treacherous companion, or possibly the only one left from a terrible tragedy . . . how, I don't know ; nor does it matter much. He searches round and finds this cave, where he stores his small supply of tinned food, et cetera. Thanks to the shelter, he is enabled to exist, despite the intense cold outside, even when he can no longer have fires. As his food-supply diminished he began to look around ; there were only two possibilities— penguins and seals. For some reason best known to himself, he decides to make friends with the penguins, and so uses the seals for food and warmth ; hence the friendliness of the former and the timidity of the latter. The natural tameness of the penguins, and the total absence of any other companionship, no doubt combined to force him to seek their company increasingly, until he began to understand their language bit by bit. The more his world became penguinized, the more he exerted a kind of dominion over them until he developed a complex that he was their king. Slowly but surely the terrible isolation and privation unhinged his brain, the past being deeply buried in his subconscious. In fact I seriously believe that he takes us for a new breed of penguin."

When the laugh had subsided, he continued : " The question is, what are we to do about him ?   I confess that the problem baffles me—perhaps some of you can suggest a solution ? "

Each tried to contribute something to the discussion, and suggestions were made varying from the advisability of shooting him to put him out of his misery, to taking him with them all the way to the Pole and back. After some time it was mutually agreed that he should be left where he was until the supporting party—who would turn back about two hundred miles from the Pole—could pick him up on their return journey, when they would take him back to the base.

But they were to learn that the recluse was not the only discovery which they had made. As soon as the discussion was over, the two boys wandered out of the cave.

" Let's see what his majesty's subjects are doing," suggested Frank, in a light-hearted mood.

Once outside, however, their attention was riveted by the sight of Mr. Walker, who was standing on the centre of the ice-sheet engrossed with a curious-looking apparatus. As they walked quietly up, he turned and spoke to David.

" Oh, there you are !   I was wishing you were here to help."

For some little time Frank watched, as he heard the physicist tell David to do this or press that. Then he saw him stand upright from his crouching position and enter some figures in a note-book.

" May I ask what that apparatus is, sir ? " he inquired, presuming that the experiment was now concluded.

" Well, I've nothing more to do until Doctor Elliot wants me, so I'll explain it to you if you like."

" You see this," he continued, touching a hammer just above a drum, " well, when I press the switch, that emits a sound which is aimed downwards ; now sound, as you know, travels at a regular and definite speed in any given medium—thus in air its speed is about one thousand and eighty-four feet per second, while in water it is four thousand seven hundred and fourteen at fifteen degrees. There is a different, but invariable, figure for ice, snow, earth, and many other media. But, and here is the secret of the whole apparatus, sound waves are reflected from the surface of every medium ; consequently, if you have layers of four different media—we'll call them A, B, C and D—a sound-wave will travel through A at x feet per second ; on reaching B, a portion will be reflected back to its origin, while some will traverse B at x' feet per second ; at the surface of C, more energy will be reflected and the speed through C will be x'' ; correspondingly, a third portion will be reflected from the surface of D and the rate through D will become x'''. Is that clear ? "

" Quite," assented David, " the downward speed changes with each substance, and you will hear one echo for each different medium encountered."

Mr. Walker nodded. " Exactly. As you may know, this is the principle of modern depth-testing apparatus. A sound-wave is started at the surface of the sea and the time interval between its start and the return of the echo—from the bottom—gives the depth. Now we cannot calculate the depth in this case unless we know what the media are ; but, and this is the point, the number of echoes will tell us the number of media, and from this we can deduce whether there is land or sea beneath us. . . ."

" Don't quite follow that, sir," put in Frank.

" No, probably not, but you will in a minute—that is, if I am any good at explaining things." Here he smiled, but went on. " Now listen carefully and I'll explain it. We know that there may be four layers— snow, ice, water, or land. We also know that snow, if any, is bound to be the first and that land will be the last. Now if all four are present there will be three echoes, from the surfaces of the ice, water, and land respectively. So three echoes will mean that the only land is at the bottom of the sea. Two echoes would probably indicate that the ice was resting upon land—in other words that we were on land and not on the frozen sea."

During a pause David put another question. " But suppose there is no snow, sir ? Here, for instance."

The physicist removed his pipe from his mouth to reply. " I was just coming to that. There is a slight snag there. In actual practice, if the layer of snow or ice, or any other material for that matter, is very shallow, the echo will return so quickly that we cannot measure the time interval. So, if the snow or ice is less than ten feet deep, we must ignore it . . . but I haven't answered your question yet, have I ? If there is no snow . . . well, let us consider the present problem. We are standing upon ice, so if there is one loud echo only there must be land under the ice ; but if we get two echoes, one will be from the surface of the water under the ice, and the second from the bottom of the ocean. That clear ? "

Both boys nodded. " Quite, thank you, sir," assented David.

" Now I'm going to try," continued Mr. Walker.

The two chums watched intently as he manipulated the apparatus. Hardly had he pressed the switch when a loud " Ah ! " escaped his lips. But it was not until he had repeated the experiment several times, and in different spots, that he turned to them again.

" Now you try," he said as he handed the earphones to David, " and let me know what are *your* conclusions."

" No doubt whatever," affirmed David, as he removed the earphones ; " each time there were two distinct echoes, so we must be standing on the frozen sea."

" That confirms all my experiments exactly," beamed the physicist. " Now there's no need to try over there,"

pointing to the well defined mountain-range on either side
of the cave ; " but we'll try a little way back towards
Wreck Point. If, as may be the case, that is only a
mountainous island projecting from the sea—such as in
the East Indies, for instance—then the remainder of the
snow-covered plateau over which we came must be frozen
sea."

Selecting a place well away from any indication of
land, but where the snow was not deep enough to affect
their experiments, all three " listened-in " and recorded
their conclusions independently.

" Then we all agree. There was only one echo, showing that we are standing upon ice-bound land."

Both of his hearers noticed the exuberant enthusiasm
of his voice, but it was left to Frank to inquire. " Is there
any special reason why that is important, sir ? "

Mr. Walker's face beamed as he replied : " Yes, there
is. You see, no one knows whether the ice-barrier rests
upon land or whether it is floating upon the sea. In other
words, although a few mountain-ranges and peaks are
known, no one can really say whether the frozen part of
the Antarctic is mainly a vast frozen sea with a few isolated islands, or whether it is an ice-bound continent.
*That is one of the points which we have come out here to
test*. Now I haven't told you before, but I have been
carrying out experiments ever since we landed on the
barrier, and all the results agree that, except in a few
places near the sea and down there," pointing back
towards the scene of their first tests, " *there is land beneath the ice*. There is still much to be done, of course,
but it is already obvious that we have discovered a vast
tract of land never before suspected, and our results may
go a long way towards proving that practically the whole
of Antarctica is one huge continent."

While he was speaking, the faces of his hearers showed
plainly that they too were rapidly imbued with the
speaker's enthusiasm. Both felt thrilled at the thought
of assisting in such an important discovery.

" Then where the penguins are is really frozen sea ? " queried David.

" Yes," consented Mr. Walker as he began to pack up his apparatus. " It means that there is an inlet from the open sea which reaches up to the cave. In other words, under normal conditions of temperature, the cave—perhaps with a nice beach in front of it—would be situated in the cliffs and would look down a narrow bay towards the open sea."

" A posh seaside resort, in fact. Let's call it ' Penguin Cove,' shall we ? "

" Call it what you like," laughed Mr. Walker ; " but unless we buck up, Doctor Elliot will be calling us in a different way."

Walking back towards the cave all three were engrossed in mental pictures of an enormous Antarctic continent lying hidden beneath its massive covering of ice and snow. The sight of the cave in the distance, however, reminded David of the recluse and so of the problem which the latter had occasioned.

" Why didn't we bring wireless with us—then we could have spoken to the base and asked them to send a small party to fetch him ? " indicating the man who was now engaged in one of his conferences with the penguins.

" It was entirely a question of load. Every sledge had to be kept strictly within a certain weight. When the absolute essentials—food and equipment, that is—were totalled up it was found that there was only twenty pounds to spare, so it became a question of *either* a wireless outfit *or* this apparatus. But the other two parties are both equipped with sets."

Doctor Elliot was impatiently awaiting their return. It was already past midday, and as he remarked rather more curtly than usual, those at the depot would be wondering what had happened to them. Now that all six were back in the cave he proposed to have a quick meal—a fresh supply of cooked seal-meat awaited them— and return as quickly as possible.

"The six of us will meet at the sledge *immediately* we have cleared up," he concluded, with very pronounced emphasis.

After the meal every one was busy tidying up the cave and returning the recluse's property. Frank and his chum were ready before the others and were about to start for the sledge when David jerked out, "Blow it all, bothered if I haven't forgotten that photo ! I promised young Alan that I would take some interesting snaps for him, and I meant to get one of the throne."

"Too late now, isn't it ? " asked Frank, gazing back to see if the others were ready.

"Let's chance it." For once David looked defiant. "They'll probably be ages before they're ready, and it won't take half a tick to sprint over there and snap it."

So saying, he led the way, and was, as usual, followed by Frank. A smart run took them to the throne, which was quickly recorded. Just as David was shutting the camera, Frank called his attention to the edge of the ice.

"Just look at that whopping seal ! " he exclaimed.

Seeing an unusually long specimen—it was quite fourteen feet from snout to tail—David set the camera again.

"Crumbs, I must get one of old Goliath ! " he whispered, walking quietly towards the monster.

As Frank walked in a semi-circular direction to get a better view of the animal, he noticed that, in addition to its great length, it had a much longer head and more pronounced neck than the usual specimens. But what he did not notice was its fierce expression.

Suddenly, to his horror, David saw it raise its head. Simultaneously, the brute slightly opened its mouth, revealing two rows of tiger-like teeth.

"Look out, Frank, it's a sea-leopard ! " he yelled. But he was too late. With a loud snarl, the monster propelled itself towards Frank, who turned tail and fled—towards the edge of the ice. To David's utter astonishment, the sea-leopard was not only able to keep pace with its quarry but was actually overtaking him.

It did not take him long to decide upon his actions. It was obvious that his chum's retreat was cut off and that he could not hope to dodge his pursuer for long. There was only one thing to be done. Knowing that he could run faster than Frank, David sprinted across the ice, rushed in front of him, and faced the snarling brute.

" Back to the cave, quick, Frank ! " he yelled over his shoulder.

Even the sea-leopard seemed momentarily dazed by his audacity ; swerving in its pursuit, it turned towards its new enemy with bared teeth, puffing loudly. Then it ignored its previous assailant—who was already making good use of his unexpected opportunity—and rushed at David. Leaping aside, he turned and also proceeded in a semicircle, but in the opposite direction from Frank.

Finding that the snorting animal was overtaking him, he glanced towards the cave and was much encouraged to see that Frank was already making a bee-line for safety. Now, he decided, was the time to use his superior speed to the full and save himself. With this object in view, he altered his direction slightly and put his best foot forward in the wake of his friend.

But he had underestimated his rival's speed. As he sprinted, so the sea-leopard increased its pace, and to his dismay he soon found that instead of merely diverting his chum's aggressor he had very effectually put himself into his place ; having saved his friend it now looked as if he would be the one in need of rescue.

Nevertheless, he refused even to admit such a possibility to himself. Gritting his teeth he set his eyes upon his goal and went all out. After the manner of the true athlete he resisted the temptation to look back and concentrated his whole attention upon his task.

Had he been forced to rely solely upon his own powers he would probably have fared badly. Urged on by its abnormal resentment at the sight of any human being—

or rather, of any *thing* resembling the killer of its fellow-seals—it showed an unusual turn of speed. Behind him, growing steadily nearer, he could hear the panting snarls of his enemy, and before he had traversed more than half the distance to the cave, it sounded as if it were almost upon his heels.

His brain was working furiously. What could he do ? He could not run any faster—in fact he was tiring much more rapidly than usual owing to the difficult nature of the surface. He had absolutely no means of defence ; legs or fists would be of little avail against the sharp tusks of the ferocious brute. Could he dodge ? This, he decided, was equally hopeless, as it would only postpone the final issue and might even lead him farther away from his goal.

The only hope seemed to lie in the possibility of outlasting his opponent. Seals, he knew, soon became winded. Could he stay the pace for the rest of the distance ?

Suddenly a shot rang out, and the snarling ceased abruptly. Turning his head he saw the sea-leopard on its back—motionless. Then, eased of their exigency, his muscles relaxed with a jerk, and he collapsed in a heap.

He was dimly conscious of being carried along and soon found himself lying on his back in the cave. In a few minutes he had recovered his breath sufficiently to hear the explanation of his rescue.

" Lucky you escaped so lightly, young chap ! " began Mr. Slater. " If it hadn't been for Ingram here," nodding his head towards Frank, who was still puffing and blowing, " you might have been in a bad way. He did a record sprint and yelled to us to help you. Fortunately I was just starting for the sledge and heard him. Popping back, I borrowed Doctor Elliot's rifle, worked along the ice until I could get a clear shot, and . . . well, as luck would have it, I aimed straight for once."

Both boys felt rather sheepish, as in addition to having already delayed the whole party for half an hour, they now had to spend further valuable time in returning to

" Lucky you escaped so lightly, young chap ! "

retrieve the camera. Consequently, it was nearly three
o'clock before the sledge, following in the wake of the
ice-yacht, started on its return journey, and although
there was no anxiety as to light, Doctor Elliot was on
tenterhooks lest those left at the depot should have
already set off to discover what had become of them.
On arrival they found that Le Brun was in a state of
great excitement, convinced that disaster had overtaken
them ; luckily for every one concerned, the other two
had pinned their faith to the leadership of Doctor Elliot
and had refused to leave the depot.

It would be difficult to imagine a more fantastic scene than occurred that night. Sitting round the supper-table—such as it was—were nine men and boys of several nationalities. The menu in itself would be strange to most people—pemmican soup, seal-steak, ship's biscuits, and hot cocoa—but their surroundings were stranger still. With the exception of the hills in the distance, all around them was a limitless plain of snow, and they were now nearly half-way to the Pole. When, added to these novel conditions, came the extraordinary account of the king of the penguins, those who had remained at the depot could scarcely believe that they were in a normal world at all.

At the end of the story, Doctor Elliot explained their plans for the picking-up of the recluse by the supporting party on their homeward journey.

" Do you think he'll still be there ? " asked Le Brun.

" You are thinking that perhaps we ought to have rescued him at once ? " replied their leader, with a touch of keen insight. " The trouble is that, if we did, it would upset all our plans. Obviously we cannot take him on with us, so two, at least, of us would have to turn back at once to go with him. . . . I don't see any great anxiety to volunteer for that task "—looking round at his hearers in turn with a smile. . . . " Besides which it would mean that one sledge would have only two to manage it. No, there seems no way of rescuing him immediately, but I do not think that it will be of much consequence. He's not likely to wander away ; he has plenty of food for a short time, and sufficient protection for the summer months. If all goes well the returning party should be back here within three weeks, when they can pick him up—possibly they may have to do that literally—and on reaching the base he will be well cared for, and I hope, be nursed back to health, both mental and physical."

" Do you think he will recover his sanity ? " asked Mr. Slater.

" That no one can say," was the uncertain response.

" Personally, I think he will. I should judge his condition to be merely a temporary phase, due to the combined effect of his privations and living for so long among the penguins. You see, his *sole* companionship has of necessity been limited to penguins and seals . . . the former externally and the latter internally," he added with a wry smile. Realizing that it was nearly nine o'clock, he summed up, " Yes, I think he'll be quite safe, and probably happy too, as far as he knows happiness, until our second sledge returns."

More time had been spent at two-ton depot than had been planned, so an early start was deemed advisable next morning. At first, the mountain range which they had discovered only a few miles ahead was the cause of no little anxiety to the leader. He had not expected to be troubled by any such obstacles until much nearer the Pole, and knew that its presence might entail a slow and dangerous climb, or even a time-wasting detour. He was cheered, however, by the thought that they had explored to the north of Wreck Point, and were already aware of the almost impassable " Penguin Gulf."

In consequence of this he gave orders to steer slightly south, and on passing Wreck Point was much encouraged to note that there were no mountains actually in sight except the range which appeared to run parallel with their route.

All were glad to be off again, especially the boys and the dogs—not forgetting Petz. With renewed energy, the last-named rushed forward to explore the way, and returned to encourage the other dogs or to speak to his human friends. David and Frank were all-eager to push on. Were they not now on the second lap to the Pole, which destination their leaders hoped to reach in about three weeks ?

CHAPTER XII

IN THE HEART OF THE POLAR WASTES

BOTH sledges and the yacht had been loaded to their full capacity from the stores at two-ton depot, but whereas the polar party rationed themselves strictly, the other sledge would be lightened of its burden by the setting up of a new depot each fifty miles.

Despite the monotony of the scenery—a vast, endless plain of white in every direction—the days were often full of interest. Doctor Elliot was soon delighted to note that all sign of mountains had vanished, and from time to time halts were called for scientific experiments.

The most important of these, as far as results were concerned, were undoubtedly those performed by Mr. Walker with his " Walker Stratoscope," as he had named it. Every test—except, of course, those on the ice in Penguin Cove—had definitely indicated land beneath the ice, and each additional result served to confirm his theory that their route lay over a so far undiscovered Antarctic continent.

Mr. Slater's eyes were constantly searching the white landscape for " nunataks "—or bare rocks projecting above the snow. On sighting one of these he immediately made for it and examined the spot diligently for mineral specimens, fossils, etc. Back at the base, he had accumulated a large number during the winter, and had already identified most of them. Also at Wreck Point and Penguin Cove he had secured a rich haul ; these he had not had time to examine fully, and they were left at two-ton depot to be picked up by the supporting party. Since then, however, his opportunities had become scarcer and scarcer; consequently, when he did make a discovery, he was like a child with a new toy.

Day after day there was little change in the scenery, for nowhere on earth is the panorama so monotonous as near the Pole—with the possible exception of its counterpart, a vast tropical desert.

The first sight which met their eyes on awakening was snow—north, south, east, and west, just one more or less level blanket of dazzlingly white snow. Above them was, usually, a cloudy sky; often this too was white with snow, but occasionally clear and blue. All day long, the same whiteness enveloped them, and as they turned into their tents at night their last view was of the sinking sun reflected back from endless white.

Except for their sleeping hours, there was no respite from the constant glare; with the lengthening of the days, darkness had decreased to a very few hours. The ceaseless strain upon their eyes caused acute snow-blindness in many cases, and the greatest relief to one and all was to stare at anything black.

Thanks to the meticulous preparations, and the expert handling of the dogs by Midoff, steady progress was made; except for the all-too-frequent blizzards—some of which prevented them from leaving their camping-place—the rate of progress averaged twenty miles per day.

Further depots were left, as arranged, each fifty miles, but a week elapsed since leaving the ninth depot before Doctor Elliot was able to announce:

"To-morrow we should reach 'Farewell Depot,' or rather, the spot where we hope to make it."

So far Mr. Hawlet was disappointed. Save for the few organisms isolated during the winter, no sign of any bacterial life could he find. Knowing that he would form one of the returning party, he felt unusually despondent on this his last but one full day with his comrades. Perhaps it was this which made him, almost as an act of desperation, decide to attempt some final experiments before retiring for the night.

In view of the fact that they were now only ten miles from the next day's objective, Doctor Elliot resolved to camp early, and as soon as tea was over Mr. Hawlet sent for Frank.

" I want your help this evening, Ingram. As you know, to-morrow *I* shall be returning, but I do not yet know who else is going. I want to take back with me a number of samples of snow for testing at the base. These will, I believe, be the nearest specimens to the Pole ever examined. Now I want you to take some from the surface at about a hundred yards north, south, east, and west from here, while I obtain others at varying depths. You must, of course, be very careful to select spots where the snow has not been disturbed, and to guard against any contamination while you are placing the material in the sterilized bottles."

An hour later Frank was able to report to his chief that the work had been successfully accomplished.

" Good," commented Mr. Hawlet, carefully labelling his latest specimen and entering details in a notebook. This done, he quickly replaced his fur mittens over his other gloves—the thermometer registered forty-five degrees of frost—and after glancing at the labels on his assistant's bottles, remarked, " They all appear to be in order, so I think that is all I shall want you for to-night."

" Excuse me, sir, but I've just had a new idea, and I wondered whether you would consider it worth while trying."

Mr. Hawlet knew his junior bacteriologist and at once looked interested.

" What is it ? " he asked.

Frank pointed to one of the snow-filled bottles. " It seems to me, sir, that there are so many opportunities of contamination in this method. It is very difficult to push so much snow into the bottle without touching it ; also, the bottle has to be kept open quite an appreciable time. . . ."

" That is so, of course," put in his hearer.

" Then there's still more risk when you open it again to put it into the tubes of glycerine or other media. It seems to me that we want some method of collection which will do away with so many opportunities of contamination."

Mr. Hawlet nodded vigorously. " I quite agree—have you any concrete suggestion ? "

Frank looked rather awkward for a moment. To make propositions to his senior of such long experience seemed almost presumption, but the sympathetic interest in the question reassured him.

" As a matter of fact I have, sir. I've been wondering why we should not put some directly into tubes of sterile glycerine so that they can be incubated straight away when you get back to the base. This would mean that each tube would be opened only *once*, and would be exposed to the air for . . . well, only about a second, I suppose."

A nod showed that his suggestion had been understood. " The objection to your method is, of course, that there will be such a small amount of snow in each tube. Whereas in each bottle there is sufficient material for about a hundred experiments, each tube will provide only *one*—hence the area of your experiment, as it were, is reduced enormously. All the same, I think your idea an excellent one, if supplementary to the more comprehensive experiments . . . in fact I cannot understand why I did not think of it before. I suppose it was one of those obvious things which one overlooks. Yes, I think it would be well worth while, and I suggest you do the job while I finish labelling and packing these," and he pointed to a number of bottles lying in the snow. " Take two dozen samples, will you ? "

Frank's " Certainly, sir," showed clearly his pleasure at the cordial reception of his idea, and he at once set about putting the novel scheme into practice. Before they turned in that night he had carefully placed two dozen such test-tubes, each securely sealed with a rubber cap, in an airtight box in one corner of the tent. Now that the temperature never rose to the freezing-point, even inside, he knew that it was perfectly safe to store them there.

Next morning dawned almost cloudless, and soon after eight o'clock the two sledges moved off across the snow in beautiful sunshine accompanied by its invariable polar adjunct—an eye-aching glare. Despite the beauty of the scene, it was a great relief when a halt was called at midday, and Doctor Elliot announced :

" This is where we shall dump the stores which will form ' Farewell Depot.' "

At this point the shadow of coming separation lay heavily upon all, and mixed with it was a feeling of tense anxiety as to who were to be selected to form the polar party. Doctor Elliot had purposely postponed his final decision until this moment in order to discover who were the most eligible. Consequently, except for Mr. Hawlet—who had specially asked to be among those to return—no one knew in which party he would be.

After dinner their leader announced his decision. " Zameneff will drive the polar sledge ; Mr. Walker will act as my assistant ; Midoff will take the homeward-bound sledge, and Le Brun must of necessity return with the ice-yacht. Mr. Hawlet wishes to accompany them, so, as the polar party has to be limited to five, one other must go. In view of their usefulness for scientific work, and the necessity of lightening the sledge as much as possible without reducing efficiency, I have decided that Somervell and Ingram will remain with the polar party."

As he came to this point, the acute disappointment on Mr. Slater's face was very noticeable, but in sharp contrast a flash of sheer joy lit up two other countenances.

In their most optimistic moments the two boys had hardly dared to hope that both would be included, although they had long since agreed that to return to-gether would be infinitely preferable to separation. And now they could hardly believe their ears as they heard that they had been chosen to accompany Doctor Elliot and Mr. Walker right to the Pole.

While David and Frank were eagerly discussing the exciting news, a message arrived to say that Mr. Hawlet wished to see Ingram.

" Ah, there you are, Ingram," he began pleasantly. " I wanted to have a chat in order to make our final arrangements. From to-night you will take my place, and Somervell will be closely attached to Mr. Walker." Then followed his detailed instructions for further bacteriological work, after which he added, " I shall take back all the experiments which we have done so far, and long before you arrive I hope to have incubated them and to have practically all my results ready. Now if you'll pack up those test-tubes of snow you collected yesterday I will make sure that all my gear is ready for an early start to-morrow."

Frank was soon busy sorting out and packing the precious samples ; at last he came to the test-tubes in question, and during a moment's rest held one up to the light. As he looked at it his gaze riveted itself on the sloping surface of the gelatine, then a soft whistle escaped his lips and he hurried outside the tent to find Mr. Hawlet.

" What do you make of that, sir ? " he jerked out as his senior took the tube.

" Looks remarkably like a growth on the gelatine," acknowledged the latter, " but of course it can't be. It must be an optical illusion."

" Why do you say it *can't* be, sir ? " asked Frank.

" You ought to be able to answer that for yourself, Ingram. In the first place, growth seldom takes place below about twenty degrees centigrade. Even then you have to incubate the tubes for two or three days before you can see much. But these have only been inoculated for twenty-four hours and have been stored at a temperature round about the freezing-point. No, Ingram, I'm afraid I must dash your hopes on that point."

Frank was fidgeting with another tube. " But look

at that, sir, and "—picking up the wire basket of test-tubes—" that . . . and that . . . and that."

Each time he took a tube from Mr. Hawlet he handed him another until the whole two dozen had been examined.

" Well, Ingram, I must own that there *appears* to be growth in every tube. There is certainly a distinct opaque film on the surface of each gelatine slope. All the same, I cannot believe that it really is a bacterial growth—it all sounds too impossible. . . . Nevertheless, there is undoubtedly *something* there which wasn't there before, and the fact that it is in every tube precludes any idea of contamination while they were open. What about the control tube ? "

Frank picked up the twenty-fifth tube, which had been treated exactly the same as the others except that no snow had been inserted.

" That's quite normal, sir," he declared as he handed it to his senior, pointing meanwhile to the perfectly clear surface of the gelatine.

Mr. Hawlet made a sound which was half-sigh and half-gasp. " To be quite candid, Ingram, I am extremely mystified. The only remaining alternative is that it is a very thin layer of snow which has adhered to the surface, and being frozen hard, appears opaque." Here the speaker walked round in a circle in deep thought. " I know," he suddenly ejaculated ; " we can easily test that point."

Without another word he hurried towards Mr. Walker's tent, at the entrance to which he beckoned Frank to follow him. Inside, he switched on a small electric heater and held the tube over this, carefully regulating the distance so that there was no fear of melting the gelatine. At the end of five minutes the whole of the snow had turned into water, but the film was unchanged. If anything it appeared slightly more opaque.

" That settles that point ; but I am afraid that the mystery itself must remain unsolved until I reach the base, or possibly even until we get back to civilization."

Frank's eyes were sparkling with the thrill of the

" What do you make of that, sir ? "

chase—or the lure of the unknown which always makes
the true scientist's pulse beat faster.

"Suppose it really *is* bacterial growth ? " he asked in
awed tones.

Mr. Hawlet switched off the battery and sat down on
a box. After placing the tube carefully in a convenient
enamel mug he turned to Frank, rested his chin upon his
clasped hands, and began slowly :

"It would mean that we had discovered an entirely
new and unsuspected class of bacteria. As you know,
all the ordinary ones grow best between the temperatures
of twenty and forty-two degrees centigrade ; there is,
however, one group of bacteria which will not grow under
forty-two, but thrive best between sixty and seventy

degrees centigrade—they are known as thermophylic bacteria. Thus if incubated at the usual temperatures these would show no growth, and hence might remain undiscovered. Now suppose that there was a similar group at the other end of the scale—it might be possible, *might*, I say, that these would *only* grow at extremely low temperatures and would not multiply at all above, let us say, the freezing-point. These also would remain undiscovered until some one had the bright idea—intentionally or otherwise—of inoculating the snow directly on to the gelatine and keeping it at a very low temperature. Then there's the snag about the rapid growth. *Usually* the higher the temperature the quicker the growth, but just as it has been proved that visible growth occurs within two hours at high temperatures, so it *might* occur unexpectedly rapidly at very low temperatures—after all, it's over twenty-four hours since you made these cultures."

Frank sat fascinated as Mr. Hawlet discoursed. After a pause he exclaimed :

"I'm frightfully anxious to know—can't we find out anyhow, sir ? "

Mr. Hawlet smiled at his eagerness. "I'm afraid not—not until I can get back to the base, at any rate. Meanwhile you must possess your soul in patience, and just . . . carry on. Well, I think that's all, Ingram, so good-night."

Frank found it harder than usual to wake up next morning. For some hours he had lain awake thinking over Mr. Hawlett's remarks ; even when he did doze off, his sleep was disturbed by dream-visions of bacteria of phenomenal size, colour, and antics. David's reminder that they were about to start on their third and last lap to the Pole, however, stirred him into activity.

"And only two hundred miles to go—perhaps less," exulted David as he left the tent to help cook the breakfast.

It was a thrilling moment as the two parties separated —one to make its way back to the base, picking up the

" penguin man " en route, while the other set off upon the final dash to the Pole, across two hundred miles of unexplored snow, ice, and glaciers.

What unknown dangers and hardships lay in front of them no one could foresee, but the five members of the little party preferred to dwell upon the possibility of unexpected discoveries and the joy of achievement as they disappeared from view on their perilous venture into the frozen south.

For the next four hundred miles they would be dependent upon the meagre supply of food which they were able to transport on their single sledge. This was still hauled by the team of dogs, all of which, so far, had successfully withstood the rigours of their task. Should anything happen to these, however, the five explorers would be forced to man-haul their entire equipment, with corresponding increase of fatigue and loss of time, the latter being the most serious consequence of all. Perhaps the worst danger to be faced was the risk of being repeatedly delayed by blizzards, some of which, they knew, might last for as long as ten days. They were much cheered, however, by the knowledge that as soon as the motor-sledges returned from their exploration these would set off again from the base to replenish the depots, and if need be, follow up the polar party.

Noting that the boys were somewhat oppressed by the strain of parting from their comrades, and not feeling any too cheerful themselves, Doctor Elliot and his assistant kept up a lively flow of conversation.

" How far do you reckon it is from here, sir ? " asked Mr. Walker, although he was probably the more capable of the two of deciding the distance.

" About two hundred miles according to our estimates. So if all goes well, we may be up the pole in ten days' time."

" Going seems good enough at present," averred the physicist, noticing that they had to do about three miles an hour in order to keep pace with the sledge. In fact, in places where the snow was specially level, the dogs raced ahead until Zameneff pulled them up for a short rest, thus allowing the walkers—or ski runners—to overtake them. Whereas the dogs preferred a somewhat jerky manner of progress, the ski runners found it better to maintain a steady and uninterrupted pace.

"And the sledge will be lighter after every depot—so we *might* even increase our speed."

No one could fail to notice his strong, if unintentional, emphasis. To any one who, like Doctor Elliot, had been on previous polar expeditions, the likelihood of the difficulties increasing rapidly became almost a certainty.

David pricked up his ears at the word "depot."

"Are we laying our own depots on the way, then, Doctor Elliot?"

"Oh, yes. Of course, we *could* take all our food with us, but, although it might be safer in some respects, I have decided to make depots about each fifty miles. This will have the distinct advantage of lightening the sledge as we proceed; in fact, when we turn back from the Pole"—it was very encouraging to hear his note of certainty—"our load will be only about two-thirds as heavy as when we started." Thinking that Frank looked puzzled, he explained, "Of course, our food supply will weigh less than half, but the equipment will be almost unchanged. We are going to decide the size of each depot in accordance with our rate of progress outwards, that is to say, where the intervening stretch is easy going" ("Could any stretch of Antarctica be called easy going?" he asked himself dryly) "we shall leave a small one, but where it is difficult a much larger one."

"What about unforeseen delays—blizzards, for instance?" asked Frank.

"It ain't goin' to blizz no more!" was the unexpected reply as their leader became a boy again. Nevertheless he glanced anxiously, if surreptitiously, at the black horizon before continuing. "But to be serious, we have guarded against that. Among our stores is a supply of a new brand of meat tablet. These are very light and very concentrated, and although we prefer not to rely upon them entirely, they would be quite sufficient to provide us with nourishment for a long time."

A short silence was deliberately broken by Mr. Walker. " Judging by your first remark, Doctor Elliot, I notice that you reckon upon an average of twenty miles per day. Will it be advisable, do you think, to do as much as that the first day or two ? " Glancing at the two boys, he continued, " We are not all as used to trudging long distances in the snow as you are. Until to-day most of us had rides on the sledge in turn, but now you want to avoid that, I believe ? "

" That is so. If only we can keep the dogs fit it will mean a lot to us ; and the sledge is heavier now than it has been before. All the same, if any one "—there was little doubt of whom he was thinking—" gets tired he can probably ride for a bit. Yes, I am aiming at covering fifteen miles to-day, and increasing this to twenty to-morrow or the day after. It looks hopeful, anyway "— glancing at his watch—" we shall pull up for our midday meal in another ten minutes, and we have already done over ten miles."

A full hour was taken for dinner, after which they started off again energetically and light-heartedly. Then the trouble began.

Owing to the hard-frozen state of the snow, it was almost impossible for Petz to gauge its depth. Zameneff had just cracked his whip to stir up the leader—who appeared to be hesitating slightly—when the sledge suddenly ran into a deep snowdrift, jerking it to an abrupt standstill and distributing nearly half of its burden in different directions. Meanwhile the driver, quite unprepared for such an eventuality, was pitched headlong into the snow, and most of the dogs sank up to their necks, their frantic struggles only causing them to dig deeper and deeper.

While Zameneff extricated himself—this was not the

first time that he had plunged head first into snow—the other four set to work to liberate the dogs, without much result except to increase the hopeless tangle of harness.

It was not until the Russian (he was really a Russian Pole) took charge that any progress was achieved. His expert eye saw at once that each floundering dog was steadily making matters worse—in fact, if something were not done quickly several of the animals would be strangled.

" Unhitch them, but no let go," he faltered.

One by one the dogs were freed from the traces, while their rescuers took good care to hold on tightly to their leashes. Once this was accomplished, a tent-pole was driven firmly into the snow and they were tied securely to this.

The next thing was to haul out the sledge. Unfortunately, owing to the depth of the snow, the workers quickly found themselves up to their knees, and the act of struggling to heave the sledge made them sink deeper and deeper. Only when two of them sank up to their armpits, while the other three failed to move the sledge a foot, did they decide upon the laborious task of unloading and digging it out.

An hour later five semi-exhausted explorers lowered the sledge on to a harder patch of snow. After a brief rest all the far-flung stores had to be sought and, together with what had been unloaded, rearranged on the sledge. Then came the tedious job of disentangling the traces. Before this could be done, and the dogs reharnessed, it was time to camp for the night ; moreover, most of the party were far too exhausted to go another step without a prolonged rest.

David often said afterwards that this incident was their " fire alarm," for from that moment all the elements seemed to conspire to exterminate them.

CHAPTER XIII

UP AGAINST IT

ALL had gone to sleep feeling rather despondent. Doubtless physical fatigue played a part in this, but to know that they had only covered eleven miles on the first day was distinctly discouraging. The night's sleep, however, coupled with bright sunshine, cheered their outlook next morning, and they set to work with lighter hearts.

" It's warmer this morning, anyhow," remarked David hopefully. " Last night there were fifty degrees of frost when we turned in ; now there's twenty-five less."

Fortunately he did not see the look which passed between the leader and his assistant, nor did he attach any importance to the disappearance of the sun—so seldom did they have unclouded skies nowadays.

It was the dogs who dashed their hopes of an early start. Mr. Walker offered to help Zameneff harness them in order to save time. But it did not take him long to discover that he had attempted more than he imagined. His lack of experience made the task extremely difficult, while the dogs realized instinctively that he was not their master. As he began to drag the second one into its place it gave an unexpected leap forward, tugged the traces from his hands and raced away across the snow. At a word from David, Petz was after him like a streak of light, but the fugitive had already gained a long lead, and it was not until nearly two hours later that the runaway was chased back to the camp by a nearly breathless Petz.

Hardly had they covered two miles when snow began to fall, while terrific gusts of wind came straight from the Pole. In a few minutes the landscape was blotted out by whirling flakes.

"We'll have to camp here," shouted Doctor Elliot after giving the order to Zameneff to halt the dogs.

"And better be quick about it," whispered Mr. Walker ominously to his chief.

A nod was the only reply.

David and Frank realized intuitively that the "atmosphere" was abnormal, and put their backs into the work of erecting the tent and making it doubly secure. Before the dogs were housed in the second tent the blizzard broke.

For some minutes the sky had been thick with driving snow, while the rapidly increasing wind forced the frozen flakes, accompanied by tiny particles of ice, into their faces like a shower of metal splinters. Everything beyond a few feet was blotted out, and it was darker than it had been recently at midnight. Before they could get inside their own tent the whole landscape—including themselves—was covered with a thick mantle of snow.

Without further warning they were enveloped in a vicious Antarctic blizzard. While the temperature ran up to nearly freezing-point outside, the warmth of their bodies melted the snow inside, causing intense discomfort. From a howling tornado the wind rose to the vicinity of a hundred miles an hour, until even Doctor Elliot gazed anxiously at the pole lest it should snap or the canvas be ripped off. Outside, visibility was reduced to nil.

With no first-hand knowledge of such storms, the boys buoyed themselves up with the hope that its very fierceness was a good sign—it must blow itself out before night—and as there was now no actual darkness, they might be able to make up part of their lost mileage later.

When at 10 p.m. the blizzard showed not the least

sign of abating, they made a mainly ineffectual effort to sleep, feeling confident that morning would bring better conditions.

Nevertheless, hour after hour the wind continued to shriek and howl, buffeting the tent with sledge-hammer blows and making both sleep and conversation impossible. For three days and nights they were prisoners in the tent —as securely confined as if chained—and when at long last the pandemonium outside ceased, and a faint but gradually increasing light shone through the top of the tent, they were all far too tired to do anything except to sleep continuously for ten hours.

Four days behind, and only thirteen miles out !

But all five were men of grit and had the true explorer's spirit ; with one accord they made light of their disappointment and joked freely as they set off at 3 a.m. in brilliant but spasmodic sunshine.

As if to make up for the cessation of the blizzard, conditions—as regards route and temperature—grew steadily worse. The deep snow made progress very slow, frequently rendering a long detour imperative, and in other places masking dangerous crevasses. Speed, even on the most favourable stretches, seldom averaged more than one mile an hour, constant delays being caused by the dogs sinking deep into the snow ; this also served to tire them much more quickly than usual, and frequent halts became a necessity.

To the ski-runners the atmospheric conditions were appalling. A pocket thermometer which Mr. Walker carried with him registered eighty degrees of frost ; this, on a calm day, would not have been too bad while on the move, but a piercing wind which came in fitful gusts cut their faces like a knife and drove the intense cold right through their clothes. Very soon both David and Frank were suffering from frost-bitten noses, while Mr. Walker, having removed his fur gloves to make a test with his stratoscope, had all the fingers of one hand nipped. Zameneff's feet were giving him trouble, and even Doctor

Elliot was experiencing acute pain in one eye, caused by the alternating sunlit glare and dullness.

By midday they had only covered eight miles. Nine hours' gruelling effort and only eight miles forward! Despite his intense anxiety to press forward, their leader knew that they must husband their strength. One invalid under such conditions might easily mean the loss of the whole party. Consequently he ordered two hours' rest before dinner.

Soon after restarting their route began to ascend gradually, and as the snow proved to be much less deep —the wind had drifted it into the valleys—their spirits rose accordingly.

"Now we'll be able to get along a bit, perhaps," vouchsafed Mr. Walker, mentally calculating how long it would be before he would be in a position to continue his tests. It was fortunate that he added the words " perhaps," for it very soon became evident that the deep snow had not been an unmixed evil.

Without knowing it, they had been travelling for many miles over numerous crevasses which were completely hidden and securely bridged by the blanket of snow. But now that they were on higher ground these became a very real menace. While a few remained visible—and necessitated annoying detours—the majority were concealed by a thin crust of frozen snow. Many presented little danger—the sledge usually passed safely over narrow gaps. Should they encounter an extra wide one, however, both sledge and dogs might be precipitated into the crevasse, probably accompanied by any of the party who were near the spot at the time.

Warned by several ominous escapes, Doctor Elliot called a halt.

"There's only one thing for it," he asserted ; "one of us must walk in front of the sledge and test the snow as we go. I will lead first and Mr. Walker can change with me each hour."

Although every one realized that his scheme was

essential, it was very irritating to have to check the dogs to about two miles an hour just as an opportunity to recover lost time appeared to be opening up. Instead of walking beside, or in front of, the sledge, it was now necessary for each one to follow scrupulously in the footsteps of Doctor Elliot. Keeping some fifty yards ahead he prodded the snow in front of him, and whenever he found a crevasse, signalled back to the party to slacken until he discovered a snow- or ice-bridge which he estimated would safely bear their weight.

Even this precaution did not save them from a very unpleasant experience, and one which might easily have been disastrous.

Doctor Elliot had discovered an extra wide crevasse, and after testing a crossing thoroughly—as he believed—signalled to Zameneff to proceed. Wishing to speak to Mr. Walker, he waited at the crossing and watched with growing admiration the driver's careful handling of the dogs.

Unfortunately, as may happen on any such occasion, the leader had misjudged the strength of the "bridge." To his horror, just as the full weight of the sledge was suspended over the crevasse, he saw the front begin to sink, and a moment later sledge, dogs, and driver disappeared from view. David, who was riding at the back, was likewise precipitated head foremost into the crevasse.

For a moment the three survivors stood speechless as they saw them vanish. A dismal howling from the earth jerked them back to reality, and Petz, who had been frisking beside Frank, rushed to the edge of the hole and alternately whined and yapped as if calling upon his human friends to buck up and do something.

As Doctor Elliot saw Frank hurrying towards the yawning chasm he waved him back and shouted:

" Keep away, Ingram ; we don't want to lose any more. The edge may give way if you go too near."

At a word from Doctor Elliot all three set about the work of rescue. For all they knew, both sledge and human beings might be lying smashed hundreds of feet below the surface or frozen in the tomb of ice. First the rope which Mr. Walker always carried for such emergencies was tied to a stock driven firmly into the snow ; at the other end Doctor Elliot tied a bowline and slipped this under his armpits. Then, with Frank steadying the post, Mr. Walker slowly paid out the rope while his leader crawled towards the edge. At last the signal came to hold tight, and they saw the doctor lying full length with his head and shoulders over the precipice.

Another signal, and they hauled him slowly backwards until he sprang up and hurried towards them.

" The sledge has wedged itself across the chasm and the dogs are hanging at the ends of the traces," he reported. " I can't see any sign of . . . the others, but we must rescue the dogs quickly or they'll be strangled."

Untying the loop, he retied it nearer the middle of the rope, and repeated his previous performance, except that this time he arranged for those behind him to lower him slowly down into the crevasse. There he tied the loose end to the sledge and was quickly pulled up again. After releasing himself, a quarter of an hour's combined effort sufficed to haul the sledge to the surface, while the dogs either scrambled to the top or were drawn up after it.

Immediately the dogs had been disentangled from any traces which threatened to strangle them, Doctor Elliot announced :

" Now you must let me down again to search for the others, but you will have to . . ."

To his surprise Frank sprang forward. " Let me go, please, sir. You've been twice already. Besides, I'm so much lighter, and it will be much easier for you and Mr. Walker to haul me up. . . . I mean, you two could pull me, and . . . another . . . up, whereas Mr. Walker and I should find it pretty difficult to pull *two* others up—though, of course, we *should* manage it somehow," he added.

His last argument turned the scale, and before long

The three survivors stood speechless.

he was being lowered over the edge. As he glanced down into the abyss he gasped. Beneath him he saw an almost unbelievable contrast of beauty and gruesomeness. The upside down ice cavern—for such it appeared—was lit up with a wonderful blue light, which was reflected in fairy-like beams from some of the projecting ledges near the top, although of the depths he could see nothing at present.

Then he found himself sinking slowly between walls of ice, surrounded by a weird bluish atmosphere which grew dimmer and dimmer as he descended. Most noticeable, however, was the feeling of warmth. Whereas on the surface there were sixty degrees of frost, down in the depths the temperature was considerably higher.

Still he could see nothing of the bottom, or of the two unfortunates whom he had come to seek. A double jerk and his downward progress was arrested, and as he dangled at the end of the rope he drew a flashlamp from his pocket and pressed the switch.

As the beam lit up the abyss and flashed from point to point, his eyes were blind to the wondrous beauty of the resulting hues. They saw only two black forms, some distance apart, on ledges less than twenty feet beneath him.

His succeeding signal was quickly answered, and foot by foot he approached the motionless figures. Fortunately one was in a line with his feet, and as he stood on the ledge he again sent up the signal to cease lowering.

He now had two alternatives. A rope recovered from the sledge was coiled round his shoulders. He could either fix this under Zameneff's armpits and take the end of the rope up with him, or he could attempt the more difficult feat of carrying him up in his arms.

The sight of David on another ledge and the realization that both would freeze to death very quickly—if they were alive even now—decided him. Lifting Zameneff in his arms, he struggled hard to adjust the bulk of the weight over his shoulders. When at last he thought that he could hold him safely he pulled the rope three times.

It was a terribly anxious moment as he felt himself beginning to ascend. There was a double load and only two to haul. Would the rope bear the extra strain? And what of the edge? . . . If there should be a sharp piece of ice it might cut the rope, and then. . . .

Long before he reached the surface the cold began to grip him, and when he stood once more at the top— with the motionless body at his feet—he was already partially numbed. But the memory of his chum slowly freezing goaded him into action, and after a brief explanation he hurried back to the edge.

Doctor Elliot was now in a quandary. It was vital that Zameneff should be treated immediately if his life were to be saved ; on the other hand, it was equally essential that Frank should be lowered to the other victim with all speed. Even so, he knew that there was a serious doubt as to his being brought to the surface alive.

A lightning decision was necessary—and made.

" You'll have to lower him alone, Walker," he shouted, and even as he spoke he began his attempt to revive the Russian.

Fortunately his patient had long since been inured to extreme cold. As Doctor Elliot saw him open his eyes he again called to his assistant.

"Warn me when you're ready to haul, Walker ; you can't raise two people single-handed."

A glance at the rope showed him that Frank had not yet reached his goal. Lifting the now conscious Russian in his strong arms he carried him to the sledge and wrapped him in a pile of rugs, then he hurried back to the edge of the crevasse.

Frank was feeling pretty bad. Thoroughly chilled by his first descent, he had not stayed long enough on the surface to restore his circulation. Moreover, his strenuous efforts had considerably exhausted him, and now he was again dangling in the icy crevasse. His torch lit up a black heap, and he rejoiced to note that he had judged the line of descent accurately. Another ten feet and he half-stood, half-fell, beside his chum.

While being lowered his brain had been working feverishly, with the result that he had decided to set about attempting to revive David immediately. Speaking aloud in order to counteract the awful tomb-like stillness of his surroundings, he argued :

" There are three reasons why it'll be best to do so. Every second is vital to Dave." Something seemed to grip his heart as the possibility of it being too late flashed across his mind. " Then it will give those at the top a chance to bring Zameneff round. Also, it may unfreeze me a bit."

With this in his thoughts, he pulled himself together and at once began to treat David as he remembered having been treated himself on a previous occasion. Rubbing, slapping, and shaking, he soon stirred his own body into a genial glow, but David remained inert. Again and again he renewed his efforts until he knew that his friends must be getting anxious. So with a final vigorous shake he lifted his chum on to his shoulder and jerked the rope three times.

He was thoroughly warm again himself, and on reaching the top almost ran with his burden to the sledge and laid him on the pile of rugs only just vacated by Zameneff. There were now four of them to treat one patient, and while two massaged him vigorously Zameneff prepared some hot drink, and Frank, after resting, helped the others.

Petz, who had been almost beside himself during the rescue, now settled down beside David and watched with a knowing look as they strove to restore him.

It was a hard, and for some time doubtful, fight. After nearly half an hour, however, the patient slowly regained consciousness, and from that moment revived rapidly.

" Better give him some nourishment," suggested Mr. Walker as he saw David sitting up, wrapped in rugs, chatting to his delighted rescuer. Almost unconsciously he glanced at his watch.

" Great Scot—it's nearly eight o'clock ! " he gasped.

Even Doctor Elliot looked astonished. " So it is ! Then it's supper-time for all of us . . . and I guess a bite won't come amiss either."

" Same here," said two youthful voices.

Another day gone ! A most hopeful start, and yet here they were—safe it was true, and all were devoutly thankful for that—only ten miles forward since the morning, and less than twenty-five miles from " Farewell Depot."

Nevertheless the snow was illuminated by the midnight sun as they turned in. Repairs to the sledge, overhauling the dogs, and repacking the stores proved to be a more lengthy process than they had anticipated.

Next morning three people found it unusually difficult to get up. Stiff and sore, each doubted at first whether he would be able to move ; but bit by bit the muscles relaxed, and all three refused to let it be known how bad they felt. Soon after breakfast, with David riding on the sledge, a start was made, each member of the party wondering—to himself—what would happen next. After such a steady tale of disasters, could anything else crop up—except in fiction ?

But they had reckoned without the extraordinary perils of the Antarctic, where danger lurks at every step, and where the argument that " because a blizzard has lasted several days it surely cannot last any longer " is untenable. *The blizzard which overwhelmed Captain Scott and his heroic companions lasted continuously for ten days !*

Immediately Zameneff had given his starting orders, it was obvious that all was not well with the dogs. Several were lame, some appeared indifferent to the driver's orders, while even those who were outwardly unaffected by their fall seemed to be listless. Under ordinary circumstances it might have been thought that they were lazy, but that this was not so was brought home to them by Petz, who made no attempt to hustle them, but contented himself with showing them the easiest route. Finally, as one dog grew rapidly lamer, Petz was temporarily harnessed in his place.

Although the temperature had risen, a biting wind continued to blow, while fine snow fell steadily from a lowering sky and drove cuttingly into their faces. Crevasses seemed to be everywhere, and after the previous day's experience many detours had to be undertaken to avoid them.

All this made the travelling extremely unpleasant. David was very soon glad to get off the sledge and walk, and his place was taken by the others in turn. Progress was desperately slow, and despite a most dogged effort they had covered but five miles by midday.

After only an hour's rest Doctor Elliot—who was becoming seriously alarmed at their slow rate of progress —decided to push on. During the pause he had examined the sick dog's foot, but could find nothing wrong with it, and decided to put the animal back into its former place. It was soon seen, however, that the animal was limping worse than ever, and just as they were rejoicing at having progressed two miles in an hour it suddenly collapsed. A brief examination showed that it had died in harness.

" True to the explorer's tradition," remarked Doctor Elliot grimly as he made a cursory examination of the animal. " Ah ! " he added a moment later, " here's the trouble—a nasty bruise on the stomach. I expect it injured itself internally when it fell, and that was what appeared to make it limp."

After burying it in the snow they pressed forward again, and as they camped for the night, Mr. Walker examined the log.

" That's better," he announced with a more cheerful face than they had seen for several days ; " we've made nineteen miles to-day."

Doctor Elliot looked up sharply. " Nineteen miles, did you say ? Good ! Then "—glancing at his notes—" we shall make our next depot to-morrow, if all goes well, eight miles from here."

Owing to the terribly bad surface it was four o'clock next day before they covered the fifty miles from " Farewell Depot," and by the time the new cache had been completed it was too late to proceed any further that night.

Previous to turning in, a brief review of their scientific progress to date was made. Mr. Walker consulted his notes.

" I have carried out ten tests since we left the other

party, and every one has shown the presence of land beneath the ice," he reported.

Frank felt very proud at having to give what should have been Mr. Hawlet's report.

" I have taken half a dozen more samples of snow for Mr. Hawlet, and of ten tubes which I inoculated directly with it, two show what appears to be distinct growth."

" And we have only made fifty miles in eight days," summed up Doctor Elliot.

Very soon after leaving " depot twelve " a marked change in the scenery was noticed. Crevasses seemed to have disappeared, and the landscape was " as level as a pancake," as David expressed it.

If their route had been monotonous before, it now became doubly so. As far as the eye—or even binoculars—could reach, there was nothing but an endless and flat expanse of snow, surmounted by a grey, sombre dome of cloud. The wind had dropped and everything was deathly silent. Except for the soft padding of the dogs' feet and the occasional scrunch of some one's boot on a more ice-crusted patch, not a sound broke the polar stillness, and if any one spoke it seemed as if his voice went travelling on and on. They were alone, *alone* in very truth—just five pawns of humanity removed from the chessboard of civilization, their individual lives dependent upon their own puny efforts.

Dependent entirely upon their own efforts ? It was during this insulated stage of their march that both David and Frank—unknown to each other—went through an experience which befalls so many explorers in the polar wastes.

The stillness was catching, and often for miles they marched doggedly on without a word. Even the effervescent Frank forbore to speak. And yet he felt no trace of alarm at their solitude, for time and again there seemed to be *six* wayfarers—companions on the same quest.

When in future conversation this fact was mentioned

by one of the party, it was revealed that each of the five had been keenly conscious of the extra Presence.

For two days splendid progress was made, and as they camped for the second time since leaving depot twelve, Mr. Walker calculated that they were half-way to the next cache—which would be their "half-way house" to the Pole.

This twenty-five miles of comparatively easy going and uneventful progress was afterwards nicknamed "the calm before the storm."

CHAPTER XIV

ON THE THRESHOLD OF A GREAT DISCOVERY

" WE spoke too soon," commented the physicist at dinner next day. He was referring to the conversation of the previous evening when all had agreed that, at their present rate, they would be able to set up depot thirteen in two days' time.

" That will be only four days for what took us eight on the first stretch, and there should be less than a hundred miles to go then," Doctor Elliot had remarked.

The morning did its best to confirm their optimism, and by midday the night camp was nine miles behind. Then glances began to pass. Zameneff refused his food !

A few words of inquiry sufficed to explain the reason. For the last few hours he had been suffering violent internal pains which rendered marching extremely painful. They had, in fact, noticed that he had ridden much more than usual, and now they saw that his face—or such of it as was visible—was greenish-white. Even as Doctor Elliot rose to dig out the medicine chest Zameneff fell sideways doubled up in agony, and soon began to vomit.

What was the matter with him was impossible to diagnose at first—Antarctic conditions and clothes are not ideal for medical work. A dose of the leader's " special," however, eased his pain, and after he had rested for an hour, warmly wrapped up, during which time the spasms became less frequent, Mr. Walker helped Doctor Elliot to make a thorough examination of the patient.

" I am afraid that it is a mild attack of ptomaine

poisoning," announced their chief, walking across to the two boys.

" Is it likely to be—*dangerous* ? " asked David.

Doctor Elliot forced a cheerful smile. " Oh no! I don't think there's any *danger*—providing he takes reasonable care, that is—but I am afraid it will mean at least two days' complete rest for him—and us."

" Rather curious, isn't it, sir, getting ptomaine poisoning in *this* climate ? I thought it was usually due to hot weather turning food bad or something ? "

The doctor could hardly suppress a smile. " Not always," he corrected. " It is due to the action of bacteria producing poisons in the food ; but it is not always due to heat . . . at least, I don't think so. We want Mr. Hawlet here to explain it to us fully. I certainly am rather surprised that it should occur at such low temperatures ; but who knows ? There may be some unknown germs which can act in intense cold."

And Frank was listening.

Although the enforced delay was disappointing, the time was not wasted. Mr. Walker, assisted by David, performed a large number of experiments with his stratoscope. While on the march he could only test the nature of the substratum on an approximately straight line, and he had been anxious for an opportunity to extend his experiments over a wide area. Now he was enabled to do this, and knowing that he would have at least two days, succeeded in tabulating the results at intervals of about a quarter of a mile on three circles whose radius extended one-half, three-quarters, and one mile from the camp. Not only did this entail about sixty experiments, but he was thus able to form a pretty reliable conclusion as to the nature of the substratum over a wide area.

Frank, meanwhile, worked mainly on his own, taking samples of snow and exposing a few tubes of sterile gelatine to the air to test its bacterial contents, if any. Doctor Elliot had, of his own volition, decided to nurse the patient.

Mr. Walker held his notebook in front of him.

On the second evening they gathered in the tent to discuss results and future arrangements. Doctor Elliot began with a piece of bad news.

"The patient is much better, but he will not be fit to start to-morrow."

Frank's report was mainly neutral. "Nothing much to report—just the usual routine tests."

It was left to the physicist to spring a surprise. "I *have* some interesting news," he began. At once every one was eagerly expectant.

"What is it?" inquired Doctor Elliot, leaning forward in anticipation.

Mr. Walker held his notebook in front of him as he

continued : " *Nearly* all my experiments yesterday and to-day prove that there is land beneath us, as all previous results out here have shown, except, of course, in Penguin Cove. But the remarkable thing is that over a space of half a mile long by about a hundred yards wide they indicated water."

" Where ? " put in the doctor.

Mr. Walker pointed slightly east of their future route. " It started just half a mile over there."

Again Doctor Elliot interposed : " But did you test to make sure *how far* the indications of water persist ? "

" Yes—very carefully. In fact, I could draw a pretty accurate map of the area, because I found a rough line, on one side of which my instrument recorded land, but on the other water."

" What about the ends ? " came the query.

" The ends ? Oh, I tested that too. The land bends round at each end and encloses the water—like a lake. There was one other point I noticed. At the south end there were indications of water again, but only for a few yards on either side of the line running approximately north and south."

" What do you make of it ? "

Mr. Walker's brow furrowed. " It's rather like an airman flying blind. The indications are clear enough, but unless you put absolute faith in the stratoscope you cannot actually *prove* anything. The results seem to me to suggest the presence of a lake, or perhaps an inland sea beneath the ice, with a river or some kind of outlet flowing south." After a pause, he added, " Now that I know that we shall not be able to start to-morrow, I think I will try to trace the outlet. It will be much easier if I can have two to help me—could I have Ingram as well ? "

Doctor Elliot looked across at Frank. " What do you say, Ingram ? You know best what work you want to do."

Frank jumped at the opportunity of accompanying his

chum. " I'll help, willingly, sir. I have finished all the experiments I need do here."

Next morning the three set off, the physicist carrying the precious instrument, while David brought a bundle of sticks for marking out the results. Frank took charge of Petz, who had been allowed to come only on the strict condition that he did not run over any of the snow near their experiments.

" You see it is as I suggested," affirmed Mr. Walker while they ate their dinner. " We have come exactly a mile from the subglacial lake, and we have followed the outlet, or inlet, for some distance. Its average width is just under twenty feet, and it is surprisingly straight ; in fact, if you look carefully,"—standing up—" you can follow the sticks almost back to the beginning."

" But we haven't found the end yet ? " queried Frank.

" No, no sign of it. This afternoon we shall carry on, but as the work of measuring and mapping turns out to be so slow, I do not expect that we shall do more than another mile. We must start back not later than five o'clock."

His estimate proved about correct. By 4 p.m. they had proceeded another mile, and it was decided to halt for tea—in the form of a little cold pemmican and still colder water.

" I'm going to rest here for half an hour to complete my notes. You two can do what you like providing you are back here by five o'clock sharp," said the physicist as they finished their meagre repast.

" Can we give Petz a run now ? " asked Frank.

So far, in obedience to orders, Petz had guarded their equipment which was usually dumped some distance away while the experiments were in progress. On hearing that it no longer mattered where the dog ran, the two chums set off southwards with Petz frisking joyfully in front of them.

" Don't go out of sight," came the final warning across the snow.

David turned and waved. " Right, sir ! " he shouted back.

For some little time the two wandered on aimlessly, following rather than leading Petz. Despite the none too pleasant conditions, both were glad of the opportunity of being together—but away from the others—and as they strolled along they chatted happily.

" It's a curious thing, Frank, that although we're probably almost the loneliest party on earth, yet you and I get very few chances of jawing privately. . . . Somehow we always seem to be cooped up with the others, or at any rate within earshot."

Frank turned a smiling face towards his friend. " Just what I've been noticing. I often want to say something about one of the others, but can't because they're there. Isn't the doctor a brick ? "

David nodded eagerly. " Rather ! And Walker . . . he's . . ."

Once the floodgates were opened, a stream of conversation on personality was waiting to be poured forth. But at that moment David's attention was drawn to the peculiar behaviour of Petz who was running round in circles with his nose to the snow.

The sudden break in the conversation made Frank look up, and he too stared at the dog. " What on earth is the matter with Petz, Dave ? "

" Dunno. Looks as if he'd picked up the trail of a prisoner escaped from Siberia."

" He's scented something, I bet. Let's pop over and see what it is."

Long before they had caught him up Petz started off again as if bound for the South Pole ; just as David— who was well ahead of Frank—was preparing to call him back, fearing that he would dash out of sight and be lost, he saw him pull up with a jerk, and nose to the snow, whine excitedly. Then he raised his head and looked back, uttering short, sharp barks to attract the boys' attention.

David put on a burst of speed and raced up almost breathless, while Petz ran to meet him and accompanied him to the spot with further barks and whines. At first David could see nothing unusual except a raised patch of snow which was slightly differentiated from the surrounding whiteness.

" What is it, Petz ? " he whispered.

In answer, the dog ran to the centre of the patch, put his nose to the ground and looked up again at his friends.

Then David saw. In front of him was a clear impression in the snow, ten inches long and varying from two to three inches wide ; before Frank hurried up he noticed further that the mark was practically flat, and about half an inch deep.

" What's up ? " panted Frank.

" Look ! " was the only reply.

" Gosh ! What is it ? "

" How do *I* know ? Petz found it."

Both boys dropped on to their knees, and after ordering Petz to lie down, began to examine the mark. For some time there was silence. Then Frank stood up.

" Give it up. Beats me."

With that he turned and glanced back in order to assure himself that he could still see the flag which they had tied to the top of a ski, stuck into the snow for their guidance. After spotting the signal, he let his eyes follow their own tracks, which were the only other marks of any kind within sight.

" Dave ! " he suddenly jerked out. " Look at *our* tracks."

" What's matter with 'em ? Yours are big enough if that's what you mean."

" No. They're just like this," pointing to the mark, " only slightly bigger."

All at once something seemed to flash into David's mind. Springing up, he examined several of their own footprints minutely and then returned to the mysterious mark to compare the measurements.

" You're right, Frank. *This is the footmark of some one wearing flat sealskin boots.*"

" But there's only one, Dave."

" Yes, I know. That's what's puzzling me. Let's scout round and see if we can find any more . . . marks. Lie still, Petz ! "

With upright ears and eager eyes, Petz watched furtively as the two boys searched for further tracks—for some time unsuccessfully. It was not until they thought of using the dog's superior powers that success attended their efforts.

" Find it, Petz ! " encouraged Frank, as he pointed to the mark and signalled to him to look for another.

Barking with delight, he bounded forward, and very soon stopped again, nose down, calling his masters. This time they saw an identical patch, except that there were two marks close together.

But Petz had now taken the matter into his own hands, and after a vigorous hunt he halted again. In this patch was only a single mark.

" Well, I'm blowed ! " began Frank ; but, seeing that Petz was about to start off anew, he ordered him to lie down. " Better not go any farther," he explained. " We shall be out of sight of the flag if we do."

The word " flag " reminded David of Mr. Walker. Hurriedly glancing at his wrist, he gasped : " Crumbs, Frank, d'you know it's just on five ? "

" Never ! And Walker said we *must be back by five at the latest*. We'll have to leave old Adam's footsteps and put our best foot forward."

Calling Petz, they started off at a fast pace, meanwhile discussing their intriguing discovery. But as they passed the first mark David turned aside. " Half a mo'. Look here, Frank, I've got an idea, and I simply must test it right now. You scoot on with Petz and I'll catch you up."

For a moment Frank made as if to expostulate. Then he turned, and with a final " Right-o, Dave ! " hurried resolutely forward, with Petz leading the way.

" Give it up. It beats me."

David at once got busy. Kneeling down, he began
to scrape at the snow close beside the mark. This operation he repeated at various points in the vicinity until,
apparently very well satisfied, he jumped up and hurried
after the figure in the distance.

Neither had sufficient breath to discuss the matter
further until, having made clear to the anxiously awaiting
Mr. Walker the reason for their lateness, they helped him
to pack up and started off for the camp.

On the way back David explained his curious action.
" I suddenly had a brainwave about the reason why there
were so few marks ; I felt I simply must test it before we

tell Doctor Elliot. Those footmarks—I'm pretty sure now that they are footmarks—were all on rocky places, well raised above the ordinary level. The rest have been covered up by drifting snow."

Back at the camp, their report caused no little consternation. The mere idea of footmarks in the wilds of the Antarctic sounded utterly ridiculous, and yet . . .

For some time neither Doctor Elliot nor Zameneff would believe that they were serious ; even when they were convinced upon this point, the fact that only the two boys had seen the marks raised serious doubts in the minds of the adults. Just before they turned in for the night, however, Doctor Elliot appeared to relent slightly.

" Well, we'll see to-morrow. Providing the weather keeps like this *the marks must still be there.*"

A distinct atmosphere of expectation was noticeable next morning, and breakfast was over much quicker than usual. Zameneff appeared to be fully recovered and anxious to get on, and with yesterday's tracks acting as a safe guide the pace was unusually hot.

" There it is ! " exclaimed David gleefully, as he pointed towards the stick which he had thoughtfully left to mark Petz's first discovery.

While Zameneff remained to look after the dogs the rest of the party hurried forward.

David arrived first at the patch and turned to Doctor Elliot. " *Now* you will be able to see for yourself, sir," he said rather daringly.

Experience at once told Doctor Elliot what the boys had only been able to guess.

" That is undoubtedly the footmark of some human being wearing sealskin boots," he announced. " One up for you," he smiled, turning to the boys.

Mr. Walker examined the mark critically and agreed with his senior. Then, while he took charge of the dogs, Zameneff was asked to give his opinion.

" Foot like Eskimo—certainly man," was his categorical reply.

Instructing Zameneff to keep parallel with, but well away from, their route, Doctor Elliot hurried the party forward. After examining the second and third discoveries, all were absolutely convinced that the marks had been made by human feet.

" What kind of person do you think it can be, Doctor Elliot? " inquired Frank.

Their leader was examining the notes which he had made of the measurements and shape of the footprints.

" It is evidently a rather short person, probably about five feet three inches ; from the fact that the impression is rather deep, I imagine that it is a man . . . but beyond this I cannot form any reliable conclusion. There is so little to go by."

It was with a very strange feeling that they pressed forward again. Instead of being alone in the Antarctic wastes — a fact which they had never doubted since leaving " Farewell Depot "—here was conclusive evidence that some one had been there recently. Question after question challenged them, but they were quite unable to answer a single one. Instead of plodding steadily ahead, chatting loudly and with eyes focused downwards, they now spoke little, or in whispers, while their eyes roved unceasingly over the landscape. The very air seemed to be filled with a tense expectancy.

The next two miles were uneventful, and at five miles from the camp Mr. Walker suggested a halt to enable him to test whether they were walking over land or water. To every one's surprise every experiment indicated water.

Their curiosity was further aroused when Doctor Elliot jerked out his binoculars and hastily focused them upon the horizon.

" What do you make of that ? " he asked, handing the glasses to David.

" Might be a bank of fog, but it looks to me more like a range of hills, sir," replied David slowly, as he examined a wide stretch, readjusting the focus from time to time.

At the end of this inspection he added, " It only seems to be a few miles long, whatever it is."

" Looks to me very much like cliffs," affirmed Doctor Elliot.

Zameneff could neither confirm nor deny his chief's suspicions, and it was decided to push on.

From that moment excitement increased rapidly. More of the mysterious marks were discovered, and they were amazed to see several pairs of tracks. Every test with the stratoscope now indicated water beneath them with almost monotonous regularity, and it made no difference whether the experiment was conducted on the line of their route or a mile on either side. Added to this was the rather disconcerting fact that every step revealed more clearly that ahead of them—and immediately in their path—was a high range of hills, probably an ice-covered mountain range. With this discovery came the unpleasant misgiving—would they be able to find a way *over* the hills ? Were they to be baffled now that they were little more than a hundred miles from the Pole ?

Doctor Elliot looked deeply anxious, but kept his forebodings to himself.

" There is little doubt in my mind that the steep ascent which you see in front of us leads up on to the Polar Plateau itself."

Mr. Walker was completely mystified. Although, until the previous day, he had found land almost everywhere, now he could not discover any land at all. As if to contradict his well-supported theory that they had been travelling over an Antarctic continent, for the last two hours they had been walking continuously over water ; moreover, the water was not just a narrow strip, but extended for an undetermined distance on either side.

" Look here, Somervell," he said at last with a determined air, " I simply must find out something more about the width of the channel or whatever it is. I'm going to suggest a halt so that you and I can tackle the problem in a more business-like fashion."

Suiting his actions to his words, he approached Doctor Elliot, with the result that a halt of two hours was agreed upon.

" This will do for dinner, rest, and experiments," he suggested. With a twinkle in his eye, he added, " Unless, of course, Mr. Walker prefers to devote the *whole* of the time to his pet stratoscope."

Zameneff announced that the dogs were not in the least tired, so the physicist decided to make use of the sledge, from which the heaviest items were unloaded. Even with three passengers the dogs sped over the snow at twelve miles an hour, so, ignoring the first fifteen minutes, the physicist made a test at three miles to the left of their route.

" Water," was his summary.

After this he stopped each mile, and at four and five miles came the same reply, which David duly noted on his chart.

" I think I will try each quarter now."

Zameneff nodded and soon pulled up again. This time Mr. Walker looked slightly doubtful. " I'll try once more to make sure . . . no, there's no doubt about it, we're over land again."

As each halt up to six miles gave similar results, it was decided to return and try in the opposite direction. On arrival at the camp there was only three-quarters of an hour left, but hearing the results, Doctor Elliot offered to stay another hour.

Conclusions to the right of their route were very similar. Up to four and a half miles the stratoscope registered water, then continuous land.

" That makes the water ten miles wide, doesn't it, sir ? " asked David, consulting his chart.

Mr. Walker was in deep thought, but heard the question subconsciously. " Yes, approximately," he agreed.

It was four o'clock before a fresh start was made, and progress was exceedingly slow owing to constant waits for Mr. Walker.

" Water," was all they heard him say after each halt.

When the log registered nineteen miles for the day the two leaders were seen to be in deep consultation. As the dogs came to a standstill, Mr. Walker turned to the boys.

" We have decided to camp here. Although we are all, naturally, on tenterhooks to solve the mystery of the footprints, we are already over fifty miles from our last depot ; so, while the dogs rest, we shall unload the stores for depot thirteen, and then turn in . . . after supper that is, of course," he added with a smile.

" And to-morrow, what ho ! for the mystery land ! " ejaculated Frank, little dreaming to what extent his words would be fulfilled.

CHAPTER XV

MYSTERY LAND

BREAKFAST was scarcely over when Doctor Elliot electrified every one. During the hours of official night a break had appeared in the gloom overhead, and just as they finished eating the sun shone across the snow. Seeing this, Doctor Elliot seized his binoculars and trained them upon the distant rise.

"Yes, they are cliffs right enough—icebound, I think—and . . . hallo ! what's that ! Why, *there's a lot of dark objects moving about !* "

His announcement came like a bolt from the blue. Had it emanated from any one else they would have doubted it, but they knew the speaker.

David glanced apprehensively at Frank ; he noted the sudden start at the mention of " dark objects moving about," but he saw with relief that he was standing resolutely erect with clenched teeth and a look of determination.

"P'r'aps it's the owners of the footsteps," suggested David.

"Or . . . Collinson and company," put in Frank.

" In that event they must have budded, for there's at least a dozen of them," twitted the doctor.

" We must hope that they will not—what you say ?—turn out to be wild animal, of a sort not before seen," added Zameneff.

Again Frank hesitated, but immediately recovered himself and remarked, with a good attempt at light-heartedness, " Just as well we've got rifles."

The leader's next words were carefully selected and
calmly spoken so as not to arouse any further uneasiness
Nevertheless they were ominous.

" See that our two rifles are ready and handy," he
said to his assistant. In the next breath he had given
orders to the driver, as the result of which they were soon
travelling over the snow at a good pace.

As each mile was left behind the footmarks became
steadily more numerous, the tracks often criss-crossing
each other. Similarly the view ahead grew rapidly more
clearly defined. They were approaching what appeared
to be a frozen over bay, nearly surrounded by the precipitous faces of the glacier or cliffs—they could not say
which—rising above the snow to a height of several hundred feet. On either side of the bay, a very steep, snow-
covered slope could be seen stretching for some distance.

Presently they began to make out the figures fairly
clearly. Several dozen upright beings, which reminded
them of their first view of the penguin man, were moving
about near the cliff, while a group were sitting or standing
almost motionless some distance away.

" They look like Eskimos to me," announced Doctor
Elliot, after examining them with the aid of the binoculars.

" Eskimos ? " protested Mr. Walker. " But there are
no Eskimos within hundreds of miles of the South Pole,
surely ? And who on earth could live out here ? "

" I did not suggest that they do *live* here," corrected
his senior ; " but what I am pretty certain of is that
they are human beings of some kind."

Pace was slackened as they approached the mysterious
beings, and although every member of the party went
forward alert and ready for any emergency which might
arise, the rifles were kept well out of sight.

When half the distance had been covered one of the
strangers, who had wandered towards the mouth of the
bay, looked up and saw the party approaching. His un-
bounded astonishment was obvious, and after a prolonged
stare to convince himself that he had seen correctly, he

turned and walked back to his nearest comrades—but without any outward sign of alarm.

Doctor Elliot now called his party to a halt. " Just as well to wait a bit and see what is going to happen," he began. Remembering that some might be feeling nervous, he added jocularly, " We may wake up in a jiffy and find ourselves in bed at home."

The next few moments were a period of intense interest not altogether unmixed with anxiety. All eyes were focused upon the little group in front of them, and again it was remarked that, although the announcement of the advancing strangers naturally caused much excitement, yet there was apparently no trace of fear. At first the group talked and gesticulated, frequently pointing towards the new-comers; then one of them turned round and shouted something. At once, not only those whom they had already seen, but a number of others—who seemed to come out of the very cliffs—gathered round the first group, and in turn stared at the visitors.

Doctor Elliot's keen eyes quickly noted one very curious fact. None of the party which he had seen squatting in a circle on one side of the bay had moved, except to turn their heads and glance across the snow.

Then, to their surprise, they saw the main group— now comprising some two dozen persons—advancing slowly towards them. There was no longer any doubt that they were human beings like themselves ; and they were dressed very similarly. As they saw them approaching, they were far too excited to note their appearance in any great detail, but several points struck them forcibly. Dressed in sealskin trousers, jacket, and hood, with their feet enclosed in wrapping of the same material, few of them were more than five feet four inches high. Nothing could be seen of their faces except a pair of fearless eyes and a very small nose, but the most noticeable features were their short legs, very small feet, and unusually long arms.

The dogs had seen them too, and began to bark

furiously, straining desperately to free themselves from their harness. As a precaution Zameneff drove the sledge back some distance, and ordering Petz to keep them quiet, left him in charge.

Apart from their fearless and placid manner, the fact that none of them carried any kind of weapon appeared to be ample evidence of their peaceful intentions. Moving behind the others, Doctor Elliot and Mr. Walker surreptitiously laid their rifles on the snow, after which they stepped forward and advanced to meet the oncomers.

To their astonishment, the only form of greeting offered as they met was a slight nod of the head accompanied by a friendly—and obviously sincere—smile ; then, as Doctor Elliot held out his hand, he saw a puzzled look of silence. Nevertheless, immediately he gripped the nearest hand and shook it warmly, a flash of understanding illumined several faces, and the whole group advanced, smiling broadly, and held out their hands.

" Friendly lot of blokes evidently, *but who in the world are they ?* " commented David.

By signs the leaders invited the strangers to accompany them back to their base, and as the mixed party strolled towards the cliffs Doctor Elliot turned to his assistant.

" Did you notice that nearly half of them are women ? "

" I thought they were, but there's so little of their faces visible that I couldn't be sure. What do you make of them ? "

Doctor Elliot grunted and glanced at those nearest to him before replying.

" Well, Walker, I've had a pretty wide experience in my time in nearly every quarter of the globe, and I'm not often stumped ; but *this* crowd—and out here of all places—simply leaves me guessing."

At closer range the cliffs were seen to be composed of the precipitous walls of a mountain range ; the top appeared to be completely ice-bound, but the face presented a mixture of ice, snow, and jagged projections of

Stepped forward to meet the oncomers.

rock. Along the base was a sheet of ice which, a short distance out, was covered with a thick layer of snow.

Suddenly the sight of smoke drew their attention, coming from a tiny cove in the corner of the bay, and on rounding the projecting rocks they were surprised to see a fire close to the cliff edge, with four attendants nearby.

Pointing to it, their hosts threw themselves down upon

the snow, and at a signal from one of the men a quantity of seal-meat was placed over the fire in a curious-looking receptacle which appeared to be made of stone.

While the meat was cooking, the visitors took the opportunity to survey the scene. Although they had evidently been expected to sit on the snow, none of them relished the idea of such a cold seat, and they chose a patch of rock near the cliff where the heat of the fire had melted away the snow.

" Wonder how they make their fires, sir ? " asked Frank of Mr. Walker, who was squatting next to him.

" It's a blubber fire — seal blubber, I mean. But how they light it—well, I'd like to know myself. And there's a good many other things I'd like to know too," was the wistful reply.

" Wonder what those chaps are doing over there," pointing to the group crouching on the ice at the other side of the bay ; " don't seem to take much notice of us anyway."

Mr. Walker looked over his shoulder. " I can't imagine what they're up to. They were there when we first spotted this place, and they don't seem to have moved since. Ah, here's our dinner."

His last remark was prompted by the sight of the cooking-pot, with its steaming contents, being removed from the fire and placed in a heap of snow in front of them. Their hosts at once closed in and gathered in a small semicircle round the feast, signalling to them to do the same. Then several crude knives were produced, and by means of these pieces of the meat—already sufficiently cooled by the snow—were cut off and handed to the visitors. A hearty appetite assisted the desire of the latter to appear sociable, and the meat began to disappear with remarkable speed, despite the entire absence of all adjuncts of civilization.

The method of ensuring a supply of drinking water was simple in the extreme. Two rough stone jars were filled with snow and kept close to the fire, thus providing a constant source of water, which their experience enabled them to maintain at just the right temperature.

None of the four attendants partook of the meal but continued to tend the fire with scrupulous care. Meanwhile they watched the pot of meat, and as soon as the supply began to grow low another portion was placed over the fire to cook.

Owing perhaps to their recent exertions, and partially to the rarity of fresh-cooked meat in their menu, the visitors' appetites were keener than those of their hosts. When they refused any more, the remainder of the party rose and invited them to follow.

David and Frank brought up the rear, and as they walked across the bay their eyes wandered round the unusual landscape and its queer inhabitants.

" Jolly good tuck-in, that," rejoiced Frank, smacking his lips.

" You're right," agreed his chum emphatically. " It's the first time I've been warm for ages."

" Talking about being warm, Dave, have you noticed how very much warmer it is in this bay than it was outside ? "

" Couldn't very well help noticing it. I feel as if I want to take off some of my things. Reason's pretty obvious, though, isn't it ? "

" D'you mean the bay ? "

" Yes. The whole of it is completely shut off from all the polar winds—in fact they never get a breath unless it happens to blow right into the mouth. Even then they wouldn't feel much because the opening is narrow and we're so low down here. If you remember, we were coming downhill pretty steeply for the last mile or so."

" Might have known that too from the ice. Except for a thin layer of snow, I suppose we are on sea-level."

David nodded. " So we are really in a cup-shaped depression, and although the actual temperature may not be much higher there's no wind, so it feels crowds warmer."

The person in front of them pulled up suddenly, and

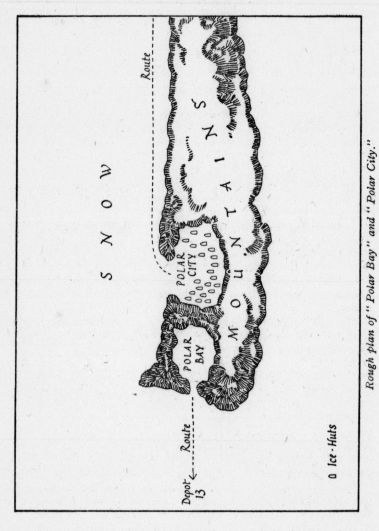

Rough plan of "Polar Bay" and "Polar City."

David nearly bumped into him (or her, he could not make up his mind which !).

" What's up now ? " he jerked out.

Pressing forward, they found that the whole party were standing round the group whose actions—or inaction —had so puzzled them.

Seven men were squatting on their haunches round a large hole in the ice. Two were dangling thin sealskin cords into the water ; two were holding long rods, with which they broke up the ice as soon as it formed upon the surface ; of the remaining three, two held nooses of sealskin, and the third a murderous-looking weapon with a sharp axe-head of stone.

. Realizing that every one was keeping perfectly still and silent the visitors watched expectantly.

While they were waiting, David's eyes wandered over the scene. Their hosts, he noticed, stood well back as if anxious not to disturb the mysterious seven ; then he saw a number of fish, one of which was still jerking feebly from side to side, lying on the ice between the two men in charge of the lines. Hardly had he realized the implication when one of the fishers began to haul up his line, at the end of which appeared a good-sized fish.

What followed puzzled the visitors at the time, although in the light of later events the meaning became perfectly clear. After a brief examination of the fish, he made a remark to the men with the nooses ; on receiving a nod he proceeded to drop the fish back into the water, still on the end of the line. Here David noticed one thing which passed unobserved by the other members of the party—whereas the fisherman had drawn up some twenty feet of line, he now dangled his catch only a short distance beneath the surface, meanwhile leaning forward and gazing fixedly down into the water. Presently he began to draw the line sideways and upwards, and, noting this, the men with the nooses grew eagerly alert. Then David saw a movement beneath the water which increased to a distinct swell. A moment later, as the fisher jerked his bait to the top, it was followed by the head of a large seal, which, in its effort to secure the prize, leapt half out of the water. In a flash two nooses were thrown, and so dexterous were the holders that both loops dropped over their quarry, while, with a united tug, the seal was dragged to the edge of the ice, where one blow from the axe effectually put an end to its struggles.

" Now we know how they feed and clothe themselves at any rate," whispered David to his chum, as the men resumed their fishing, while the noose-men completed the killing of the seal and returned to their previous positions.

Several dark looks warned the boys that, for some reason quite unknown to them, this was no place for conversation—even for whispering. After witnessing the further haul of a number of fish and several seals, they were wondering how long they would be expected to stand and freeze. Although there was no wind, their arms and legs—especially the extremities—were already becoming numb. But the spectacle, which was beginning to pall, was suddenly enlivened by what Frank described to himself as " a change of guard."

Unobserved, seven other men (or were any of them women? David asked himself as he tried hard to judge from their faces) had approached. Halting in an outer circle, they chanted something in their native tongue and were immediately answered by those at the hole. As the inner circle stepped backwards, the others took their places, but remained standing erect. Then one of the first party raised his arm towards the water and began to intone. Simultaneously, the remainder joined in his benediction and swayed their bodies rhythmically from side to side. After this the new-comers took up their duties at the ice-hole in the same pious silence while the relieved party vanished quietly.

Apparently their hosts presumed that they had seen enough and began to move away, but before they did so one of them approached Doctor Elliot, shook him by the hand and slowly waved his arm in a circle, then pointing to each of the visitors in turn, he again circled his arm, shook the doctor's hand and walked away. Seeing that the party which had accompanied them so far was now splitting up and undertaking various duties, Doctor Elliot turned to his fellow-explorers :

" As far as I can make out from that rather picturesque signal, they mean that we are welcome to wander anywhere round the bay we like. They evidently want to get on with their jobs."

David and Frank, intrigued by what they had seen and heard so far, made full use of their opportunity ; while Zameneff went off to bring back the sledge and the two scientists strolled about in earnest conversation, they explored round to see what the natives were doing. One group they found cutting up the seals, while the next party were cleaning the skins which had been removed. A third group were preparing the fish—doubtless for the evening meal—and in another place a number were sitting in the snow making garments from some recently cleaned and dried sealskins.

David nodded towards the group and remarked, " Guess we're pretty safe in presuming they're women, but I'm blowed if I can tell one from t'other when they're mixed."

" I'm not so sure," argued Frank. " Everything seems topsy-turvy here, so p'r'aps the *men* make the clothes."

And so they strolled from place to place, deeply interested in all they saw, although often quite unable to explain the meaning of some of the weird happenings. Just as they were standing still, undecided which way to go next, Frank pointed to the middle of the bay.

" What's that chap up to ? "

David saw one of the natives, whom he had several times noticed as taking a leading part, detach himself from a group and turn towards the cliff. As he halted, he cupped his hands to his mouth and shouted something. His voice, which might not have reached some of the

others under ordinary circumstances, was echoed back
by the cliff ; this, as the result of its curved face, reflected
the sounds clearly to every part of the bay.

At once eleven individuals separated themselves from
the others and divided into two groups, one of which
proceeded towards the ice-hole, while the other four made
for the fire. Anxious to solve the new mystery, the boys
stood and watched. As each party reached its destination
a similar ceremony was performed to that which they had
witnessed at the ice-hole.

" Seems they're changing over duties," concluded
Frank.

" But it's only a short time since we saw them swap
over," remonstrated David, glancing at his watch.
" Phew ! " he exclaimed, as he saw the time. " It's two
hours since then—jove, doesn't the time fly ! "

" Then p'r'aps they change guard regularly every
two hours ? "

David frowned as he nodded his assent. " Probably.
Seems to be a sort of religious ceremony about it too—
jolly mysterious I call it."

" Wish young Alan was here to see it. Wonder what
he's doing now, and whether the others are back yet."

" Same here. Anyway, I'm getting some fine snaps
for him. I've taken several here already—but I don't
know what to autograph them. I've numbered them so
far, but I must put a name to one to show where it
was."

" Let's call it ' Polar Bay,' " suggested Frank.

" Jolly good idea—' Polar Bay ' it shall be. Any one
who's been there would guess that."

At this moment Petz came bounding over the snow
and hurled himself at the pair with joyful barks. Then,
hearing the sounds of the incantation in the distance, he
suddenly became rigid and bristled with desire to rush at
the strangers.

" Down, Petz ; it's all right, they're friends."

Whether actually understanding the words or not,

Petz gathered their meaning, and relaxing, sat down between the boys.

Two hours later the same ceremonial changing of duties was witnessed, and soon after this Mr. Walker beckoned to David.

" They've just made some weird signals to the doctor, and I believe they intended to tell us that supper's ready," he explained, adding almost as a warning, " We'd better not keep them waiting if that's their idea."

Following their informant, they met Doctor Elliot and Zameneff accompanying some of their hosts towards the fire, where a plentiful supply of seal-meat and fish was already cooked.

At the end of the meal, in response to further signals, the five visitors followed their hosts across the snow towards the eastern headland. To their surprise they were led round the point ; there they saw another sheltered but less protected bay.

All at once David, who with Frank was walking slightly in front, turned to Doctor Elliot.

" Look, sir, what on earth's that — those white mounds, I mean ? "

In the distance they could see what looked like a large number of oblong hummocks of snow.

" 'Spect it's their burial ground—hope we're not going to be invited to stand for hours to watch a polar funeral," whispered Frank.

As he spoke he shivered. It was much colder where they were, and the biting wind seemed to cut right through them after the stillness of Polar Bay.

Meanwhile Doctor Elliot was making good use of his binoculars. " I believe those are their snow-huts. I can see a number of them crawling in and out, but they are such a curious shape," was his somewhat ambiguous verdict.

Pressing on, even Frank soon veered round to his opinion. Several dozen natives could be seen walking about, and now and then one would crawl in or out of one of the snow-mounds.

David was busy counting. " Crumbs, what a mob of
'em. I make it twenty-two."

" Same here. Go up to the top of the class," agreed
Frank. " Then, as our Yankee friends would say, ' Mr.
Somervell, meet Polar City.' "

A further surprise awaited them. On reaching the
huts they found that these were constructed on a very
novel plan. Instead of being built like the typical Eskimo
snow-huts—resembling a beehive—these were bullet-
shaped, the point aiming towards the mouth of the bay
and the blunt end towards the cliff. The middle of each
was about six feet high and broad, but the length varied
from ten to fifteen feet. On closer inspection it was found
that they were constructed of blocks of frozen snow, the
outside being plastered with loose snow which had been
pressed hard and smooth, giving them the appearance
of gigantic white slugs.

Mr. Walker was specially intrigued with the shape.
"Clever little chaps these ! Seem to have streamlined
their houses. I wonder why ? "

There was no time to discuss the matter. Their guide
led them to one of the large huts and pointed to the five
explorers in turn and then at the doorway.

" That's our night quarters evidently," translated
Doctor Elliot to his friends, nodding to their guide.

Then they were led to the next one, a much smaller
hut. Pointing to it, the man looked at Zameneff and
went down on all fours, finally running along the snow
in this position.

" That's for the dogs evidently," laughed Doctor
Elliot. " Very thoughtful of them."

At the blunt end of each hut was a low doorway
covered with a sealskin curtain. Putting this aside, they
saw that the one for the dogs was a compartment about
eight feet long and five broad, but on glancing into the
other they could distinguish nothing at first. It was not
until the physicist produced his flash-lamp that the true
nature of the interior was revealed. Across the middle

" That's for the dogs evidently."

was a partition of snow with a curtained-off doorway, and a space near the roof to admit air and light to the inner apartment.

"We're in luxury! A two-roomed hotel and nice and snug," commented David, as he and Frank prepared to turn in for the night, while the two scientists awaited the return of Zameneff who had set off to fetch the dogs.

On the floor was a pile of sealskin rugs, and very soon all five were sleeping restfully, warmer than they had been since leaving Penguin Cove. So soundly did they sleep that no one stirred until one of the natives crawled in and shook Zameneff, who awakened the others. Then, led by their guide, they returned to Polar Bay.

"Hallo!" exclaimed Frank, as they rounded the point. "They've got the fire going already! Wonder how they light it?"

" And they're fishing too ! " added David.

While they were enjoying breakfast, Mr. Walker turned to Frank. " You said just now that you wondered how they relight the fire ? "

" Yes, I've been thinking hard, but I can't make out."

" And how in the world do they break the ice over that hole ? " put in David. " It must freeze jolly thick during the night, and yet I've seen no sign of any tools. What's more, I strolled over just now and there were no lumps of ice. In fact, the hole looked exactly the same as when we left it last night."

Doctor Elliot paused in the act of eating a mouthful of fish and looked up interestedly. "I must own, Walker, that I also am puzzled about those two points."

Mr. Walker smiled as he replied, " You all slept too heavily last night evidently. Try keeping awake a bit to-night and you should be able to solve your problems."

CHAPTER XVI

AN UNKNOWN PEOPLE

NEITHER David nor Frank forgot the physicist's words, and the day proved to be a busy one. Three meals were supplied by their hosts, who took them on short tours of exploration—round the western headland and also to the village, where they saw inside many of the other huts. In between these occupations sledge excursions were made to enable Mr. Walker and David to perform further tests.

To their surprise, never once during the day did they see less than seven people at the ice hole and four round the fire, and both boys retired for the night determined to try to solve the puzzle.

"Let's both keep awake and see if we can hear anything," suggested David.

In order to avoid dropping off to sleep, they conversed in low whispers.

"From what we saw to-day," began David, "it seems as if they spend the day in Polar Bay and the night in this place."

"Dining-room and bedroom, in fact," put in Frank.

"Yes. And they don't seem to go anywhere else at all. There's no bay where we went this morning, and if you notice, there were very few tracks there."

From their new friends, their conversation turned to those at the base, the members of the three other parties, and then to home, finally reverting to their future plans.

"Has Doctor Elliot said anything about going on to-morrow?"

David shook his head. "No. I think we're going to stop here a bit, although I can't quite understand it. I thought he was in such a hurry to get to the Pole."

"Perhaps. . . ."

At that moment David held up his finger. "Ssh! What's that?"

Listening intently, Frank heard a voice outside, as if giving orders.

"Come on, let's see," whispered David.

Very stealthily he pushed the curtain aside and glanced into the outer room. It was too dark to see much, but he could hear from the regular breathing that all three occupants were sound asleep.

"All clear," he called back softly, leading the way between the shadowy forms.

Crawling flat, so as not to awaken the others by a sudden flood of light, they crept out into the open. Here they found that, owing to the dense clouds, it was much more like twilight than the glare which they had expected. Crouching on the snow they listened intently.

Again they heard the voice, this time quite close. Peeping round the corner, they saw two men emerge from the next hut and join two others standing near-by. Then the four moved off towards the headland, while the native who had called them returned to his own hut.

"I vote we follow and see what they're up to," proposed David, putting his mouth close to Frank's ear.

A nod approved this suggestion, and carefully keeping away from the hut into which the "caller" had disappeared, the two crept stealthily after the men. As they saw them round the headland they broke into a trot and kept it up until they could obtain a clear view of Polar Bay, while being hidden themselves by a projecting rock.

The four men had now separated into two groups; one pair was making for the ice hole and the other for the "kitchen," as Frank called it.

"Dave! The fire's still burning!" ejaculated Frank.

David quickly saw that his chum was right. From where they stood they could see two men tending the fire which was dull, but well alight.

Each pair timed themselves so as to arrive simultaneously, and at each place all four joined together in a short ceremony, raising their arms above their heads and chanting something, although very little of the latter was audible at a distance. Then the new arrivals took over their duties, while the four who had been relieved joined forces and made for where the two boys were hiding.

" Look out," warned Frank. " If they find us spying on them there may be trouble."

David pointed to a niche in the cliff. " Right-o, come in here. Don't suppose they'd care one way or the other, but ' safety first ' is the motto of the day."

Stepping into the niche they found that they were completely hidden from the bay, although they would be visible after the men had passed.

" Crouch down . . . that's right," David pushed Frank farther into their hiding-place. " We'll be O.K. here till they turn towards the village, and they're hardly likely to look round then; even if they do, I doubt if we should show up against the cliff."

Despite David's cheery optimism, both felt a little anxious as they waited for the two to pass. So far there had been nothing to suggest anything but the most friendly disposition on the part of the natives. Nevertheless, they had heard so many stories of people being misled by outward friendships; and even if they were amicably disposed under ordinary circumstances, this was not to say that they would be so if they found their visitors spying upon them.

After what seemed an interminable wait, the sound of voices reached them and grew gradually louder; then, very faintly, came the scrunch of padded feet upon the snow. Almost simultaneously two forms hove into sight, and breathlessly the trackers watched them as they proceeded towards the huts . . . fortunately neither looked round, and as soon as the cliff hid them David and Frank slipped from their hiding-place and crept back to Polar Bay to see what was happening.

In the distance they could discern two forms standing near the fire, while two others squatted at the edge of the ice-hole.

"What are they playing at—can you make out?" queried Frank, shading his eyes with his hands.

His companion shook his head. "Not much. Queer lot of chumps to get up in the night to look after the fire and do fishing. The only thing I can gather is that, apparently, four look after the fire and seven do the fishing during the day, but only two are on duty at each place at night-time. And they seem to change over every two hours day and night."

"What's it all for?" asked Frank with a puzzled look.

David waved his hands as if dismissing the subject. "It's all gibberish to me. 'Spect they've got some idea in those sealskin-hooded heads of theirs, but what it is I haven't the foggiest. P'r'aps Doctor Elliot'll be able to ferret out something; I know he's made a special study of the science of races. What on earth do they call it? —some ology or other."

"Ethnology, I think."

"That's it. You always were a glutton for long words."

"Why use seven words when one will do?" bantered Frank.

"*Seven?*" Why seven?"

"'The study of the science of races'—that's seven in *my* arithmetic, although I expect Einstein'd make it six point seven three nine eight two five four, all recurring."

A mighty yawn from David drowned the end of the sentence. "I'm for bed right now, despite all Einstein's ethnological prognostications," he stammered, determined to have one up upon his chum.

Two forms standing near the fire, while two others squatted at the edge of the ice-hole.

David was quickly asleep after their uneventful return journey. Frank, however, continued to puzzle over what they had seen and the little they knew of their eccentric hosts. Presently his thoughts were interrupted by sounds outside ; as far as he could distinguish, the same voice as before was giving similar orders. Glancing at his watch he saw that it was exactly two hours since then.

Once more he crawled noiselessly to the doorway and peeped out. Yes, there stood the one who was evidently the " caller," and two men were in the act of emerging from the hut in front of him. Then Frank watched him proceed to the next " house " and repeat his call. As soon as two more had appeared, the four set off towards Polar Bay, and the caller vanished into his hut.

Frank returned to bed to sleep fitfully ; each time another pair were turned out he awoke with a start, and every time his watch showed him that it was just two hours since the previous call.

During the second day experiments were continued. " Water everywhere," summarized Mr. Walker, as he and David met Frank—with a box containing more specimens of snow and ice, also a few samples from the cliffs—who was on his way back.

That evening, as the explorers gathered in a group, David turned to Doctor Elliot.

" How long are we going to stay here, sir ? "

" Mr. Walker and I have just been discussing that point," was the unexpected reply. " We were, of course, anxious to press on to the Pole, because prolonged blizzards might cause serious delays, and so upset our calculations as to food ; but now that we know that we can obtain as much seal-meat and fish as we want here, there's nothing much to worry about.

" What I think we shall probably do is to make two more depots at twenty and forty miles from here before we leave for the Pole. By that means we shall be able to start from the second depot with a full sledge-load, which, we reckon, is equal to full rations for a month. As, however, it will be only about a hundred and twenty miles from there to the Pole and back, the new arrangement should relieve us of practically all anxiety upon that point. Moreover, we shall now be able to procure plenty of food for the dogs.

" But there is another point. There is not the slightest doubt in my mind, and Mr. Walker agrees with me, that we have made a most important discovery, and one which will, I believe, rank very high in the annals of ethnology. No one has ever suspected the existence of human beings near the Pole, and I venture to think that we have discovered an entirely new race, though whether they are related to those in any other part of the globe we cannot, of course, yet say. I feel, however, that as a student of ethnology—quite apart from being an explorer—I must do some research into the matter. We have decided, therefore, to stay here until I have learned something about their history."

David held the curtain aside for him to enter the hut. Inside, they sat down to continue the conversation, and were almost immediately joined by Zameneff.

"If I may ask, sir, why do you want to do it now, rather than on the way back ? " asked David.

Doctor Elliot hesitated as if groping for a suitable reply. "Life is uncertain in the polar wastes, but written notes usually survive," was his somewhat enigmatic reply.

"How are you going to find out anything if you can't understand their lingo—I mean language—sir ? " put in Frank.

"Research workers have to *find* a way out of difficulties," emphasized the doctor ; "but, as a matter of fact, we have a scheme," glancing at Zameneff, "though whether it will succeed or not we cannot yet forecast."

"It would not be Doctor Elliot's scheme if it didn't," commented Mr. Walker quietly.

Without replying, Doctor Elliot began to collect his rugs and consulted his watch. "Something seems to tell me that it's bedtime," he said with an air of finality.

Fortunately for every one the weather favoured them for several days, during which the two scientists concentrated upon their self-imposed task of ferreting out as much as possible about the inhabitants of Polar Bay, while Zameneff spent most of his time exercising the dogs. The boys were allowed to continue any experiments which they thought worth while, and occasionally went off in the sledge to points several miles away.

Nevertheless they had a great deal of time on their hands, during which they noticed that the life of the natives was, in the main, machine-like. Night and day the same routine was observed—seven at the ice hole and four at the fire from breakfast to supper, and two at each in between, while the watchers were changed regu-

larly every two hours.   Exactly what the remainder did
they could never make out, as there always appeared to
be some standing about in Polar Bay, and whenever they
walked across to the village they invariably saw natives
going in or coming out of some of the huts.

Strangely enough, it was a blizzard that gave them
some much-desired information which would have been
difficult to obtain otherwise.   The novel shape of the
huts had puzzled them all, and several times Doctor
Elliot had cogitated, both aloud and to himself.   " What
on earth do they do in a real polar special ?   How do
they feed ? "

When they had been there a week, an ominous rise
of temperature and leaden skies heralded an interruption
in their work.   Before long snow was falling heavily,
while the wind increased with amazing speed.

" Back to shelter, quick ! " ordered Doctor Elliot.

The weather-wise Zameneff had already kennelled the
dogs ; it was fortunate that he had, for as they rounded
the headland they realized that the gale was blowing
directly into the bay.   With a forty-mile-an-hour wind
behind them, it did not take long to reach the village,
but their last vision of Polar Bay was of a general stam-
pede for shelter, except for four men, two of whom were
lying prone near the fire while the other two were prostrate
on opposite sides of the ice hole.

As they approached their hut the whirling snow was
like a dense fog, except that it was being hurled towards
the cliffs with ever-increasing force.

It was then that they learned the first fact.   The snow,
instead of being piled up against each hut, eventually
burying it, was deflected by the hard-surfaced bullet-like
structure, until it was finally driven towards the cliff,
there to pile up in a deep snowdrift.   Moreover, the wind,
which, as they were soon to learn, sometimes reached well
over one hundred miles an hour in this part, was likewise
veered off, instead of levelling the huts as it must otherwise have done.

Once inside they felt remarkably secure. Not only did the walls cut off all sight of the wild conditions outside, but the eerie shrieking and moaning of the tempest was largely muffled. Moreover, the smooth walls around them gave an impression of great strength.

" Now what's going to happen about dinner ? " asked David ruefully.

Frank saw that it was already past midday. " They were cooking it when we left Polar Bay."

David was thinking regretfully of the excursion which he and his chum had planned only yesterday, during which they hoped to map out the land to the west of Polar Bay as a surprise to Doctor Elliot. " Yes, blow it all, and now the fire'll be put out and we shan't get any. Expect we shall be cooped up here for days and days."

Doctor Elliot knew how easy it is for grumbling to spread under such conditions and strove to check it at its source.

" Cheer up, hungry one ! I expect we shall get some dinner alright. Very likely this storm will turn out to be one of the short-and-sharp variety."

Part of his prophecy was quickly verified. All five men were not a little astonished when a native pushed aside the mat and handed in a dish of hot meat.

" Phew ! Good egg ! " exclaimed Frank.

David regarded the steaming meat with a look of bewilderment. " Well I'm blessed ! How in the world did they ever manage to cook it—still more bring it all that way through *this* ? "

Mr. Walker was dividing the contents of the dish into five portions. " Perhaps it *was* cooked when the storm came on ; if so, all they had to do was to serve it out and bring it over—though how they did that without it getting cold I can't imagine."

No one worried further about the problem until later. The most interesting thing at that moment was the appetizing smell and taste of the portions in front of them.

Later in the day the subject recurred. There had been no sign of any abatement in the storm—in fact it had steadily increased in fury.

Prompt at the usual time, however, the curtain was lifted to admit a dish of cold seal-meat for supper, and much surprise was expressed that night when they went to bed at the unfailing regularity of the natives' arrangements.

Each day their mystification grew. Seldom had they experienced a worse blizzard, and all five were confined to the hut or its very near precincts. Yet, as regular as clockwork, cold food and drink arrived three times every twenty-four hours.

On the fourth day Zameneff decided to try to solve the problem. Standing just outside the door, he found that he was partially sheltered from the gale and that the snow had abated slightly, enabling him to see three or four huts away and, very dimly, the base of the cliffs. He had deliberately chosen his time—the midday meal was due to arrive in less than half an hour.

At first the village appeared utterly deserted, and his —rather melancholy—view comprised only eight snow huts, the blurred outline of the cliffs, and whirling snow —and more snow. Then he heard a shout, and from one of the huts crawled two men who, to his surprise, made straight for the cliff, followed by another pair from the adjacent hut. On arriving there they turned to their right, and with bodies bent almost double, forced their way against the terrific wind. With straining eyes he watched them until they were lost in a pall of white. They had, he noticed, found their direction by following the cliff, and when last seen, were apparently making for Polar Bay.

Before he recovered from his surprise, two more shadowy figures emerged from the whiteness and entered what was the largest hut of all, built in the centre of the village. His alertness was soon rewarded by seeing the pair emerge, each carrying several lumps of seal-meat, which they proceeded to distribute among the various huts. The arrival of their own dinner prevented him from seeing anything further at the moment.

Hardly had he taken his stand outside again when he witnessed another party of four make for Polar Bay by the same route. Half an hour later four figures crept along the cliff base from the opposite direction, eventually vanishing into their huts. Thoroughly intrigued, Zameneff continued to watch and established the interesting fact that—presumably only during storms—the parties on duty in Polar Bay were reduced to two each, but were changed every hour.

Noticing that there was a distinct lull in the fury of the blizzard, Zameneff decided to make an attempt to satisfy his curiosity as to why the men went to Polar Bay in such terrible weather. Returning to where the rest of his party were grouped round Doctor Elliot, enthralled by a vivid account of one of his trips to the Arctic, he waited for a pause, and then informed his leader of his plans.

For a moment Doctor Elliot was inclined to forbid such a hazardous venture, but on second thoughts he concluded :

" I suppose you are more acclimatized to such weather than any of us are, and better able to look after yourself. But take care, Zameneff, and avoid any unnecessary risk. Remember, none of us can drive the dogs ! "

As the Russian turned to go David called after him, " Why not take Petz with you on a lead ? If you should get lost he could always find the way back."

" Good idea, Somervell. Yes, take him, Zameneff," endorsed Doctor Elliot.

A moment later the pair were gone. Even the hardened Zameneff, however, soon found that the task was far harder than he had anticipated. Towards the cliff, going was fairly easy as the wind almost carried them along ; but, near the wall of rock and ice, the snow had piled up deeply, and his legs sank in at each step. On turning, conditions became rapidly worse. To walk against the wind was a gruelling effort in itself, but the exertion of forcing one's way through the knee-deep snow, while the icy flakes lashed relentlessly against one's face, was exhausting in the extreme. Even Petz whined occasionally and had the utmost difficulty in keeping up with his friend.

With grim determination the pair kept doggedly on, and at last experienced a measure of relief as they turned the corner. Once in Polar Bay they seemed to have stepped into a new world. Although the snow still whirled about their heads they felt as if the wind had dropped suddenly, and yet they could hear it whistling above the cliffs. So wonderfully was Polar Bay protected from the prevailing storms that, in comparison with the conditions outside, it resembled a dead calm within its shelter.

At the end of the bay a surprise awaited them. The fire was still alight—tended by two of the guards—and at the ice-hole he saw the other pair. Making his way across, he discovered that conditions were much worse on the other side, as a powerful, biting down-draft was caused by the rush of wind above. On reaching the ice-hole he saw that both natives were lying practically flat, to avoid the force of the wind, and that their sole occupation consisted in keeping the water ice-free, which, with seventy degrees of frost and a piercing wind, was no light task.

That night the storm blew itself out, and next morning the explorers were able to resume their experiments, while the natives returned to their normal routine.

Both boys were beginning to feel the monotony of their present life and were much relieved when, a few days later, Doctor Elliot announced at supper :

" To-morrow we shall make our last two depots. Mr. Walker and I shall ride on the sledge, and Zameneff is confident that with the light load which will be necessary for two small depots, the dogs will be able to cover the forty miles in a day, even with three passengers. You two boys will be quite safe here—eh ? ''

" Rather ! " agreed David, adding in a crestfallen tone, " Shall you be long away, sir ? We're both dying to start off again."

" Oh, no ! " was the laughing rejoinder. " We shall camp for the night, and if all's well, be back the next day. Then we shall start for the Pole the following morning."

" Good ! " came a very emphatic duet.

For once everything favoured the depot-makers, and their estimate proved over generous. Just before midday, on the day after they had left, Frank was astounded to hear his chum exclaim :

" Great snowflakes, Frank, here they are back again ! "

Both hurried forward to greet them, and David inquired with a touch of anxiety :

" Anything wrong that you're back so soon ? "

" Quite the reverse," was the cheering reply ; " the dogs pulled so well that we had finished both depots by five o'clock ; so we erected our tent, had a good night's rest, and started for home at four o'clock this morning. We've very little to do this afternoon except to reload our sledge and make sure that everything is in order for our final polar dash." At these words two pairs of eyes lit up with youthful expectation. " So I think that, after tea, I will give you a brief summary of the conclusions to which Mr. Walker and I have come—as regards our queer hosts, I mean."

Needless to say, it was a very excited group which waited for Doctor Elliot to begin, as they sat in the hut after tea. All were eagerly anticipating their start next morning, and the two boys had the additional allurement of their leader's promised talk.

Once they were comfortably settled he began.

CHAPTER XVII

NEARING THE POLE

"WHEN we arrived it was obvious to me that there were two alternatives—either these people had somehow become temporarily separated from the main body to which they rightfully belonged, or they were an entirely new and undiscovered race. The problem was to discover whether they were indigenous to the Antarctic, or, well"—with a smile—"only marooned there. I realized at once that here was a really important field for research to which it was well worth while devoting a week of our rapidly decreasing time.

"It did not take me long to see that they were no strangers to polar life, and the wonderful way in which they have adapted themselves to its demands, coupled with their powers of resistance to its rigours, convinced me that they have been here for many generations.

"You have no doubt noted that fear—of other people, that is—is entirely absent. The facts that they can lie or sit on the snow for long periods, walk against a wind which would blow us backwards, eat the same food—seal-meat and fish—without any variation, and resist such intense cold, all support the theory of a very long period of acclimatization. Again, did you notice their exclusive method of greeting—just a nod and a smile ? I remarked that at once and made my own deductions—namely, that they never see strangers ; as they are constantly meeting during the day, a nod and a smile suffices each morning, and this has become their recognized form of greeting.

" The first real problem which I encountered was the apparent anomaly that, although they are entirely cut off from civilization, they are very highly developed in many respects, especially in the art of hut-construction. After a good deal of thinking, it suddenly dawned upon me that this was additional evidence of their insularity ; in other words, it is just because they have nothing else to do that the few opportunities of self-expression which do present themselves are so highly developed. Their only object in life is to live, hence the continuous fishing and cooking ; but here again arises an interesting point. Worship of some kind is an inherent part of all life ; in fact, every known tribe worships *something*. It is only natural, therefore, that these people should worship the two things which form their staff of life, viz. food and the means wherewith to cook it—fire.

" It did not take me long to learn that both the ice-hole and the fireplace are sacred to them. The fire is never allowed to go out day or night, nor is the ice-hole ever allowed to freeze over except. . . . Here I have to own that there is a link missing in my chain of argument. I am puzzled to know what happens during a blizzard such as we experienced the other day, or during the winter, and how they relight the fire and break the ice after such periods."

Here Zameneff began to look rather pleased with himself. It was not often that the driver could tell his leader something which he did not know, but at last an opportunity offered.

" I can tell that," he said somewhat hesitantly.

Rather incredulously, it must be owned, Doctor Elliot looked across at him and replied, " You can ? Then let us hear anything which will help to elucidate this point."

In concise, but often rather halting, English, Zameneff told of his visit to Polar Bay during the blizzard and of what he had seen. While he was speaking it was easy to read in Doctor Elliot's expression a deepening interest in the account. Immediately he paused their leader broke in :

"*Thank you*, Zameneff, that is a very valuable contribution, and just supplies the missing link in the evidence. It also adds considerable weight to my statement that they are hardened to an extraordinary degree. So, you will see, it appears that the fire is never allowed to go out, nor is the water allowed to freeze over. It is, no doubt, as I suspected. It is part of their religion to tend the fire and the ice-hole. Possibly they know that if the fire went out they could not relight it, and if the fishing-hole once froze over thickly they could not break it again ; in that event they would quickly starve. All this is strengthened by the short religious ceremony which takes place at each change over ; it also helps to explain the unvarying number in each party—two, four, or seven. No doubt these are their sacred numbers.

" There was another point which puzzled me, but thanks to Zameneff I am now beginning to see daylight. Why was the village not built in the other bay which is so much more protected ? This, I am beginning to realize, is due to some kind of belief that the bay is sacred, or taboo, at any rate for sleeping purposes.

" That, I think, explains a good many points, but the biggest problem of all still remains a mystery. *How did they come to be here in the first place ?* " Here the speaker paused, smiling to himself, evidently in deep thought. " I can hardly imagine," he continued, " that God created a second Adam in the polar regions. That being so, they must have migrated from somewhere at some distant period, or . . . could they possibly be the only surviving descendants of a once-numerous polar race—I mean, the inhabitants of the Antarctic continent ? "

So engrossed was he in his mental wanderings into the sphere of ethnology that he ceased to talk to his hearers and continued to argue with himself, meanwhile uttering strange remarks which acted as sign-posts to his deliberations.

" Continent . . . well populated . . . breaks from main-
land . . . isolated . . . die off . . . survival of fittest . . .
remnant," they heard him mutter.

Suddenly he looked up and laughed. " I beg your
pardon, I was dreaming. I think I have told you everything necessary—no, wait a minute," another pause, " yes,
there is one more point. One of the first things I tried to
do was to establish some means of communication. In
this I failed dismally, so I set to to study their language.
There has not, of course, been nearly enough time to do
this seriously, but—and this may prove very important—
I have noted a stray word here and there which very
closely resembles the Eskimo tongue ; also, Zameneff has
recognized several akin to Russian. We think that, with
more time at our disposal, we may—*may*, I say—be able
to collect these words, and by means of our combined
knowledge of some ten languages, hit upon some kind of
intercommunication. *That we propose to attempt on our
way back from the Pole.*"

Not only did his account interest his hearers deeply,
but they were one and all intrigued by his hint of the
possibility of finding out something from the natives
themselves.

" There is still time to do any final packing or, if
that is already done, to stretch your legs before supper,"
concluded Doctor Elliot with an air of finality.

Next morning, after they had breakfasted and done
their best to say farewell, in the language of signs, to their
hosts, five eager explorers set off with a heavily loaded
sledge. It was not until they had been walking for some
time that the boys realized that they had not climbed
the hills as they had anticipated, but were still travelling
over practically level ground.

" We shall climb later on," explained Mr. Walker, in
answer to David's inquiry. " If you look, you will see
that the mountains turn south after leaving what I think
you nicknamed Polar City, and we have been walking
parallel with them. This we shall have to do for about

forty miles—until we reach the second depot, that is. Then the range turns east abruptly, so we shall have to climb up on to the Polar Plateau, and *that* will not be exactly a picnic, I can assure you."

In many ways this was one of the easiest stretches encountered so far, the snow being level and fairly free from crevasses, while the route had been clearly marked by the depot-laying expedition. Moreover, they were subconsciously helped by the knowledge that the way had been previously explored, and the consequent lessening of anxiety as to unforeseen dangers.

Halting for the first night at " depot fifteen," as they marked it upon their map (Polar City being known as depot fourteen), they started off again next morning with light hearts, and after another twenty-mile walk camped at depot sixteen.

At this point the scene ahead was anything but alluring. Above them, mountainous glaciers rose to a height of several thousand feet, apparently barring all further progress—for the range bent back at right-angles from the point at which they stood. Nowhere could they see the slightest sign of any possible ascent, and all turned in with decidedly foreboding thoughts—except Doctor Elliot.

Although he said nothing to his two companions on the previous day, as he did not wish to risk raising their hopes groundlessly, he had noted a peculiar formation at one point in the cliffs which had given him confidence. Next morning, before awakening the others, he and Mr. Walker explored along the base of the glacier.

" We shall be starting upon our most difficult patch yet," he announced at breakfast, " and one which will test all our powers of endurance."

He had intended his statement to refer only to the actual climb up to the Polar Plateau, but they were to learn that it could equally well be applied to the whole of the sixty miles which stood between them and the Pole.

Led by the two scientists, the now lightened sledge was driven along the base of the glacier until they reached a spot where a projecting buttress hid the cliffs immediately beyond and made it appear as if there were nothing but a continuous precipice. On rounding the buttress they saw a steep pass leading up the mountainside, and it was up this that Doctor Elliot proposed to proceed.

Never had David or Frank visualized anything like the climb up that awful glacier. In places their route was mainly a sheet of ice, and in others a mixture of ice-furrows and snow. Worst of all were the only too frequent stretches of deep snow, into which the sledge sank until the combined efforts of dogs and men failed to move it a yard. From the start the dogs had been unable to pull the sledge up the steep slope, and supplemental man-hauling became necessary. But in the deep snow they were often forced to unload it, carry the contents bit by bit to the next " navigable " stretch, and then reload all over again. Crevasses formed a constant source of danger, while exhaustion and snow-blindness added seriously to their hindrances.

Besides all this, there was the appalling influence of the wind and cold. Every yard they ascended the shelter grew less, and with eighty degrees of frost the piercing wind cut them through and through, causing agonizing frostbites on any exposed or thinly clad parts.

It was a heavy blow to find that, after struggling on for ten hours through such awesome conditions, they had only progressed four miles towards their goal. Never since leaving the base had they gone to bed with such heavy hearts, although in two cases the depression was lightened by the memory of previous apparently insuperable barriers overcome.

The next day proved little better. Increasing wind and deep snow made conditions almost impossible, and time and again both boys felt as if they simply must give up ; indeed it was only the recollection of one fact which enabled them to plod grimly on. Doctor Elliot's words on the true spirit of the explorer recurred to them again and again, and the energizing effect of these was augmented by the knowledge that they were the first boys to be chosen to accompany a polar party ; this could only mean, they argued, that some one had great faith in them, and this faith they must not, at all costs, disappoint. Nevertheless, twenty hours' gruelling effort with only nine miles to show for it was not exactly a sleep-inducing pillow.

Still worse experiences awaited them on the third day. After making a mile in two hours, the sledge hit a submerged ledge of ice, leapt into the air and dived into a deep patch of snow ; the sudden jerk as it was brought to a standstill—while the dogs continued to pull—snapped several of the traces, resulting in a sideways lurch which turned the sledge upside-down. Meanwhile the six dogs which were thus set free celebrated their unexpected freedom by vanishing in different directions, deaf to the shouts of Zameneff, who had been left nearly buried in the snow. To make matters worse, the lashings of the food and equipment also gave way, leaving the sledge's burden distributed piecemeal on and under the snow.

So complete was the catastrophe that no one did anything for some minutes except stare disconsolately. No one that is, except Petz. Owing to the necessity for every available ounce of hauling-power, he had been hitched to the sledge ; fortunately, or so they thought at the time, his trace was also snapped, and he tore off —presumably to round up the runaways.

Four of the party were jerked back to reality by the voice of their leader.

" Leave the dogs to Petz and see to the sledge—sharp, all of you ! "

Inspired by the example of their leader all set to work with renewed energy. The sledge had to be dug out and the stores retrieved and carried to a more auspicious

The sledge had to be dug out.

starting-point, there to be reloaded and strapped firmly into position.

"And now it's dinner-time!" remarked Mr. Walker ruefully as, having made the last knot secure, he glanced at his watch to see that it was nearly one o'clock.

"No dogs back yet?" asked Doctor Elliot of Zameneff.

"None," came the disheartening reply.

Dinner was eaten almost in silence; no one had any energy to spare for talking. It was past two o'clock when Zameneff suddenly raised his arm and pointed.

"Dogs, coming back," he asserted.

"Probably Petz," suggested Frank.

Anxiously they watched the tiny blur in the distance,

and as it grew nearer, Zameneff began to call. Immediately the indecisive, searching gait of the dog changed to a fast, straight run, and it was soon near enough for the driver to recognize it.

" Kresor," he announced.

Almost tired out, the dog allowed itself to be re-harnessed. While they were all discussing what had caused it to return and why Petz had not come back, Zameneff's keen eyes saw another blur in the opposite direction.

Again Frank was disappointed, but before long a second dog was back in the traces. And so, during the next two hours, more blurs appeared, and at last the whole team was in its place once more at the head of the sledge.

But still no sign of Petz.

By this time all were worried as to what could have become of him, especially so Frank and David.

" I'm going to look for him," announced Frank at last in very definite tones.

No amount of argument could dissuade him, so, seeing that he was prepared to risk his life to find Petz, all except Doctor Elliot set off towards the four points of the compass, each undertaking to be back within two hours, and not to go out of sight of their leader, who erected a flag-staff—improvised from skis and a red pullover—to guide them.

Frank left last. Before starting, he carefully examined the tracks of the runaway dogs ; two, he noticed, led off together, but in no case had two returned from the same direction. Moreover, he fancied that he recognized something in the footprints of the second dog. Then he hurried off as fast as it was possible to proceed over the treacherous surface, finding no difficulty in following the double tracks.

Presently he noticed that the two trails separated. Whereas one turned sharply to the right, the other swerved to the left and then in a semicircle to the right.

Wondering what to do, he stood still to think, and began to call loudly for Petz.

To his joy there was an answering half bark, half whine, and racing forward, he found Petz nearly buried in the snow. On dragging him out he saw the reason. The broken trace had trailed behind him as long as he ran more or less in a straight line ; but, when the other dogs tried to dodge, instead of following immediately, he had made a wider detour so as to head his quarry back towards the camp. In doing so the trace had become entangled with his legs, depositing him in a heap in the snow. There, his frantic struggles only served to enmesh him more securely and bury him deeper in the snow.

An hour later all were back at the camp, Petz being the main centre of attraction.

" Nearly seven o'clock, so we must camp here for the night. Better luck to-morrow," asserted Doctor Elliot, carefully avoiding any mention of the fact that they had only covered one mile that day.

Three days' provisions consumed but only ten miles on ! It was a terrific relief when, after two more days of fighting against the natural barriers of the Antarctic— during which they pushed forward twenty miles—the top of the glacier was reached, and they saw the Polar Plateau stretching away in front of them.

" Thank goodness ! " exclaimed Doctor Elliot. " At any rate there should be only another thirty miles or so to the Pole, and that probably will be fairly level."

" Curious how different it is on this side of the Pole," remarked Mr. Walker, glancing at his leader. Seeing that the latter was not quite clear as to his meaning, he added, " On Scott's route it was nearly three hundred miles from the top of the glacier to the Pole, but here the mountains are much farther south than any one suspected, and we shall have only about one-tenth of that distance on the Polar Plateau."

" It seems curious, I agree," replied Doctor Elliot

with a nod. " But it is not extraordinary when you come
to think it out—especially if you do so with the help of a
map. As you have no doubt already noticed, some maps
show a range of mountains, which is, of course, a con-
tinuation of the Queen Alexandra range, extending
towards the Pole on this side ; but this range is only
known for a short distance. We have to remember, however, that we are well beyond that point, and it is evident
from what we have found that the range bends back
towards the Pole. We met one bend where we ascended
the glacier, which accounts for forty miles, so there is
presumably a further bend somewhere else which will
account for the other seventy miles or so."

Their relief was short-lived. That night they camped
on the Polar Plateau and settled down with a sigh of con-
tentment, rejoicing that there would be no more climbing ; from what was already known it seemed probable
that the last thirty miles would be over deep snow, and
that the slope would be slightly downhill most of the
way to the Pole.

Next morning a bitter disappointment awaited them.
During the night a terrific blizzard had set in, and while
they slept the sleep of exhaustion the wind had been
roaring across the plateau, driving an impenetrable
blanket of snow before it. Immediately Doctor Elliot
awoke—at 4 a.m.—he was conscious of the fearful blows
which threatened to destroy the tent, and on looking out,
found that he could see nothing but a wall of whirling
snowflakes. The tent was already partially buried in a
rising mound of snow.

Without awakening the others, he did what he could
to strengthen the tent, and as each one roused he joined
him in the difficult task.

Hour after hour and day after day the blizzard raged,
proving easily the worst they had experienced. Cooped
up in a small tent, life was monotonous and irksome in
the extreme, and it was only the indomitable pluck of
one and all which made the delay bearable. Whatever his

The tent was partially buried in a rising mound of snow.

personal reactions to the crisis, each kept a brave face and made jokes at every opportunity.

To the dogs, too, it was a terrible time; to them, although the actual danger meant nothing, the period of inactivity was galling.

On the seventh evening Mr. Walker was consulting his

notes and comparing them with those of his leader. "Surely I've made a mistake, Doctor Elliot. According to my figures this is the thirteenth day since we began to climb the glacier and yet our total mileage only adds up to thirty."

Doctor Elliot glanced at his own records. " I'm afraid your figures are quite correct, Walker. Thirty miles in thirteen days and another thirty miles to go. Pretty awful that ! At the present rate it will take us exactly twenty-eight days from Polar Bay to the Pole—allowing for the two which it took us to reach the glacier. That means," with a grim smile, " that we should have just enough food to reach the Pole, then . . ."

" Sit down and starve. We'd be up the pole in more ways than one," put in his hearer.

" Between you and I, our position is pretty desperate unless the future treats us very much kindlier than the past. In fairness to the others "—with an involuntary glance at the two boys, who were deeply engrossed in a desperate encounter over a pocket set of chess-men—" we must not take impossible risks. *If* there were any likelihood of this snail's pace continuing, I should say at once ' turn back.' It would obviously be foolhardy—and useless—to press on just to starve at the Pole. What do you think ? "

" I quite agree with all you have said. All the same, I should vote for going on. We are already half-way there. This blizzard has now been blowing continuously for seven days, so it is extremely unlikely to last much longer ; nor is there any probability of being held up again for so long, as prolonged blizzards are unusual at this time of the year. Again, we *should* have better conditions from here to the Pole and back, and it will be much easier to descend the glacier than it was to come up. Once at the bottom, we have depot sixteen."

Doctor Elliot was nodding as he listened. "Then I propose to put it to the others and see what they say."

Waiting until Frank had checkmated his opponent,

their leader put the whole question before them, purposely omitting none of the threatening dangers and hardships. At the end, he asked for their considered views on the subject.

" Go on—our luck'll turn soon," was the emphatic decision.

Their optimism was rewarded the very next morning. During the night the storm subsided, and they awoke to a calm but very cold morning. As if to lure them on, the sun made one of its rather rare appearances, beautifying their surroundings but increasing the glare acutely.

By eight o'clock they had breakfasted, cleared the snow away from the huts, packed up, and harnessed the dogs. A few minutes later a joyous chorus of barking greeted Zameneff's long-deferred order to the animals, who pulled so eagerly that, despite the soft, deep snow, the special skis which were fitted to the sledge enabled it to glide over the surface at four miles an hour.

At this pace, however, it was impossible for the ski-runners to keep up with it, and Zameneff wisely adopted his old tactics. When a halt was called at eleven o'clock for a mid-morning meal, the physicist quickly got busy with his stratoscope.

" Every test has shown land since we reached the glacier," he reported.

Before resting, he consulted the log, and a moment later turned to the rest of the party with a beaming face.

" We've done eight miles already."

" Good," was his leader's only rejoinder.

David and Frank continued to jubilate, and many were the facetious remarks about, " calling in at the Pole Café for a cup of tea," " the danger of overshooting the Pole at such a breakneck speed," and "whether the road was decontrolled or not."

By dinner-time the log registered thirteen miles, and so elated was every one that at two o'clock they were off again. Speed then began to diminish considerably. The dogs were feeling the effects of their dash—especially after a week's enforced idleness—but even their reduced speed was too much for the humans. Moreover, conditions were less favourable, the snow being very rough in places and the surface bad.

Despite this, a happy party halted for tea, and the physicist's report sounded like music to their ears.

" Eighteen miles—we are now only twelve miles from the Pole."

Enthralled at the idea of seeing almost to their goal, David borrowed Doctor Elliot's binoculars and gazed hungrily at the horizon. Then, as he swept the intervening stretch of pure white, he suddenly gasped out :

" There's a flag sticking up out of the snow over there, *and it's red !* "

" What's that ? " ejaculated Mr. Walker, seizing the binoculars. " He's right, doctor . . . and Collinson was dropping *red* flags."

CHAPTER XVIII

THE GOAL REACHED

DESPITE their fatigue the two scientists left their tea and hurried through the piercing wind. Half an hour later they struggled back and dropped into their seats, surrounded by six news-eager eyes.

"It *is* Collinson's flag," reported Doctor Elliot; "and there is a message attached. It just says:

" ' Believe somewhere near the Pole, but flying blind. Terrible blizzard. All well at present. Outlook pretty hopeless.—Collinson.'

"The date is the day on which he started."

Tea was considerably delayed by this totally unexpected find. Frank wanted to begin searching for the aeroplane at once; David was for starting after tea; while the other three avidly discussed the new possibilities opened up by the discovery.

It was in just such dilemmas that Doctor Elliot's leadership and clear thinking made all the difference between sane action and what might be fatal rashness. Suggesting that their immediate task was to restore their flagging strength—otherwise to have tea—and setting the example himself, he summed up his conclusions between the mouthfuls.

"It would be useless waste of time to search here. They were flying rapidly when the message was dropped, and would be far away when it fell. If the 'plane or its occupants are anywhere near here we may see them as we proceed. To delay now might be critical to the success of the whole of our party—and, even if they had come down, there would not be the ghost of a chance of any of them still being alive in these parts."

After a pause, he continued, " If you all feel fit, we will press on a bit farther after a rest and then camp— for the last time, I hope—before the Pole."

By eight o'clock he saw that several of the party were exhausted, although no one would admit it, and ordered a halt.

" Twenty-one miles to-day—isn't it great ! " exulted David, five minutes after they had turned in for the night.

A snore was the only reply from his chum, and the speaker decided to follow his wise example. That night all five reached the Pole in their dreams and spent many happy hours—so it seemed—rejoicing at their triumph. The nature of their dream-pole varied enormously with the personality of the dreamer.   To one it appeared as a pillar of snow.   To another a wooden pole fixed through the earth and revolving rapidly with the globe ; a third saw it as a hole waiting to swallow the intrepid explorers, while a fourth visualized a mighty volcano, forming the safety-valve of all the pent-up energy in the centre of the earth.   Frank was, perhaps, the most original. Arriving at the Pole, he found Collinson's 'plane, into which all five—and the dogs—jumped and flew back to the base, arriving in a terrific storm.

Both dreams and nightmares came to a sudden end, however. The storm was more real than Frank imagined. All five awoke with a jerk, their hearts palpitating unpleasantly for no apparent reason. Before any one could speak a loud roar heralded the approach of a cyclonic blast of wind which forthwith struck the tent with battering-ram blows, tore it from its fastenings, and whirled it away like a balloon, leaving the five occupants —and a dog—exposed to the full fury of the blizzard.

Apart from the immediate danger of being frozen to death, the loss of the tent was serious enough. Unless they could retrieve it there would be only one tent to

Half an hour later they struggled back.

shelter all the dogs and five human beings—an almost impossible situation. Without the tent they would not dare to lie down.

Leaving Petz to guard the sledge—or, rather, to guide them back to it if necessary—the whole party set off on a frantic hunt.

To find a white object lying on a blanket of snow would be no easy task at the best of times, but with all distant vision obscured and the bitter polar wind half blinding them, their difficulties were increased tenfold. Yet they knew that their case was desperate and that their very lives—or those of the dogs—depended upon finding it. For the first time they were thankful that it had picked up so much dirt, in fact, against the pure white it might appear almost brown.

Although they watched it sail away—*how* intently their eyes had strained to follow its progress !—the falling flakes blotted it out long before a temporary lull allowed it to settle. All they knew was the approximate direction in which it had disappeared, but how far it had gone it was impossible to say.

On Zameneff's suggestion they separated until each was only just within sight of the next one and advanced in this spread-eagled fashion. Doctor Elliot, who was in the middle, consulted his compass frequently as a safeguard against losing their way back.

It was fortunate for them that the blizzard had abated slightly. What now was a gruelling ordeal would have been a sheer impossibility had a real polar storm persisted. As it was, only the exigency of their search enabled them to carry on.

David's thoughts were far from pleasant. Were they to be balked by such a chance accident when only a few miles from the Pole ? After all they had endured in the cause of science, was a trivial incident such as this to nullify all their efforts ? Were they to be frozen to death by the result of a mishap which none of them could foresee ?

Frank was reviewing the same possibilities from a different angle. As he strode eagerly forward his mind was full of a picture of Grenfell marooned on an ice-floe, but saved from being frozen to death by the skins of his dogs which he had so reluctantly killed. After all *they* still had plenty of dogs. Moreover, if it came to man-hauling the sledge . . . every man-Jack of them was now as tough as leather.

Almost subconsciously his gaze became riveted upon a darkish patch on the snow several hundred yards ahead, and his pace quickened accordingly. At each step the blur grew clearer and became more distinct from the surrounding glare. Then it resolved itself into a triangular patch, and his pulse began to beat faster as he felt sure that he had sighted the priceless piece of canvas.

But as the last three words flashed through his brain his heart rose into his mouth. What if the tent had been ripped into shreds when it was wrenched so violently from its moorings and whisked away by the gale? Suppose it were damaged beyond repair?

At once he broke into an apology for a run, but at the same moment he noticed that the others had also changed their direction and were already converging upon the same spot. His start, however, enabled him to arrive there first, and he examined the tent with the utmost concern. Apart from several bad tears—which he knew Zameneff could mend—he saw to his joy that it was still whole, and as the others raced up, he joined in their jubilation.

Back at the camp the dogs were tethered outside while their tent served for shelter for the humans. By supper-time the tent was repaired and re-erected, and when they crawled into it later on all felt very thankful for its recovery.

Next morning the whole party set off with renewed hopes. A dull, bitterly cold day, but no blizzard—and only nine miles to go.

Before long Doctor Elliot began to sweep the horizon with his binoculars. The second time his report mystified his hearers.

" I can see a flag of some sort, though whether it is one of Collinson's or one of those left by previous explorers I cannot determine at this distance."

A little later he reported, " It certainly *looks* red."

At midday Mr. Walker calculated their position carefully. " Only two miles from the Pole now."

Buoyed up by the news, despite the terrible conditions of loose snow and a wind which penetrated to their very bones, they increased their pace ; meanwhile their eyes were fixed upon the tiny flag ahead.

Again their leader halted and examined it. " It's a

Union Jack," he announced in more than usually thrilled tones.

His words proved correct. As they reached the spot they saw the tattered remains of the British flag flying from a short pole stuck in a cairn of snow.

With one accord the whole party came to attention and saluted, after which their leader turned towards them, and pointing to the cairn, said in solemn tones :

" That must be the flag left by the Scott expedition in nineteen-twelve. . . ."

" What's that, then ? " broke in Frank, pointing excitedly across the snow.

Less than a mile away a dark triangular object was visible. Seizing his binoculars, Doctor Elliot soon gave his opinion.

" There is *another* flag . . . and something which resembles a tent."

Again the party hurried forward, while Petz remained with the sledge, and very soon they were able to distinguish a small dark flag flying from a thin pole above a nearly black triangular tent.

At first the flag appeared to be black, with a few shreds of white beneath it. This time it was Zameneff who was the first able to interpret the scene.

" Norwegian flag," he announced.

" Amundsen," added the physicist laconically.

Turning to the boys, Doctor Elliot filled in the gaps.

" That must be the tent and flag left by Amundsen and his party who reached the South Pole only thirty-five days before Captain Scott. You can see now that that," pointing to the tattered remains, " was once a Norwegian flag and that there was a white flag, or piece of material under it."

Inside the tent they found written records of both Amundsen's and Scott's arrival at the Pole, but there was no time to linger over the sad relics as there was much scientific work to be done, and their leader was anxious to start on the return journey as soon as possible.

Experiments with the stratoscope still indicated land, and while David assisted Mr. Walker, Frank was busy collecting samples of snow and taking photographs for Alan.

Doctor Elliot joined the two physicists, and as soon as Zameneff had brought the sledge to the required spot, helped them to unload and assemble the most up-to-date apparatus for the determination of the exact position of the Pole. For several hours the three worked under most trying conditions, and not until they were entirely satisfied with the results did they desist. Then Doctor Elliot called the party together and dropped a bombshell.

" You will doubtless wonder why I called you over here. We are nearly a mile from the flag of either of the previous explorers. *But we are now standing exactly at the South Pole.* Mr. Walker has just proved (" typical of him to give *all* the credit to some one else " thought Frank) beyond all possible doubt that this is the true geographical south. So we are, after all, the very first people to reach the *actual* South Pole."

Here the speaker paused to allow photographs to be taken of him making the announcement. It was indeed a thrilling moment for David and Frank ; unknown to the other, each was thinking exactly the same thing—how he wished Alan were there to share in their jubilation. But their well-merited pride was interrupted by the speaker's voice.

" Although we are naturally delighted and proud to know that the honour of locating the exact Pole now belongs, in actual fact at any rate, to Great Britain, yet I would not have you imagine that our triumph in any way detracts from the honour due to Amundsen and Scott. It was they who first reached what, so far, has been acknowledged to be the South Pole, and as far as the accuracy of the instruments of that time would allow, they did apparently attain it. It is only thanks to our more modern apparatus that we have been able to correct their reckonings . . . and after all, what is a mile or less in these vast distances ? Moreover, they travelled under much greater difficulties than we have done ; each of the other parties only had the backing of its own nation, whereas we have all the influence of the League. For this latter reason we shall not be able to claim our success for Great Britain *officially* as the expedition was assisted in its earlier stages by several other nations. And we must not forget Russia—what could we have done without Zameneff ? "

" And Petz," chimed in Frank with a laugh, stroking the dog's head fondly.

" Then again," continued their leader, " we have been blessed with excellent health. Had it not been for the absence of that factor, and phenomenally atrocious weather conditions, Scott and his party might have lived to tell their tale."

" What really happened to them ? " asked Frank.

Doctor Elliot looked astonished at the question. " Surely you don't mean to say that you have never read the story ? "

Frank shook his head.

" Then read it at the very first opportunity," advised his leader with pronounced emphasis. " Among all the epics of polar exploration—and they are many—the account of Scott's heroic expedition to the Pole, and more especially of his tragic return journey, when, after pressing forward in the teeth of almost impossible odds, the whole party perished only eleven miles from a depot, is without exception the most moving and yet the most stimulating of all—but I suppose the South Pole is hardly the most suitable spot to rhapsodize," he added with a broad smile, " so now to work."

Each knew exactly what he meant by " work," as all duties had been thoroughly planned out beforehand, and the rest of the day was occupied in making many kinds of scientific observations. Two days were spent at the Pole while Mr. Walker, driven by Zameneff on the unloaded sledge, explored for miles around to carry out tests with the stratoscope. At the end of his investigation his report to his senior was brief and to the point.

" Land everywhere within ten miles, sir."

" Then we start for home early to-morrow morning," was the welcome reply. " To-day is the seventeenth since leaving depot sixteen. This allows us only twelve days to cover what actually took us fourteen and a half coming out, so we had better not dawdle."

Doctor Elliot was up long before the others and had scrupulously examined everything by the time the first ones began to stir. At nine o'clock Zameneff gave the word to the dogs and the whole party moved off, knowing that all had been left in perfect order. The exact position of the South Pole had been suitable marked, records left of their observations, and everything possible done to preserve the relics of the former expeditions for as long as possible.

David and Frank always said afterwards that it was obvious that the clerk of the weather did not approve of their expedition to the Pole. On the way *out* almost every possible barrier had been placed in their way, whereas from the morning of their departure everything seemed to favour them. The wind dropped, leaving a thin layer of cloud to obscure the sun and reduce the intensity of the dazzle. Temperature rose to five below zero, and there was no snow. In fact, they experienced what Doctor Elliot called " super-Amundsen weather."

Both dogs and humans reacted to the better conditions (although Frank said that it was " the old, old tale of the donkey and the carrots ! "), and with the light load, two were able to ride in addition to the driver. At eight o'clock they were astonished to hear Mr. Walker report :

" Thirty-five miles from the Pole."

" Of which you and I have only walked about ten," commented Frank to his chum.

Doctor Elliot glanced at his watch and spoke to Zameneff before addressing the others. " Then we will camp here for the night. This excellent progress means that we are only twenty-five miles from our depot, and with similar conditions we *might* be able to do that to-morrow."

His "might" became fact. Although they had camped on the very brink of the glacier, rapid progress was made. In places, owing to the downhill nature of their route, all five were able to ride—Petz running well ahead and proving an excellent guide. Just as Doctor Elliot was thinking of halting for tea, his binoculars showed him the depot at the bottom of the glacier.

"The question now is ' shall we stop for tea and have a big meal at night, or would it be better to press on while the going is good and have a tea-supper table-d'hôte ? ' "

All voted for the latter. After nearly three weeks of strict rations—of a very monotonous nature—the lure of a plentiful supply of varied kinds of foodstuffs was irresistible. Consequently, at seven o'clock David and Frank were ransacking the depot for its choicest contents.

"What shall our menu be ? " smiled Frank.

David thought for a moment. " I think we'll start on hors-d'œuvre. There's a few small fish which we brought from Polar Bay—we'll call 'em sardines."

" Then water soup, I suppose ? " suggested Frank.

David was rummaging among the stores. " O.K. We'll miss the fish course and pass straight to entrée—what about fricasseed pemmican ? "

" Fine ! I vote for seal-steak for the joint."

" Then there's sweets . . . what on earth . . ."

Frank produced some ship's biscuits. " Oh, cut out the sweets—let's have a savoury. I propose soft roes on toast—at least, I'm not sure whether seals have roes or not, but we've got biscuits instead of toast, and we'll have a look inside this lump of seal and see what we can find."

The two boys had volunteered to prepare the evening meal while Zameneff attended to the dogs, and the two scientists erected the tents and made sundry scientific observations.

Promptly at 7.30 p.m. the towering ice-cliffs echoed back the very un-polar-like sound of a gong. When, however, the physicist saw the metal container of his precious stratoscope in one of Frank's hands and a spanner in the other his smile changed to a look of aggrieved concern.

Nevertheless, very soon, five hungry and expectant persons—and a dog—gathered round the festive table—in the form of an old box. One by one they stared, seized a piece of paper and burst into laughter.

In front of each was the " menu " as arranged by David and Frank. Unknown to his chum, Frank had added at the bottom :

WINE LIST

Champagnes	Iced Polar Special.
White Wines	Aqua Pura.
Red Wines	L'eau à sang d'explorer.
Spirits	Courage à la Doctor Elliot.

It was a happy and much better fed party which left next morning, after carefully restoring the depot, " For future explorers," as Mr. Walker expressed it just as he completed a series of experiments which corroborated those on the outward route—water all round the depot from the edge of the cliffs, although every test from the Pole to the end of the glacier had shown land.

No definite plans were made for the return journey to Polar Bay. All anxiety as to food had now vanished as, in addition to the two depots, there was still a week's supply on the sledge. Consequently, it was nearly midday before they started, and travelling by easy stages depot fifteen was reached in plenty of time to camp there for the night, while by tea-time on the twenty-third day since they left, the familiar headland of Polar Bay came into view.

An hour later they were being warmly welcomed by their former friends—the mysterious native inhabitants.

Next morning Doctor Elliot outlined his plans :

" Mr. Walker and I are going to concentrate upon our special investigation, namely, to try to find some means of communication with the natives. Zameneff will help us in between his duties of looking after the dogs. You two boys can assist me by making a scale-map of as much of the district as possible, and when you have explored on foot I will arrange for you to use the sledge. I shall rely upon you not to take foolhardy risks, and to adopt every possible precaution to avoid getting lost—otherwise, you will have a free hand."

This scheme suited David and Frank admirably— not to mention Petz—and they thoroughly enjoyed their task of exploring and mapping, as far, that is, as it was possible to enjoy life under such bleak conditions. Meanwhile the two scientists made unexpectedly rapid progress. Using the slow method of pointing to an object, pronouncing the Eskimo (or Russian, etc.) name and looking inquiringly at a native, they were very soon able to pick up a rapidly growing vocabulary. Practically the whole day was given over to this, and during the evening the three sat in their tent and wrote out the words phonetically, later discussing and memorizing them. As the dictionary grew, they were able to establish beyond any reasonable doubt that the language of Polar City was an offshoot of the Eskimo tongue, mixed with words closely allied to the various languages of Russia and Siberia.

With their combined knowledge of languages, and a novel method evolved by Doctor Elliot, the three were able to converse with the natives in a remarkably short time, using signs where words failed.

In this they were greatly helped by their hosts, who, having very little to do apart from their routine in Polar Bay, put themselves entirely at their visitors' disposal, and entered into the scheme with great zest.

At the end of a week David reported to his leader

Frank picked up a stone axe.

that they had mapped the district to a distance of ten miles in each direction.

"We knew that there was no need to explore back along the route we came, so we confined our survey to the mountain range, sir," he concluded.

"Quite right, and to-morrow you can have the sledge —and for as long as you need it," replied Doctor Elliot.

With the sledge, taking only a few pounds of food in case of accidents, they found that they could travel surprisingly long distances and still rely upon returning safely to camp the same night. After three days' exploration towards the glacier it was decided to penetrate as far as possible along the western side of the hills. By dinner-time they had covered over forty miles, so David suggested that they should spend the afternoon mapping and exploring on foot.

Frank agreed, and while David sat on the sledge to start the diagram, he proceeded towards a hummock which hid the cliff immediately beyond.

Presently David heard a shout and saw his chum beckoning eagerly to him. Handing the map to Zameneff he jumped up and hurried towards the spot.

" Hurry up, Dave ! " urged Frank. " There's a cave round there," pointing to the rocks.

In silent expectation the two rounded the point to find that the cliffs turned sharply back. Less than fifty yards from where they stood David saw a large cave, and as they entered Frank picked up a stone axe.

" How's that for a find ? " he gloated. " But that's not all ! "

CHAPTER XIX

AN UNEXPECTED MEETING

BEFORE they left the cave Frank had shown him several roughly made axes, a number of rods resembling those used at Polar Bay, and the remains of what appeared to be sealskin clothes. Thrilled by the finds, they hurried back to tell Doctor Elliot, who, after listening intently to all they had to say, replied mysteriously :

"You appear to have found the missing link in our evidence. I will accompany you there first thing after breakfast to-morrow morning."

Back at the cave their leader examined everything with the most scrupulous attention ; then he started to explore, only to find that there was a series of small caves. In the second one he came to a sudden halt, dropped on to one knee, and began to scrape at the dusty surface of the rock.

"Unless I am very much mistaken," he concluded, " there has been a fireplace here at some distant—probably far distant—time."

Not until he had satisfied himself that he had thoroughly examined every part of the caves did Doctor Elliot sit down just inside the entrance and beckon to the other four to do likewise. Then he began :

"I have been working things out and find that we must leave Polar Bay as soon as possible. Not only will the others be getting seriously anxious at our long absence, but there is the much more important question of that mineral deposit to consider. Unless we can find that and leave the Ross Sea well behind us before the winter sets in again, we may be frozen in and delayed for another six months. I have, therefore, decided to start on Monday ; that will give us to-morrow and Saturday to complete our investigations and pack up.

"In view of this, and the momentous discovery of the contents of these caves, I thought I would give you all a very brief summary of our conclusions with regard to the inhabitants of Polar City. For some days now Mr. Walker and I have been in constant conversation with several of them, among whom were two of the oldest. From this we have learned the following basic facts "—consulting his note-book.

"One—they have lived in the two bays for as long as they can remember.

"Two—they know nothing of any other human beings except themselves, or of any animals apart from seals and fish.

"Three—they have never—as far as they know—let the fire out or the ice-hole freeze.

"Four—they worship the spirit which gives them food and the power to cook it. Hence their most sacred spots are the place where they imagine the spirit lives—the ice-hole ; and the place where he sends them fire—the kitchen.

"Five—Polar Bay is sacred, and they think that to sleep there would desecrate it.

"Six—their only ambitions in life are to keep warm, procure sufficient food, and propagate their race.

"Seven—their sacred numbers are two, four, seven, and eleven.

"Eight—they have never been far from home ; very occasionally a spirit of wanderlust—probably some form of insanity—seizes upon one or more and they go off in search of the unknown—but seldom come back."

"That explains the mysterious footprints," whispered David as he paused.

"Incredible as it may seem, *that* is all they actually *know* ; they have, however, a most interesting folklore. I think I have enough notes to write a book on this when we get back to civilization," continued the speaker with a smile, " but I have no time to tell you much about it now. I will confine myself to one or two specially cogent points.

" This tradition—which is handed down by word of mouth—tells of a time when they were part of a very large race, spread over a vast area. Then, in the dim past, their spirit became angry with them and caused a great split across the earth which developed into an impassable stretch of water. Thus they were completely cut off from all mankind, and began to die out. In order to preserve their race they were forced to seek shelter by migrating to the mountains. According to the tradition the main body used to live ' over the mountains,' but when they were reduced to a few hundreds they moved to their present position, because of its more sheltered nature.

" Now the interesting thing is that whenever they are talking about the place where their immediate ancestors lived, they point over here, or ' over the mountains ' as they call it, and this discovery—thanks to Somervell and Ingram—appears to provide us with very strong evidence of the truth of their tradition."

Noticing that it was nearly time to return, he hastened to conclude :

" Perhaps all this mixture of fact and tradition may seem a little muddled to you at present, but I feel sure that if you think it over methodically in the light of what you already know, the probable explanation of the existence of these queer people will be clear to you. What is more, I think that this solution will appear a perfectly reasonable one."

Although they were sorry to say good-bye to their hospitable friends, every one was glad when Monday came, and nine o'clock saw them waving a final farewell to the specks in the distance.

Setting out on the return journey was a very different undertaking from the outward venture. Not only did they know the nature of the route and its probable dangers, but there was little anxiety as to food. In addition to the seal-meat and fish which their hosts had insisted upon giving them, they knew that there was a depot approximately every fifty miles. Depot thirteen was soon left behind.

As they plodded over the snow the two chums were chatting eagerly.

" Seems funny to think that we're really homeward bound at last," reflected David.

" Just what I was thinking," agreed Frank. " Wonder how every one is at home ? "

" And Alan, and all those at the base," added David.

" Hope Hawlet and Co. got back all right."

" Talking about them, I *would* like to know what's happened to the Penguin Man."

" Gosh ! So would I ! Still more poor old Collinson."

" Yes, and one mystery leads to another. Wonder if we shall ever find out who that poor chap was we saw in the block of ice."

" And the wreck. Ugh ! Makes me squirm now when I think of those ghastly grinding and cracking sounds."

" Crumbs, so it does ! Hope Captain Baker and his lot are back safely—and Lieutenant Carmen and his party."

" I'm simply dying to hear what Hawlet has found out about those bacteria."

" I'm more anxious to see heaps of that precious new mineral in our hold," chipped in David.

And so they discussed their hopes and fears until dinner-time when, owing to their good progress during the morning, two hours were allotted for rest.

An hour was enough, however, for the boys, and they were soon exploring around their camping-place. Just as they were about to turn back David pointed to his right.

" What's that, Frank ? Something black on the snow."

On reaching the spot both gasped. " Well I'm jiggered ! " began David. " Bothered if it isn't a specimen of the black snow Walker told us about. Never thought we'd see any."

But there were more surprises to come. Near where they were standing were several masses of rock—mainly covered with the ever-present white mantle—projecting above the snow. As he rounded one of these, Frank pointed eagerly.

" Golly, look over there ! Thought it was another rock."

David followed as fast as the rough ground would allow him. He, too, at first sight concluded that the brown patch was a flat slab of rock which had somehow (he did not stop to imagine *how*) remained clear of snow. He was quickly disillusioned, however, on reaching Frank's side. At close quarters it was obvious that there was no rock there, and picking up a handful of the brown material, he found that it was ordinary snow except for its colour.

" That's interesting ! " he exclaimed as he waited for his chum to bottle a specimen, which was placed in the same pocket as the black variety.

" Let's look round and see if we can find any more." Frank pushed down the top of his glove. " We've got just twenty minutes before we start off again."

His optimism was well rewarded when, only a short distance away, they discovered a small area of green snow, some of which was duly transferred to a third sample jar.

" We'll just have time to show these to Walker if we hurry up," mused Frank as he hastily screwed on the top, " and they'll be useful to Hawlet too."

The physicist was very interested to see the specimens. " First I've ever come across, although I knew that they existed," he summarized.

" What are the colours due to, sir ? " asked his assistant.

Mr. Walker was shaking the bottle of brown snow and examining it with a pocket lens.

"I am afraid I cannot answer that question—definitely, at any rate—because they are so seldom found. I doubt if any one knows for certain. I believe that it is sometimes due to dust—rock dust, for instance. If you like I will examine them fully when we get back to the base— that is, if the bacteriologists leave me any to test," he laughed, turning to Frank.

Further discussion of the interesting problem was precluded by Doctor Elliot's signal to proceed, but the monotony of the next few miles was very greatly minimized to three people by a keen outlook for further specimens. The only discovery made, however, was a small growth of lichen on the sheltered side of a rock.

Although progress was much more rapid than on the outward route, considerable delay was caused by the physicist's wish to repeat his stratoscope tests in these parts. All results confirmed those on the first journey, and while he and David were away, Frank used the opportunity to good purpose by photographing as many of the footprints as he could find.

For this reason it was not until 3 p.m. on the third day that they sighted depot twelve ; next morning they embarked upon the ill-omened fifty-mile stretch which, outwards, had taken them eight days to cover. Fortunately, despite the bad surface, nothing untoward happened to the sledge or dogs, and no blizzards were encountered, with the result that only seven days after leaving Polar Bay, Petz came rushing back—after an unusually long run ahead—and barked excitedly.

"Something interesting ahead, sir," explained Frank.

Doctor Elliot soon had his binoculars trained upon the horizon. "We're in sight of 'Farewell Depot'; I can see the flag on top," he announced with evident glee.

"Good old Petz !" commended David, patting him approvingly. "But how in the world did you know it was there !"

Neither the dog nor any one else ever answered his question. All were far too excited to trouble to decide whether his sight was keener than theirs, or whether his triumph was due to some special canine faculty.

That evening the two chums diligently rifled the depot, and again prepared a table d'hôte for the hungry party.

"We've done the hundred miles from Polar Bay in exactly half the time it took us going," exulted the physicist as they sat down to their repast.

Doctor Elliot was obviously enjoying the change of food, and spoke with a note of cheery optimism. "Another two hundred miles and we shall be at two-ton depot ; then we're over half-way to the base."

Less than twenty-four hours later he was thinking sarcastically of his optimism. He was lying in the tent next to his assistant ; both had that morning fallen into an unsuspected crevasse, and although not seriously injured, each had so badly twisted his ankle that it had swollen up to several times its normal size.

"If we are able to start again inside a week I shall be pleasantly surprised," was his carefully considered verdict.

It was a very irksome delay for every one. All the experiments which they had set out to accomplish had been completed, and apart from the utter monotony of their position there was the grave possibility of running short of food. Owing to the depots being only fifty miles apart they carried a bare two weeks' supply on the sledge. Should a long blizzard delay them—and autumn was rapidly approaching—the result might be serious.

On the second day Frank suggested to David that they should ask Zameneff to take them for a ride so as to mark out the safest route ahead. This would save much time when they were able to start, and might avoid further disasters.

Doctor Elliot willingly agreed, especially as he realized that it would make a break in the monotony of their enforced delay for the younger members of the party. By 9 a.m. the sledge was nearly out of sight of the camp and David prepared to mark the route. After a brief halt for dinner, the journey was continued.

" We'd better turn back about two, don't you think, Zameneff ? " asked David.

" Slower going back—dogs tired," was the non-committal reply.

" We're nearly twenty-five miles out now," shouted Frank.

David nodded. " Right. Watch the log, Frank, and we'll turn at twenty-five."

Twenty minutes later they heard Frank announce, " Twenty-five up ! " and David leant across to the driver.

" Time to go back now, Zameneff."

They had already turned when Frank glanced back to make sure that he had marked the route clearly.

The next moment both David and Zameneff were convinced that he had gone mad.

With a bound he leapt off the sledge—a risky thing to do with crevasses about—and stood as still as a statue, staring back along their route as if demented.

" There's something black coming towards us ! " he shrieked in terror, trembling at the knees.

Zameneff jerked the dogs to a standstill, and, while David leapt off to join his chum, looked round.

" Motor-sledge," he said laconically.

" What ? " shrilled David, " motor-sledge ? You're dreaming, Zameneff "—staring back. " No, by gum you're right ! At least, it's the motor-*trailer* coming to look for us." With a beaming face he shook Frank vigorously, " Buck up, Frank ! Oh boy, we're rescued—it's Lieutenant Carmen with the motor-trailer, not the motor-sledge ! "

Frank—who might well be excused for mistaking the huge unwieldy machine for a nightmare monster—quickly recovered, and all three gazed at the oncoming party in the greatest excitement. There was no longer the slightest doubt that it was one of the motor-trailers which had laid the first series of depots, though whether it was manned by Lieutenant Carmen now no one could yet say.

Holding up a dark garment they waved frantically and were overjoyed to see an answering signal. Then, as they began to halloo for sheer joy, visions filmed rapidly through their minds. How good it would be to see some of their friends again. . . . They would start immediately for home, as the trailer could carry them all in addition to sufficient stores to last from depot to depot. . . . Their homeward journey would be reduced by one-half—or more—and there would be no more walking, other than voluntary, or shortage of food, or risk of crevasses, and a hundred and one other dangers. In fact, if all went well, they might reach the base in a week. Further visions of reunion and of the thrilling tales which all would have to tell were interrupted by the arrival of the motor-trailer within hailing distance, and very soon it pulled up only a few yards away from their sledge, to the accompaniment of an ear-splitting babel of shouting and barking.

In order to avoid carrying large supplies of food the search-party had been reduced to three—Carpini and the driver in charge of Lieutenant Carmen. On hearing of Doctor Elliot's accident, Zameneff was left to bring back the sledge by easy stages while the other five—and Petz—clambered on to the motor-trailer and returned to camp. Here news-telling occupied the rest of the evening, and next morning the two invalids were made as comfortable as possible on the motor-trailer. All stores were then transferred from the sledge to the larger vehicle so that Zameneff would be able to keep pace with the motor, although it was later found possible, on occasions, to take all the dogs on to the trailer and to pull the empty sledge behind.

In this way splendid progress was made. Most of the party now had very little to do, and much of the time was whiled away by relating their adventures. In view of the importance of the polar party's work, Lieutenant Carmen insisted upon hearing their story first, and Doctor Elliot kept them all fascinated by his inimitable account of their thrilling adventures.

But when his story, often supplemented by Mr. Walker, was ended, he turned to Lieutenant Carmen :

" And now for *your* thriller, please."

The motor had come to a standstill in order to allow the dogs to catch them up. This was too good an opportunity to stretch their legs to be missed. Even the two invalids were able to walk for a few yards, but were thankful that they would not have to face long stretches of fifteen to twenty miles over the rough surface.

Allowing the dogs to get well ahead, the party climbed back, and as soon as they had restarted the narrator began :

" As you know from our messages, all of which I hope you found, we had a good deal of trouble with the motors at first. Later, however, they worked well, and we made excellent progress, often covering a hundred miles in a day. Despite one or two bad patches we reached the Bay of Whales, on the Ross Barrier, in three weeks. Except for a few isolated nunataks, nothing of any special interest was discovered on the way, so, after a short rest and some fishing to make a variation in our menu, we turned inwards and explored along behind the Alexandra Mountains. Here we made some important additions to the cartographical knowledge of that region." Remarking a puzzled look on Frank's face, he added, " Cartography is, of course, the science of map-making. Although we did not make any hair-raising discovery, our expedition proved well worth while, as we have added nearly three hundred miles of land—mainly mountains—to the map. We were also able to prove that the Alexandra Mountains contained several volcanoes ; these did not appear to be active, but we could not settle that point finally.

" Biologist Gutzberg made a number of interesting observations on penguins, seals, killer whales, and other Antarctic fauna, as well as discovering several new marine animalculæ and one previously unknown species on land.

" Physicist Carpini did some valuable work on temperature, wind velocity, and the structure of the Ross

Ice Barrier, while geologist Ardenholdt's work may prove to be the most fruitful of all. During our journey he was constantly stopping us to examine some nunatak or other, and I believe he found evidence of a number of unsuspected minerals. When we explored along the back of the Alexandra Mountains he was just like a schoolboy let loose. Geology is a bit of a mystery to me, so I must leave him to speak for himself, but I do know that he found a large bed of coal, one area which I understood him to say consisted of the carboniferous remains of a prehistoric forest, traces of gold and platinum, and one mineral which he cannot yet identify."

" Not a bad haul ! " laughed Mr. Walker.

" No, but that is, of course, only a very sketchy outline of what we did." He seemed about to pause, but suddenly continued, " There was just one other thing— it may be of no importance whatever, but one day it might prove to have some bearing upon some one else's discoveries. We had one abnormally warm period which not only cleared many inlets of ice but opened a large number of channels. One of these started from Biscoe Bay and turned south-east, bending back towards where you were, that is."

Unseen by the speaker, Doctor Elliot glanced meaningly at physicist Walker, and a vision of Penguin Cove and its outlet formed in each mind.

" I think the only other thing," continued Lieutenant Carmen, " was that, as the result of the large number of evidences of land which we came across—either in the form of nunataks or actual mountains—physicist Carpini is strongly of the opinion that the whole of the Antarctic —the frozen part, that is—is one huge continent."

" His opinion will probably be strengthened considerably when he hears all about our stratoscope work," whispered Mr. Walker into David's ear.

" Did you go back to the base, sir ? " asked David, who had been absent during Lieutenant Carmen's previous talk.

258 POLAR PERIL

"Oh yes, Somervell. We arrived back at the base only two days later than the date we suggested, and left again five days ago. When we heard that you were already several weeks overdue we decided to set off to meet you. Not that we were over-anxious, but I knew that it would be a help to you to have a lift and plenty of stores, and if anything had happened to delay you—as, curiously enough, it did—then our presence might be welcome for other reasons."

"What's happening at the base? Are they all well . . . and has Captain Baker got back all right?" put in Frank.

Lieutenant Carmen's face clouded momentarily. "No —at least, we found them well and quite safe at the base. But Captain Baker's party has not returned . . . and they were due back over three weeks ago."

"Where are they—they're in touch by wireless, I suppose?" queried David a little anxiously.

"That's the trouble. No wireless message has been received from them for over a month."

Although no one made any comment, it was obvious that the news was disquieting to one and all.

"What did the last message say?" persisted David.

Lieutenant Carmen hesitated for a moment before replying that they were six hundred miles from the base, and that one sledge had been giving a lot of trouble. Previous to that they had a rather unintelligible message to say that Hill had been badly bitten by some animal. But the message seemed to be more atmospherics than English.

CHAPTER XX

BACK AT THE BASE

THE disquieting news of the third party cast a temporary gloom over all, but this was soon largely dispelled by the excitement of seeing two depots each day. On reaching two-ton depot they felt specially elated, and talked about being " nearly home," although three hundred miles still separated them from the base, and three hundred miles in the Antarctic—well, *many* things may happen.

To their pleasant surprise very little did happen, and exactly a week after leaving " Farewell Depot " Doctor Elliot lowered his binoculars and shouted back :

" The base ! I can see the wireless mast."

Hardly had he spoken when they saw the ice-yacht skimming towards them. Instead of being piloted by Le Brun, they noticed that Alan formed the sole crew, and a few moments later the three youths were doing what Frank described as a " Polar War Dance," to celebrate their reunion, accompanied by the delighted barks of Petz.

Then came the second motor-trailer, followed by the other dog-sledge, each crowded with their friends from the base, in whose uneventful lives the return of one of the expeditions was an occurrence of great importance.

For the remainder of that day the camp was filled with the wagging of tongues, as every one tried to exchange news with every one else. Except for the one shadow—that they were still without news of Captain Baker—all were riotously happy. That evening they sat down to the most varied spread which any of them had faced for many days.

Next morning those at the base were anxious to show the new-comers what they had done during their absence. To Alan's disgust, Mr. Hawlet dragged Frank—although, in actual fact, he needed little persuasion—off to the bacteriological laboratory, and the physicist asked David to help him in tabulating the results of his stratoscope tests. Doctor Elliot joined Lieutenant Ransome to discuss plans for the immediate future, the other scientists paired off to their respective laboratories, while the drivers gave their attention to their charges—motor or canine.

In the bacteriological laboratory Frank was being thrilled by his senior's account of his work after reaching the base with the supporting party.

" I have succeeded in isolating several more organisms from the samples of snow and ice which I brought back with me," he began, taking down tube after tube and handing it to Frank. When these were all examined, he went on in a voice full of suppressed excitement, " But the part which will interest you most is that which concerns the snow which you inoculated directly into the tubes. I have spent quite a long time on these, with the result that I have confirmed my—almost joking—suggestion that we have discovered an entirely new group of organisms which thrive best at a temperature of minus ten to minus twenty degrees centigrade. I could not detect any growth above the freezing-point, but it was impossible to find a minimum temperature of growth owing to my lack of apparatus for producing extreme cold."

" I suppose you will make a full report about it when we get back, sir ? " asked Frank.

Mr. Hawlet was replacing the tubes in a wire basket. " Yes, I shall certainly make a detailed report of our discovery, but it will go in under our combined names. Had it not been for your idea of inoculating the snow

In the laboratory, thrilled by his senior's account of his work.

directly on to the gelatine, Ingram, we might never have discovered them."

" Did you test their chemical reactions at all, sir ? "

" Yes. That is one of the remarkable things about them ; they show distinct chemical action at their optimum temperature."

" Did you try them on meat or other food ? " continued Frank.

" No—why do you ask ? "

Frank related what had happened to Zameneff, concluding, " It might be interesting to test this point, sir."

Mr. Hawlet nodded vigorously. " Certainly. *Most* certainly. I wish we could do it now, but Doctor Elliot has given orders that all new experiments must be postponed until we get back."

At this Frank returned to the work in hand, but a look of acute disappointment was detectable in his expression.

Mr. Walker and David were kept busy for some time tabulating their results, and consulting maps and records of previous explorations, and collating these with physicist Carpini's discoveries. Later in the day they began to pack up the books and papers; meanwhile, Mr. Walker announced to his fellow co-workers:

" I think that whoever compiles the expedition's report upon this subject will have ample material to support the statement that there is quite definitely an Antarctic continent, and that the majority of the ice barrier and polar plateau rests upon land, and not water."

It was not until that evening that any one remembered the mysterious Penguin Man. Just before supper, however, the three boys were busy photographing and being photographed when a familiar figure emerged from one of the tents.

" Great Scot, there's the old Penguin Man ! " exclaimed David.

At once everything else was forgotten, and a lively discussion broke out.

" What happened when you arrived back at Penguin Cove ? " asked Doctor Elliot of Mr. Slater.

" Nothing much. We found him chatting away to his subjects. We had to kidnap him, as it were, and pretend that we were coming back for the penguins. He was convinced that they would all die without him, I think."

" And who is he ? Have you been able to find out anything about him since he has been here ? " put in Doctor Elliot, turning to Lieutenant Ransome.

" I'm afraid not, sir. We have done our best, but without much success. He had quite a bad breakdown after he got here — became quite wild, in fact. He's always talking about his subjects and saying he must get back to them. We had to undress him and wash him, though which were his clothes, which his skin, and which dirt it was hard to say. However, we got him fairly clean at last, shaved him, cut his hair, and put him to bed. Had to keep him in hospital for a fortnight, then he began to recover very slowly. Occasionally he has periods when he's almost normal, but the curious thing is that, at these times, his mind becomes a blank. He has at last learnt to eat in a more civilized manner and to talk English—after a fashion. No one can do much with him except Alan ; for some unaccountable reason he always seems happy in his company. When we got him here we thought he would soon come round because, when he saw the camp, and the ship in the open sea beyond, a sudden gleam of recollection came into his face . . . but it was no go."

" Supper-time ! " broke in a voice at the rear, and their thoughts soon reverted from the Penguin Man to penguin steak.

Much to their disappointment, it was several days before the boys had any chance to revel in the joys of united excursions or even of prolonged discussion. At every opportunity the scientists dived into their laboratories, where they remained buried except for meal-times. This usually entailed the presence of David and Frank, while Alan was frequently required to assist in the photographical department. Even when they were not occupied at their tasks, so much help was needed with the cooking, washing-up, journeys to and from the ship, and umpteen other jobs, that they were seldom together.

During this time the thoughts of David and Frank were often far away, wondering what had happened to Captain Baker and his party. But what haunted them still more was the face of their chum. Although he said nothing, Alan was obviously—to those who knew him intimately— worrying acutely about his father. Frank especially tried his utmost to cheer him up, but the sole result was that Alan displayed a forced cheerfulness when in his presence, but whenever he thought that he was out of his sight relapsed into a state of brooding.

Sunday was their first opportunity to get together and discuss things. After morning service the three boys strolled towards the sea with the comforting knowledge that they would have a full hour to themselves before dinner. There was only one thought in each mind. Unknown to the others, each had been deeply stirred by Doctor Elliot's prayers for the safety of their companions and the way in which he had guided the course of his simple talk on faith towards the same objective.

" Isn't Doctor Elliot going to search for them ? " asked Frank, quite unconscious of the ambiguity of his question.

David was staring at the bridge of the *Queen of the Antarctic*, but came slowly back to reality. " Not yet," he answered dreamily.

" *Why ?* " put in Alan emphatically.

His tone cleared David's brain at once. " Because we don't know where to look for them. All we know is that they intended to make for the Weddell Sea and explore that region. But as they might go several hundred miles in either direction, or return by quite a different route, it's pretty hopeless to set out. Very likely we should spend weeks searching in one direction, and all the time they might have come back by another route and be back at the base just after we left."

Alan was clearly unconvinced. " But," he protested, " Carmen went to look for you."

David was quick to follow the trend of his thoughts. " Yes, that's true, but it's quite a different case. He knew that we were going straight to the Pole and back. Also, he was familiar with the first three hundred miles because he'd laid the depots himself. But we know absolutely nothing of the other route—the kind of surface I mean—and they may come straight back or make a huge detour." Seeing an opportunity to raise his chum's hopes, he added, " *That* is probably the explanation of their delay. They have returned by a longer route than they intended, and that might easily add hundreds of miles to the distance."

" Ye-es . . . I suppose it might," drawled Alan.

" Look, Alan, there's a crowd of killers out there. What about a snap ? " Frank saw his chance to create a diversion and he seized it.

As soon as the photographer was out of earshot, he turned impatiently to David :

" Look here, Dave, it's all very well to talk like this in front of him," with a nod towards the distant figure ; " but I'm just about fed up with it. Here's six people— including our leader—five weeks overdue, and yet nothing is done."

" What *can* we do ? " protested David.

Frank's reply was very definite and reflected a momentary flash of his old self. " Do ? We can go and look for them. I can't stand this uncertainty any longer, and if Doctor Elliot won't send out a party I vote we three go. The ice-yacht would take us, and enough food for a week, I reck'n."

" What ? Go *without* the Doctor's permission, you mean ? "

" Ye-es, if necessary."

" Nonsense, Frank. You know perfectly well that you'd never do that—not in your saner moments, at any rate. Don't forget that he relies on our loyalty."

Frank's face was a picture as the conflicting emotions fought for supremacy. Slowly the sullen look gave way, and he compromised.

" Then let's see him and get his permish. I'm sure he'd see our point."

More in order to pacify Frank than with any hope of success, he agreed. " Right-o, we'll ask him first thing to-morrow morning."

In more ways than one it was probably fortunate that

the suggested interview proved unnecessary. All three
boys had been soundly asleep for several hours when
Alan was awakened by Petz, who was licking his face and
whining anxiously.

" What's the matter, Petz ? " he asked, knowing that
the dog never acted in this way without good cause. Even
as he was speaking, he became conscious of another noise
—a chorus of barking in the distance.

At first Alan was puzzled to know what to do. He did
not want to disturb the others unnecessarily, but when
Petz ran to the door of the hut and whined to be let out,
he realized that there must be something amiss.

Shaking David gently, he whispered, " Dave, there's
something funny going on ; d'you think we'd better go
out and see ? "

Sitting up with a start, David listened. In a moment
he had taken in the ominous signals, and after creeping
softly towards the door without disturbing the sleeper,
he opened it and peeped out. The chorus of excitement
coming from the dogs' hut convinced him that something
very unusual was happening, but when he noticed that
Petz had vanished he hurried back and awoke Frank. A
few minutes later all three had thrown on additional
covering and were standing outside. The dim light told
them at once that it was past midnight.

Alan's first thought was for Petz, and he began to call
him by means of the special whistle which the dog seldom
disregarded. This time the only answer was a sharp bark,
and all three stared in the direction from which it had
come. Although nothing unusual could be seen, a distinct
hum vibrated faintly through the clear night air.

By this time most of the other sleepers were stirring,
and one after another came out to inquire what was wrong.
Louder and louder grew the roar, and visions of earth-
quakes, aeroplanes, and a massed attack by unknown
animals filmed through the minds of the more nervous
ones, many of whom were still half asleep.

Suddenly Carpini turned to Doctor Elliot. " Sounds

. . . like . . . motor-sledge," he suggested in halting English.

" I *wonder*—is it . . . ? " began his hearer.

The sentence was never finished. At that moment a blur came slowly over a slight rise, and in the rapidly increasing light resolved itself into a motor-sledge.

" It's Dad ! " yelled Alan, making a frantic dash forward.

Very soon there was a confused mêlée as the entire population of the base mixed themselves inextricably with the occupants of the sledge, and for some moments there ensued a babel of questions and greetings in five or six different languages.

At last Doctor Elliot succeeded in detaching himself from the crowd and ran his eyes over the five new-comers. Evidence of their hardships was not wanting—Don Miguel's arm was in a sling and Mr. Hill's leg bulged noticeably below the knee—but he was overjoyed to note that every one had returned, except the second sledge and its driver.

" Where's the other sledge ? " he asked Captain Baker.

" Just behind," was the comforting reply, and as he spoke Doctor Elliot remarked a twinkle in the speaker's eye.

His words were quickly verified. A second hum was heard above the babel, and attracted by the increasing noise they paused to look. The other sledge was just visible.

Then they stood and gasped. The oncoming vehicle, instead of being loaded with stores, was crowded with human beings !

CHAPTER XXI

MORE MYSTERIES SOLVED

EVERY one—except the five recent arrivals—was too flabbergasted to move, and the whole crowd awaited the heavily burdened sledge in silence. Even when Lieutenant Carmen put a question to Captain Baker, the latter continued to study the expression of utter bewilderment upon the faces of the watchers with evident enjoyment, but said nothing.

At closer range it was seen that the occupants of the sledge were all men of foreign appearance dressed in tattered clothes, their faces largely obscured by hair. Then some of the crew of the *Queen of the Antarctic* noticed articles of seafaring attire, which suggestion received immediate confirmation when the new-comers jumped off the sledge and commenced to walk with a rolling gait towards the main party.

Only then did Captain Baker turn to his friends. " Let me introduce to you some of the survivors of the Russian schooner *Stalin*. Three cheers for our fellow-explorers ! "

Three resounding cheers rang out, and very soon the two parties were greeting each other warmly. Captain Baker, knowing that the rescued men were in dire need of food, had secretly sent a message to the kitchen, and remarking that explanations could wait, marched off the whole of his party to have the first good meal for many weeks. After that he insisted upon every one turning in for a long sleep before attempting to clear up the mystery.

Next morning all was hubbub and excitement. Needless to say, Zameneff and Midoff were in their element, and even forgot the dogs—for the first time during the expedition—in their absorption in the delights of chatting freely to their compatriots.

When the commotion began to die down, Captain Baker gave his promised explanation of the mystery.

" I propose to give you only the barest outline," he began ; " you can fill in the rest by degrees. On our way back—we were already several weeks late, and our wireless had broken down—we suddenly came across a party of half-starved men living in a snow-hut. Thanks to Vosziche, who knows a little Russian, we found that they were survivors from the wreck of the *Stalin*, a ship fitted out for polar exploration by the Soviet state. Unfortunately they were caught in the ice and their ship was pounded to pieces and sank." His next sentence electrified his hearers. " *That* was the ship whose destruction we witnessed while we were imprisoned in the ice. The majority of those on the ship left in boats before the ice closed entirely, intending to make for the nearest land. Our friends here were the skeleton crew who stayed on board to the last, hoping to save some of the valuable equipment. That blizzard foiled them, however, and the only remaining boat was smashed by an iceberg. When the ship sank they decided to try to reach safety on foot, living as best they could on seals or anything else obtainable. When we discovered them they had already covered over four hundred miles, and were utterly worn out and half starved. Rescuing them, and the consequent slowing-down owing to the extra load, delayed us still further."

Captain Baker refused to give any general account of his trip. " That can wait," he affirmed. " We have no startling achievements to record unfortunately."

Nevertheless, facts leaked out bit by bit, and it was soon common knowledge that his party had made heroic efforts in the face of almost impossible odds. The motor-sledges had given constant trouble until one broke down completely, necessitating a week's delay for repairs. Several accidents—due to the large number of unusually wide crevasses—and terrible blizzards had caused further delays, while the zoologist was severely bitten when trying to capture a fine specimen of sea-leopard, as the result of which his life was despaired of for nearly a week. Owing to the unexpected delays, food had run short, and their rescue of the marooned Russians, when in dire extremities themselves, was a masterpiece of leadership and dauntless optimism. Nevertheless, in the face of all these odds, they had traversed nearly a thousand miles of unexplored Antarctica, charted a new mountain range, the coastline of the Weddell Sea, and a large number of nunataks. It was also rumoured that the scientific results of the trip might cause a furore of excitement in the world of science when they were published.

Captain Baker now took over command from Doctor Elliot, although in actual practice the two co-operated in all their arrangements at the base. During the first few days every one was so busy trying to find time in between his duties to hear the adventures of the others, that no one thought to tell Captain Baker about the mysterious Penguin Man, who, ever since his arrival, had kept almost entirely to himself—or " moped," as Frank expressed it—and seldom left his tent. Meals were always taken to him, but owing to the excitement his supper was overlooked on one occasion.

The signal for this meal had just sounded, and all were hurrying towards the dining-room, led by Captain Baker. At that moment the Penguin Man emerged from his tent in search of something to eat. Then the onlookers witnessed a scene which remained fixed in their minds for years afterwards.

Without the slightest warning he gave a yell and hurled himself at Captain Baker. Thinking that he had suddenly become demented, several stepped forward to defend their leader. But, to their amazement, he just uttered one word and gripped the outstretched hand firmly between his own.

" Eric ! " he gasped.

" Walter ! " was the only reply, yet one which spoke volumes.

Seeing that the two were lost in the joy of their mutual rediscovery, the remainder melted away to discuss the dramatic scene round the supper-table. Not until the meal was nearly over did the two appear, and as the Penguin Man sat down beside Captain Baker they saw another miracle. Except for his clothes he was no longer the Penguin Man, but a sane human being, talking normal— though at times somewhat halting—English. No one attempted to disturb the two brothers in their happy reunion, and after making sure that they had everything that they were likely to require, the crowd dispersed silently.

Later it transpired that his brother and a friend—at least, he thought he was a friend—flew out to the Antarctic to explore the feasibility of an aerial route between Cape Horn and New Zealand via Graham Land. When over the bleakest part, however, the engine failed, and they planed down, hoping to land on the snow or ice. Just at the critical moment they were caught by a terrific gust of wind and driven into a snow-covered hill, where the wreckage was found later by the boys. There the 'plane caught fire and was destroyed ; fortunately not before they were able to rescue most of their reserve food supply and a small sledge which they had taken in case of emergency.

At first they wandered about for some time until they found the spot where the Penguin Man was eventually discovered. Here they started to kill all the seals they could find in order to supplement the rations saved from the wreck, preparatory to an attempt to reach the coast, man-hauling the sledge.

Two days before they had arranged to start the captain's brother fell and hurt his head, delaying their departure. One morning he awoke to find that his so-called friend had vanished, taking the sledge and most of the provisions with him. In desperation he took up his abode in the cave and lived there until discovered by the polar party.

All that was known about the sneak that deserted him was that *somehow* he reached the coast, was picked up, and taken home. There he pitched a yarn that his friend had died in the Antarctic. Eventually he went to sea—since when Captain Baker had heard nothing of him.

Very soon, in view of the oncoming autumn, energetic preparations were made for a start for home. Originally Captain Baker had planned to proceed direct to Ross Bay to search for the new mineral, but in view of a possible rescue of the remainder of the *Stalin* survivors he decided to proceed first towards Graham Land.

It was a strange feeling as they left the base, the only sign of which was now a depot of surplus stores, left for chance wayfarers in the future, and steamed across the newly christened " League Sea," through the narrow opening and out into the pack-ice. Threading their way with much less delay than on the previous journey, drift-ice was reached, and finally the open water of the Southern Ocean. Here they turned east along the edge of the ice barrier, and a constant look-out was kept for the missing men.

Excitement increased as, on approaching Peter I. Island in the early hours, the look-out reported some one signalling from the cliffs. Very slowly the ship was navigated as near the shore as possible, when it was seen that the " some one signalling " was only a flag fluttering from the top of a pole on the highest point—four thousand feet above the sea.

Despite the disappointment hopes rose high, and Captain Baker blew a series of blasts on the siren. A moment later several wrecks of humanity came tumbling out of a large cave, and after staring incredulously, waved frantically. Hearing their shouts, a crowd of their fellow-shipmates appeared from the cave.

Three hours later the castaways—who proved to be the remainder of the survivors of the *Stalin*—were safely

Several wrecks of humanity came tumbling out.

on board. While they were hurried below to be nursed back to health and strength, Captain Baker heaved a sigh of relief at the—comparatively—short delay, and ordered " Full speed for Ross Island."

" Just a year since we came along here, but what a difference in our speed ! " exclaimed David as the *Queen of the Antarctic* ploughed its way through the ice.

His remark was called forth by the fact that their return journey round the ice barrier was much more rapid than on the way out. For one thing the exact route was now known ; even more important than this were the weather conditions. So far, the temperature had not dropped low enough to create large areas of ice, while a gentle breeze from the land kept the drift-ice in a loose condition, through which they were able to proceed with little difficulty. The result was that Captain Baker gave orders to crowd on as much sail as possible, and kept the engines going at full speed, except during the lengthening periods of darkness when, by the aid of searchlights, quarter speed was maintained.

In view of the necessity for light during their mineral hunt, the favourable conditions—and resulting speed towards their goal—caused universal satisfaction, and when, near the end of March, the look-out reported Ross Island, excitement grew to fever pitch.

A thrill passed through the watchers as they saw the twin peaks ahead, each over eleven thousand feet high and snow-covered except near the summits. With the island slightly to their left, the ship was steered through the McMurdo Sound until a convenient spot was found to anchor it to a sheet of ice—an offshoot of the Barne Glacier—near the Delbridge Islands.

It had been touch and go whether they would be able to anchor before dark, and having accomplished it safely, every one was glad to turn in for a long rest, preparatory to what might prove to be an arduous task.

Next morning, amid feelings of tense excitement, the occupants of the *Queen of the Antarctic* divided themselves into parties as planned by Captain Baker. Doctor Elliot led the group of scientists who were to search for the deposit. Lieutenant Carmen was to supervise the digging operations, and Zameneff was appointed leader of the sledges, all of which might be needed to convey the mineral to the ship. Lieutenant Ransome was left in charge of the *Queen of the Antarctic*, thus freeing Captain Baker to co-ordinate the whole task.

Several days were spent in prospecting, but the honours finally fell to geologist Ardenholdt. Following his own line of thought—which he had purposely kept to himself—he examined the sides of the crater for traces of lava, and on discovering them, began to dig down

through the hard-frozen snow. On reaching a stratum
of what once had been a stream of molten lava, he secured
a number of specimens and rushed them to the laboratory
on board ship. After an anxious wait he was rewarded
by hearing Mr. Slater report:

" I think you've hit it. These specimens all contain
a so-far-unknown metal and its oxide."

Immediately after a second report—that all analyses
agreed in classifying the powder as an unknown mineral,
closely resembling a platinum ore, but with slightly
different properties—orders were given to start mining.
While a large gang worked hard to lay bare a long stretch
of the lava deposit, most of the scientists hurried back
to the ship to make fuller analyses of the new substance.

That night Doctor Elliot announced to his co-workers,
" I have now received the reports of all the analyses, and
I am glad to tell you that they definitely confirm the fact
that we have discovered the mineral deposit which we
came so far to seek. Mining operations will begin in
earnest to-morrow morning."

Loud cheers—among which those of the three chums
made up for any deficiencies—rang through the vessel,
and dreams that night were more than usual " on the gold
standard."

It was now a race against time. Any day—probably
immediately upon a change of weather—the sea might
begin to freeze over. On the first signs of such an eventuality they must pack up and fly, or risk the alternative
of being frozen up where they were for another winter.

Despite the feverish efforts of all concerned, progress
was tantalizingly slow. The lava was exceedingly hard,
and from this the mineral had to be separated. Only a
limited number could work on the restricted area which
had been cleared of snow and ice, and transport was
dangerous and difficult. More than once a load of the
precious material was lost through the treacherous ice
giving way beneath the sledge, and the work was several
times held up by sudden blizzards. Not only was the ore

lost by these disasters, but on one occasion the dog-sledges fell through the ice and both sledge and dogs disappeared.

On the tenth day after their arrival Ardenholdt succeeded in laying bare a second deposit of the mineral, which, judging by the preliminary analysis, was twice as rich as the first one.

A squad was at once transferred to the spot, but just as they commenced to dig, four blasts from the ship's siren came wailing across the snowy wastes—the signal for all to return to the vessel at once.

With looks of dismay, tools and apparatus were hurriedly collected. Before they could start, however, a message was signalled from the bridge :

" Change of wind.   Ice closing in."

Many a wistful glance was cast at the towering snow-white peaks as the *Queen of the Antarctic* sped northwards, but in a very few hours there was ample proof of Captain Baker's wisdom in leaving their treasure behind.

Urged on by a steadily increasing wind, ice-floes were being rapidly massed together and driven into the bay. A sudden drop of temperature and snowy clouds added to the ominous signs.

Full speed could not be maintained for long, and it was not until the third evening that they sighted Cape Adare.

The scientists were busy in the laboratories ; most of the crew were on duty or asleep. The three boys were engaged on deck, scrubbing, polishing, and clearing up.

Suddenly Alan, who had borrowed his father's binoculars to have a final look at the cliffs of Antarctica, yelled out :

" There's some one waving from the top of the cliffs ! "

CHAPTER XXII

HOME AGAIN

THE thrilling news spread like wildfire, and plans were at once made to rescue the castaway. Owing to the oncoming darkness it was obvious that nothing could be done that night, but the officers sat up until a late hour discussing possible—and many impossible—schemes.

Every one was roused at dawn, and sleepiness was quickly forgotten in energetic work. After steaming as close to the rugged cliffs of ice as they dared, signals were made to the lonely figure on top. Even through the most powerful binoculars nothing could be seen of the person except a small portion of his face, and the only data they had to go upon was that he (or she) was of average height and build.

Something in the actions of the castaway seemed familiar to Captain Baker, and he fired a shot at random. Snatching up his semaphore flags he spelt out :

" WHO ARE YOU ? "

His heart beat faster as he saw the answering signal that his message had been understood. But he gasped with incredulity as he read the reply :

" COLLINSON."

Had it not been for the fact that there was more than enough work for every one, much time would have been wasted in discussing the astounding news. Subsequent messages from the signaller, however, indicated that a speedy rescue was absolutely vital, as he was in the last stages of starvation and exhaustion.

As the officers had foreseen, the process of rescue proved extremely difficult and hazardous. Taking their lives in their hands, the crew lowered the lifeboat and threaded a tortuous way through the ice until they reached a ledge projecting from the cliffs. Snow was falling, coupled with a biting wind, and the subsequent journey on foot of nearly a mile over slippery ice was fraught with danger at every step.

Even on reaching the precipitous wall of ice they knew that they might be balked, unable to find any way of reaching their friend. Here Collinson was able to help, and almost too weak to stand, to point out to his rescuers a part of the cliffs where, although too steep and slippery for him to climb down, they might be able to ascend by means of ropes and ice-axes.

And so it proved. When volunteers for the dangerous task were called for, every man stepped forward. Doctor Elliot chose his men with the eye of experience, and insisted upon leading them up himself.

With hearts in their mouths the boys watched from the deck as the three intrepid climbers—all of whom were amateur mountaineers—ascended the dangerous incline step by step. At last they saw them on top. . . . Collinson was lowered slowly to those below. . . . Doctor Elliot held the rope while the other two descended, then faced the perilous descent alone.

After Herculean efforts Collinson, now in a state of utter collapse, was brought on board and carried below, then without further delay the *Queen of the Antarctic* was steered for home.

It was some time before the aviator could tell his story, and it was the general opinion that another twenty-four hours on the bleak headland would have settled his fate. As it was, they had left the Ross Sea far behind, threaded their way—sometimes with great difficulty and no little danger—through ice-floes and between monstrous ice-

bergs, and were ploughing slowly through drift-ice only
about a hundred miles south of Macquarie Island, before
he was considered fit to be questioned. Even then, only
Doctor Elliot and Captain Baker were allowed to be
present, and David and Frank had to rely upon what they
heard from Alan to satisfy their curiosity.

Knowing that Alan would be off duty after tea, his
two chums completed their tasks in record time and
joined him in the bows. This was their favourite haunt
when off duty ; all three loved to feel the steady rise and
fall of the ship as it ploughed its way through the swell,
and to stare across the watery wastes with the tang of
the salt spray against their faces.

" Heard Collinson's story yet ? " burst out David as
soon as they were settled.

" Bits of it, but Dad hasn't had time to tell me a great
deal—says he'll tell me the whole yarn when we get
home."

Frank's face was eager with anticipation. " *Do* tell
us all you know," he urged.

Alan thought for a moment. " Expect you know more
than I do 'bout the first part. We all heard the wireless
messages, and you two lucky beggars helped to find the
notes they dropped. It seems that they ran into a
howling blizzard before they reached the Pole, and had
to fly blind. They knew they couldn't land—it would
have been certain death to attempt it under such conditions—so they just flew on. Then the magnetic storm
upset their compass, and as they couldn't see more'n a
few yards they had no idea where they were going.
Collinson knew he'd got a big store of petrol, so he pluckily
held on and took the only possible chance—to keep on
flying until either the petrol or the storm gave out.
Luckily the petrol won, and after flying for hours and
hours they suddenly shot out of the storm ; but instead
of popping out into daylight they saw stars above them.
This was a bit of a blow and put the kibosh on any idea of
landing, so they just flew on at reduced speed until it

got light again. They spotted a nice stretch of snow and came down. Of course, they hadn't the vaguest notion where they were—all they knew was that they must have flown nearly two thousand miles. The rest is a bit misty. I think they scouted round and found some high hill, from the top of which they saw a range of mountains, so they made for these. On following the hills—they had to carry all their stuff on their backs, so their progress was pretty slow, and I guess even more painful than slow— they discovered that the range suddenly turned south. This gave Collinson a hint, and he guessed that they were in Victoria Land, so they climbed up to the top to see where they were and spotted the Ross Sea. This encouraged them tremendously, because they knew that they would find penguins and seals to eat there and that there would be a good chance of being picked up by us on our way back. Then, just as they thought they were saved, the other two fell down a crevasse and Collinson never saw them again."

" Sounds like a tuppenny thriller," put in David.

" Not too thrilling for the two in cold storage," added Frank.

" Shurrup ! " countered the teller. " Well, to cut a long story short, Collinson struggled on alone and reached the place where we picked him up. When he got there he found that he couldn't get down to get the seals and penguins, so he just had to watch them making faces at him from below and to exist on what he had left. When we arrived he'd got one biscuit and a few tablets left."

" Crumbs ! " ejaculated David, " if that's the odd bits of the yarn, I'd like to hear the whole thing from his own lips."

" Land ho ! " came a shout from the crow's-nest.

At any time this warning is a thrilling one, but on such a trip as this it vibrated through the hearers like an electric shock. At last they were again to see land free from snow. And was not Macquarie Island the outpost of their home regions ?

All the stores which they had left on the outward journey were found intact. Fortunately, they were not required, so it was decided to leave them for any who might be less fortunate than they were. No one felt any great regret at leaving this bleak and barren island, especially when they remembered that in three days' time, if all went well, they should be back in Hobart.

Although very heavy seas were experienced, these seemed mere child's play after all they had gone through, and the look-out's last cry of " Land ho ! " found a large group of eager spectators huddled in the bows. For some time only those with binoculars could see anything of their goal, but at last the familiar coastline came into view and the seas echoed with hearty cheers from the throats of the home-hungry wanderers.

" Safe back at last," remarked David tritely.

" All but three," corrected Frank with a tinge of sadness.

David was too busily occupied with thoughts of the future to think clearly. " Three ? Let me see, the observer and wireless op. of Collinson's 'plane, and. . . ."

" Poor old Bob," supplemented Frank.

" Of course, old Bob Harker. Wonder what really happened : whether the berg hit him or whether he was just drowned ? "

" And don't forget we've lost ten dogs during the whole expedition. Thank goodness old Petz came back from the Pole all right," added Alan, squatting down beside his pet and fondling him. " Ought to have a medal for all the lives you've saved, old chap," he mused.

If their send-off had been enthusiastic and noisy, their welcome back can be better imagined than described. Every one from Captain Baker to Petz was the hero of the hour, while the crowd was a League of Nations in itself. The brief wireless reports which had been broadcast on their way back had intrigued the scientific world, and in addition to all the official welcomes, friends and reporters of nearly twenty nationalities were there to greet them.

Immediately he could free himself from his admirers, Captain Baker hurried off to report the loss of the three members of their expedition, which had already been done in brief by wireless.

On arrival a shock was awaiting him. The death of the two members of the aeroplane's crew had been duly registered and their relatives informed, explained the official.

" But," he went on mysteriously, " we cannot trace Bob Harker. No such person lives at the address you gave, and none of his so-called relatives appear to exist."

For the moment Captain Baker was flabbergasted, then his naturally quick brain deduced the probable solution.

" Perhaps he wasn't Bob Harker at all. Very likely he signed on under that name and gave a false address so as to hide his identity. Maybe he'd made a mess of things in the old country and wanted to be forgotten." Suddenly he remembered the scene at the iceberg. " *But Bob was a fine sailor* whatever he might have been before," he affirmed.

The outcome of the discussion was that Captain Baker offered to examine the few personal belongings which Bob had left behind and which had been locked up in a chest ever since.

Accompanied by an official, he made his way to where the box had been stored. On unlocking it he found the usual seaman's miscellanea, including a spare coat.

" Better go through the pockets," suggested Captain Baker, proceeding to carry out his suggestion.

His search was fruitless, however, and he began to fold up the garment. As he did so he heard a faint crackling noise and felt something stiff in the middle of the back. Thinking that it might be part of the lining, but deciding to make sure, he unrolled the coat, slit down the lining with his jack-knife, and inserted his hand.

" Peter Illerton ! " he gasped.

To the astonishment of both he drew out a packet consisting of an envelope, addressed to Captain Baker, carefully wrapped in a piece of oilskin.

Hardly had he torn open the envelope and pulled out a crumpled piece of paper when the official heard him whistle and noticed that he was staring hard at the message.

" Peter Illerton ! " he gasped.

With a set expression Captain Baker handed the letter across. As the official read it his eyes opened wide.

Some of it was in the nature of a personal message to the addressee, but one sentence riveted his attention :

"Bob Harker is my assumed name. I am really Peter Illerton, who murdered your brother Eric."

"So he thought he had murdered Eric by deserting him in the Antarctic!" cogitated Captain Baker almost to himself. As he spoke his face set into a hard mask, but suddenly relaxed, and he exclaimed with an air of finality :

"Ah well, fortunately he was mistaken, and *Bob Harker* was a splendid seaman after all."

.   .   .   .

For many weeks David and Frank, in addition to all the scientists, were kept very busy. Doctor Elliot lectured before several learned societies on the new Polar race which they had discovered. Mr. Walker was in great demand by the Geographical Societies to explain his theory—now so well substantiated by actual experiments —of one vast Antarctic continent. Mr. Hawlet was the lecturer of the moment on bacteriology, but always insisted upon coupling Frank's name with the isolation of the new "low-temperature bacteria."

It was some time before the mineral could be removed from the hold and its properties fully investigated. At last, however, the report came through.

Doctor Elliot called his scientists together for the last time. "Our hopes are fully justified," he began. "The deposit which we brought back with us from Mount Erebus contains a rich percentage of an entirely new ore— an oxide of a new element which will almost certainly prove far more valuable than platinum—of which, incidentally, it may be an allotropic form. There was also a small percentage of the metal itself. Gentlemen, I thank you for your loyal co-operation in making this important discovery in the cause of science."

It was typical of the man that he omitted to mention that the proceeds of the sale of the deposit would enable every member of the crew to enjoy a long holiday and then to put by a substantial nest-egg for the future.

Both David and Frank were offered good posts with Mr. Walker and Mr. Hawlet respectively, but before starting each was granted a holiday.

" Guess I'll hop off to my cousins in the country, after I've been home for a bit, and revel in *green* trees, *green* grass, and . . . well, *anything but white*," smiled David as he and his chum met for the last time before parting for several weeks. To his surprise Frank did not reply.

" What are you going to do, Frank ? " he asked.

" I'm going home too." Then as the speaker turned to leave he added, " I think I shall pop into the Zoo each day for a bit. Good-bye, Dave ! " And with that he was gone.

David stood baffled for a moment, but the excitement of the next few hours put the problem out of his mind. Nevertheless the mystery of Frank's reply recurred to him frequently, and he missed his chum's company acutely after having lived with him for nearly two years.

On the third day of his holiday he startled his parents by blurting out at breakfast :

" I'm off to the Zoo to-day."

Although he hurried into the Gardens, an observer might have noticed that David did not seem the least interested in the animals, but made for any enclosures where there was a crowd and scanned the individuals closely.

Suddenly he came to a halt. Only twenty yards in front of him were the open-air cages of the lions, while close to the rail of the third one stood Frank, staring at the finest lioness of the whole collection—only a few feet away !

Then he understood.

THE END

Printed in Great Britain at the Press of the Publishers
Thomas Nelson and Sons Ltd, Edinburgh